TRUST BUT A FEW

TRUST BUT
A FEW

THOMAS M. JOHNSSON

Matador
9 Priory Business Park
Kibworth Beauchamp
Leicestershire LE8 0RX, UK
Tel: (+44) 116 279 2299
Fax: (+44) 116 279 2277
Email: books@troubador.co.uk
Web: www.troubador.co.uk/matador

ISBN 978 1784622 558

British Library Cataloguing in Publication Data.
A catalogue record for this book is available from the British Library.

Typeset in Aldine401 BT Roman by Troubador Publishing Ltd
Printed and bound in the UK by TJ International, Padstow, Cornwall

Matador is an imprint of Troubador Publishing Ltd

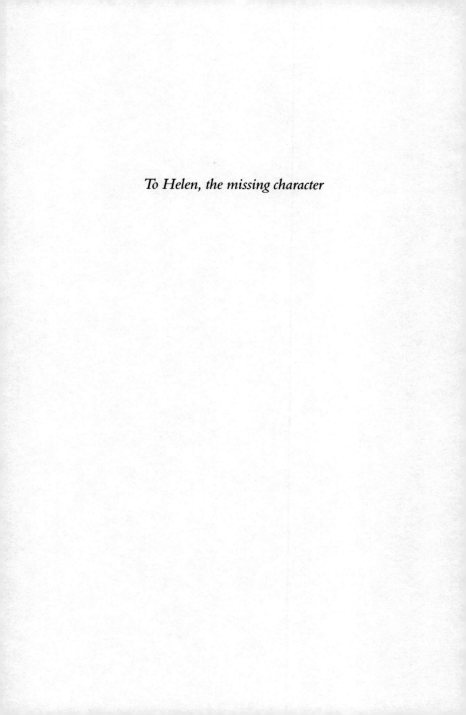

To Helen, the missing character

Love all, trust a few,
Do wrong to none.

Shakespeare, *All's Well that Ends Well*

1

The housekeeper placed the tray on the coffee table. She was aware of a tension in the room so withdrew quickly. It was unusual for her boss, Mr McBain, not to acknowledge her. She could see that his aide-de-camp, Rab Donald, was bursting with indignation.

Rab was unusually bold. He got up from his seat and jabbed his finger at Alex McBain. While he was a good nine inches shorter than McBain, he exuded the same menace and power as his employer.

"Sonny's got to be reined in, Loco. He's getting out of control. We need to keep the cops sweet, but they'll not turn a blind eye for much longer. He nailed that boy's hands and feet to the floor."

McBain looked up from the sofa. He started:

"But he'll never grass again, Rab. Sonny's my lad, I can't be too …"

The theme from *Mulholland Drive,* McBain's mobile ringtone, cut in. He listened, held up his hand to Rab, and said "Wait." He went into his study, closing the door behind him. Rab faintly heard McBain repeating details of an appointment and then abruptly ringing off. After a pause, McBain shouted for Rab. When he went into the study, McBain seemed to be three inches shorter than his six foot three. His complexion was pasty. He was diminished.

"Not good news," said McBain. "We need to go to Edinburgh. I have to see a specialist. At the Murrayfield

Hospital. Must be near the rugby ground. I've got to be there at four."

"I know where it is, Loco. Next to the zoo. Well, we better start now. The M8 can be a nightmare. Why not see someone here in Glasgow?"

"Here's a village. I don't want my problems discussed at some golf club. Anyway, this guy's supposed to be the best."

The Mercedes ate up the dreary miles past derelict steel works, pit bings and other remnants of Scotland's abandoned industrial heritage. As soon as they could see Arthur's Seat in the distance, they were in a more prosperous environment. As Rab got out of the car in the car park of the private hospital, he was aware of the big sky stretching out south from Corstorphine Hill to the Pentlands. It was good to be alive. His boss had sounded solemn after the phone call. He'd clearly been suffering breathing problems for months, and Rab had pressed him to do something about it sooner, but the boss had always found an excuse to put it off. Now he had to face up to hearing about the test results, but would McBain confide in him, Rab wondered.

They walked together up the short flight of steps to the entrance. McBain turned to face Rab.

"Wait in the car. It's safe. No one knows me here."

"Good luck, boss."

McBain walked along the corridor to the outpatients waiting area. How ordinary things seemed here. He towered above the two receptionists. The chubbier one greeted him brightly, but a glimmer of concern crossed her face when she noticed the scar line on his cheek. There was a momentary pause in the well-rehearsed greeting.

"Mr Stewart will see you soon. He's running a bit late, I'm afraid."

McBain sat down next to an assortment of injured sportsmen and elderly couples discussing digestion problems.

Ten minutes later, a portly middle-aged gent wearing a three-piece pinstripe suit breezed round the corner, called his name, shook his hand and guided him into the furthest consulting room.

Mr Stewart said he had the results from the tests, which had been carried out by a colleague, and there was no need for any further tests to be carried out today. The results were disappointing.

"Forget the patter, doc", said McBain. "Just give me the bottom line, as it were. What's the damage, and can it be fixed?"

McBain fixed his gaze on the consultant, and tried to read his expression. But Mr Stewart wouldn't keep eye contact, and busied himself shuffling his papers and opening out a graph showing the results of an ECG. He spoke as if dictating a letter:

"I could give you some false hopes, Mr McBain, but that wouldn't be fair to either of us. Your arterial disease has spread to the point where treatment is pointless."

McBain felt a tightening in his chest. It took a minute for him to recover:

"How long have I got?"

"A year, probably. Oddly enough, you won't suffer any more than you have already, and your GP can prescribe some new drugs to help. So to the outside world you'll be just as you are. All that will happen is you won't wake up one day, or you'll pass out suddenly. No drama, no hospice. Quite a good way to go, considering other possibilities. I'll let your GP know what to prescribe. I'm very sorry. Please feel free to get another opinion. There are people doing excellent pioneering work in Leeds."

McBain had expected this, though he had been hoping against hope that the first readings taken by his GP had been inaccurate.

"No, I don't think so, doc. I guess I'm lucky in a way to know in advance. I'll just settle up now."

Mr Stewart looked blank.

"Your fee, doc. How much?"

"Er, my secretary deals with that. Would you like another appointment? Or maybe you should think about counselling."

As soon as Mr Stewart mentioned the word counselling, McBain narrowed his eyes and gripped the armrests so tightly his knuckles whitened.

He snarled, "No thanks, doc. We're done here."

McBain strode out without shaking hands, walked along the corridor past the waiting area and out into the sunshine. Rab drove the car up from the car park to meet him. McBain climbed into the passenger seat.

"What's the news, boss? You look bad." Rab looked straight ahead as he asked this.

"I've got about a year," McBain sighed and turned to face Rab directly. "Now look at me and listen. This is how I'll be up to the end. No one's to know. Not Sonny, not Irene, not Joe. No one. Comprende?"

"Whatever you say, Loco."

The journey back to Glasgow passed in silence, both men reflecting on the news. There was one big issue McBain had to deal with, but he was at a loss to work out how. For Rab Donald, the prospect of Sonny as his new boss didn't fill him with enthusiasm, but it was possible he could turn the situation to his advantage.

2

The barman had just come on shift. He wiped the mahogany bar in a desultory fashion as he watched the two men chatting in the corner of what had at one time been the smoking room of the Northern Cross Club. Now smoking in the club was outlawed, and the room was used by members and their guests as a coffee lounge. In the mornings the tables were usually occupied by single retired gentlemen catching up on the financial news or the racing tips for the day, or three or four lady members taking a break from shopping. After one o'clock, in came the professionals – lawyers, accountants and surveyors – for a quick coffee and a chat after lunch in the dining room. It wasn't at all busy the rest of the day, unless there was a function of some sort taking place in the evening. Few members stayed overnight, indeed the bedroom accommodation was mostly used by High Court judges sitting on circuit in Glasgow. At six o'clock, it was a safe place to have a private discussion.

The older man sipped his gin and tonic, turned in his seat, making sure no one was nearby. He was jowly, florid-faced, hair almost over his collar. The barman knew the type. Probably a merchant banker, definitely London. He was clearly the more sophisticated of the two, and his appearance indicated he was used to the good things in life. His chalk-striped suit was pure Savile Row, and the dark red handkerchief in his breast pocket showed he wasn't a Glasgow man. He also had an easy familiarity with the club environment, the way he'd summoned the waiter for more drinks. His companion stopped talking and drained his glass of warm bottled lager. He was slimmer, and his closely cropped hair made him look much the younger, which he was.

The Londoner shifted on the red leather armchair and leaned towards his companion:

"Well, all I'm saying is that's how it *could* be done. I've heard that there are quite a number of wealthy individuals in India and the Far East who have arrangements in place to use *hawala*. There are lawyers in the West Indies and even the Channel Islands who document the transactions. It all looks very innocent. They set up what's called a pilot trust with something like the Red Cross as the only beneficiary, then the real people, who'll get the money, are added later. So you really want to entrap this character? You'd better be careful you don't stray offside. Why him, in particular? Is he not just one of many?"

"He's a big fish up here," the younger man said. "This isn't London, you know. I need a name. Someone you've come across, or maybe heard about. A lawyer or an accountant who knows his way around the offshore scene. Someone from Glasgow; or Edinburgh, at a push. Someone totally kosher, no history. Also, I need to know how the mark would access the cash when he went abroad. Presumably you just can't turn up with millions without some sort of credible explanation."

"There is a way you can do that using structured financial products. Think of it like an each-way bet. You buy a put and a call option. One goes up, inevitably the other goes down. You use a network of companies to place the bets, and produce a holding company with all the subsidiaries that made a profit. Liquidate the losers. It would cost about 10 per cent, but with an accountant who's – shall we say – imaginative, it could be done."

The younger man became insistent. "Is this all just a theory, or does it work in practice? I still need a name for the first part, getting the money washed clean."

The Londoner turned and looked out onto Royal Exchange Square. He leaned forward and cradled his chin in the palm of his right hand. He mused, "Funnily enough, I worked on a supply agreement up here for the Saudis which involved a Jersey company and some tricky transfer pricing issues. I was dealing with the tax partner, but I saw the work which had been done by the corporate department. It was quite impressive. I never met the lead partner, though. Easton … Easter … Eastman – that's it, Eastman. From the papers I saw, he would be someone who could help you."

"He sounds ideal, so long as he's never met you or got to know your name. Would he know about how all this works?"

"Oh, yes, I'm sure of it. What we were doing was very much on the edge of legality. In the papers he referred to a Jersey firm he dealt with all the time. But how could you persuade Eastman to be – what do you call it – a plant, an inside man?"

"We may not need to. Everyone has a weakness, don't you think? My people'll find out what his is, and maybe he'll volunteer."

"This all sounds most – how can I put it? – irregular. But if you insist."

"I need chapter and verse about *hawala* and the options."

The Londoner leaned back in his chair.

"Are you sure about this? … Well, if you are, I'll email you Eastman's contact details and the mechanics of the scheme. Now I must dash."

"No emails. Send me an old fashioned letter in your own fair hand. There's to be no record of this anywhere."

"As you wish, bro. As you see, I've picked up the patois."

The Londoner gave the barman his name and the address of the London club which would settle his bill. There was no question of cash being required. The barman offered to arrange taxis, but the two men declined. They walked along together to Queen Street, stopping at the junction with Ingram Street, by the statue of Wellington on his horse Copenhagen. As usual, a drunk had scaled the statue and deposited a traffic cone on Wellington's head.

The men shook hands and the older one flagged down a taxi. The door slammed shut and the taxi sped off.

As the younger man walked on along Gordon Street, he spoke into his mobile. "It's coming together. He'll tell me how it could be done, and if McBain has a year, I'm sure it can be done. He's sending me the details of a solicitor here in Glasgow who should be able to set it up. You get someone to do a full background check on the guy, find his weak spot and con him into it."

★ ★ ★

Two days later, Rab Donald made his way into the Mitchell Street office of Colin Scott Investigations. The building was tatty, last upgraded about 1900. The ancient lift creaked upwards to the sixth floor, through an ever-changing palette of rank aromas that combined with those of urine and disinfectant in the lift itself. Colin Scott liked to keep a low profile. The grubby red carpet and cheap oak desk showing decades of cigarette burns added to the seedy effect. Colin still sported a 1970s moustache, hair over his collar and a kipper tie. He sat with his size tens on the window sill.

"So, what do you have for me, Rab? A background check on a lawyer? Not your usual scene."

"James Eastman practises in Glasgow but stays in Inverleith, an upmarket area in Edinburgh. I think he could be useful to us. We've some commercial deals coming up and I'm not too happy about the lawyers we're using just now. Alex wouldn't change without me giving him the gen on Eastman. It's all a bit preliminary at the moment – in fact, I haven't even mentioned this to Alex. If he's no good to us, I won't bother Alex about it, so don't bill this separately, just roll the cost into something else for us. Understood?"

"OK, Rab, but what am I looking for? Credit report and the like, or a bit deeper?"

"Well, we may want to put a bit of pressure on him, so dig deep and see what you uncover. Websites he visits, any bits on the side. Boys, girls … you never know."

"How long have I got?"

"A week should do it, don't you think?"

3

James Eastman sighed as the blinking stop lights indicated a traffic snarl-up ahead. He was on his way from Edinburgh to Glasgow on the M8. Just past the giant wire horse, near Easterhouse, the traffic slowed to a standstill. He quite liked the sculptures which had been placed alongside the motorway, though he wasn't sure about the thinking which lay behind them, as they were definitely distracting. It was safe enough for passengers, but what about the drivers? As usual, he thought about everything in terms of the law. Here they were, banning adverts at the side of motorways, but pyramids, giant red heads, coloured sheep and wire horses were allowed. If a driver new to the area was admiring these sculptures and ran into another vehicle, could the roads authority be liable? Interesting? Maybe not to most people.

Anyway, Hot Chocolate were playing "It Started with a Kiss" on Radio 2, just after a news report that two Palestinians had been shot in quick succession by a sniper in the Gaza Strip, as Eastman hit the stationary traffic. He had travelled this stretch of motorway for fifteen years, so he knew what to do. Take the next turnoff and head into town on the Old Edinburgh Road, using a few side streets as rat runs. Simple. A twenty-minute delay, but so what? His first meeting was at ten and it was now just before eight.

He turned left off the slip road, right at the second lights, left, right again onto Carntyne Road. This would take him into the centre via Duke Street. The traffic was light here, and he was able to make good time. Just another day in the life of a Corporate Partner in a Glasgow law firm, he thought, as he glanced at the houses on this street. He remembered when they'd all been owned by the Glasgow Corporation, pre-Thatcher, but some had now been bought by tenants under the Conservatives' Right To Buy legislation.

He'd been brought up in Haddington, a few miles east of Edinburgh, on a private housing development near a council estate just like this. He had always marvelled at how the people who lived in the council houses accepted the uniformity dictated by the Local Authority. In the avenue where his family lived, everyone, including his parents, had expressed their individuality with differently coloured doors and windows, wooden or iron gates and the like. On the council estate, all the house doors and windows were green, until one summer all the woodwork on every council house was painted yellow. The shock! But friends who stayed there seemed unaffected. It had been a bonus to get the houses painted at all, apparently.

Eastman didn't know he was being followed, of course. Someone had been on his tail since he left Edinburgh that morning. Colin Scott's report on Eastman was almost finished, following a couple of nights sitting outside his house beside the Botanic Gardens in Edinburgh, logged into Eastman's network. It was pretty clear to Colin which user in the house was logging onto the barely legal pornographic websites, and confirmation came when the same user logged into the Scottish Courts website and something called Westlaw. Colin noted down that the eminent lawyer – "A powerhouse, one to watch!" according to something called *The Legal 500* – had a weakness for young girls. Nothing illegal, just something he might not want broadcast to the world. Recently, two judges had had to resign because they frequented saunas in Edinburgh and Glasgow.

Eastman decided to stop at the line of shops halfway along Carntyne Road to buy a newspaper and some mints. As he pulled in, the private detective drove past and stopped fifteen yards further on, watching in his rear-view mirror. As Eastman came out of the newsagents, a commotion broke out as a dog was struck by a Volkswagen Golf just beside the shops. The dog was clearly dead, and the driver who emerged from the Golf took one look at it and threw up. Unfortunately, the accident had boxed in Eastman's car.

The shop window reflected the scene, and Eastman saw just how out of place he looked. All the locals looked stunted; he towered above them. No one here wore a grey suit, white shirt, blue and green tie, Barker shoes. Just a sad collection of fatties in shell suits and slimy anoraks, acned complexions, greasy hair and scruffy trainers. A collection of motorised disability scooters was scattered on the pavement.

"You wus speeding", screamed an old crone, waving a tattered umbrella at the driver of the Golf from the pavement. She turned and pointed to Eastman. "You're a witness – you, the toff in the suit! Poor Buster. My dug never stood a chance!"

There was a murmur of agreement from the onlookers, whose numbers were being swelled by the arrival of a pack of rather sinister-looking schoolchildren, all dressed entirely in black – not in uniforms as such, but in what looked to Eastman like a rag-bag of weird garments. It was as if they'd raced round "What Everyone Wants" picking up every piece of black clothing they could find. Their darkness was accentuated by the bright white trainers which all of them were wearing; that, at least, seemed to form a self-chosen uniform.

"Look," said Eastman, "I was in the shop, and I didn't see anything." He most definitely didn't want to get involved.

Buster lay stretched out full length across the carriageway, as if he'd been making one last spectacular leap for freedom before he was hit. Already an informal "stop–go" arrangement had been devised by some of the older passers-by for getting the traffic moving, and the Golf and Buster had become just another obstruction.

The crone was now babbling about poor old Buster, and a couple of the older schoolgirls were comforting her. Eastman thought one of them was quite a looker, great tits, blond hair, her full lips looked good enough to … He smiled at her, and she smiled back. She must be at least eighteen. Down boy, he thought, this is not the moment.

But this exchange had been photographed by Colin Scott. He smirked as he added this to his report. Mr Eastman definitely had an eye for the ladies, the younger the better. He'd a penchant for websites featuring teenagers, and now here he was eyeing one up. It shouldn't be too difficult to put a bit of pressure on him, quite apart from the money problems which a trawl of his bank records had disclosed. For a moment Colin thought of getting the girl's address, for if Rab had blackmail in mind, she looked like the ideal temptress and a hundred quid should be enough to sign her up. She certainly didn't look like an innocent. But just then Eastman managed to manoeuvre his Audi out, so Colin followed him all the way to his office.

★ ★ ★

The next day he and Rab Donald looked over the report. On the financial side, Eastman's house was worth a lot, but it was in joint names with his wife, mortgaged to the hilt, and his bank records showed he was working on overdraft to pay three sets of school fees. They agreed it was clear that Eastman was living way beyond his means. On the personal side, Colin had found out that there was speculation in his office of a relationship between Eastman and his secretary, Natasha. In addition, based on the website visits and the photographs, Eastman was obviously interested in young girls, though there was no evidence that he did anything about it.

Colin sighed:

"Nothing much to help with your proposal to Alex, then?"

Rab said nothing, which was very unusual, so Colin raised his voice.

"Rab, am I wasting my time here? I don't see where this is going. None of it's relevant to your cock-and-bull story about Alex changing solicitors, so if this is your private initiative to blackmail Eastman, I don't see you getting much out of him, even if you set him up with some Lolita. He's strapped."

Rab looked up at Colin and smiled.

"You're just too smart for your own good. OK, it may be a bit more complicated than I said, but it's all to help Alex, so keep your trap shut. The main thing is Sonny mustn't know. I'll think this over and get back to you. We might need a girl, right enough. But not from Glasgow. Can you get someone from London, if need be?"

"Sure, Rab. Whatever. Black, white, legal, not … just say the word."

4

Two weeks later, Jenny Eglinton squinted into the mirror in the Boutique Hotel in Bath Street. As she added the finishing touches to her makeup, she thought this was going to be the easiest five grand she'd ever earned. She'd never been to Glasgow before. She usually worked the Park Lane hotels, Arabs mostly. A maximum of two clients at a time, with lots of protection. What good had that degree done her, she thought? Since she'd left university and become an escort she'd made ten times what she could earn on any graduate recruitment scheme. She was always in demand, especially for what the boss called covert assignments which usually involved some sort of sting, maybe trapping a suspected adulterer or setting up a blackmail operation.

In fact, the degree had been of some use, she mused, to pass herself off as almost anything but a high-class prostitute, which in reality was what she was. She'd kept away from drugs and the plan was that after five more years, she'd have enough to open a small restaurant in the West Country. She sighed and thought she'd done some weird things in the past two years, but this was a bit different.

The specific instructions had been to fly to Glasgow on Thursday. She'd been given an identity – business suit, demure style. There was an invitation to a conference on Friday with a briefing note about it, but she didn't need to go. The main thing was to attend an art exhibition opening on Thursday evening. She was to find Mr Eastman (a photo was provided), compliment him, tease him, get him relaxed and talking about sex (the instructions included suggested topics). Tempt him but *do not sleep with him*. Most important, she was to get his business card – she could give him one of "hers" if he asked. She was to write up a full report of what he said, verbatim if possible, and leave it in the envelope provided, together with Eastman's business card, at hotel reception on Thursday evening before returning to London on Friday.

An hour later, all heads turned as Jenny breezed into the exhibition. She'd made herself up to look younger than her twenty-five years, to look like the girl in the photograph she'd been given with the instructions.

Graham Yorke, the gallery owner, had been looking out for her, as he'd been warned that a young lady from London called Jenny was writing a piece on Scottish galleries and would be attending the reception. He'd been told not to reveal her reason for being there to any of the other guests, especially not to James Eastman. Graham was a bit troubled about that. Eastman was one of his most loyal customers, who almost never missed the monthly receptions. But the gentleman who had called in to the gallery to advise Graham had been most insistent – that, and the fact that he'd purchased a fairly average Scottish watercolour, with a promise of further business in future, had persuaded Graham to go along with his instructions. As the man had left, he'd added that while Eastman wasn't to know the purpose of Jenny's visit, it was important that he be introduced to her.

Graham scuttled across to greet Jenny, and, as Eastman had not yet arrived, introduced her to some accountants discussing VAT. Jenny immediately lightened the conversation.

After about ten minutes one of the accountants spoke over Jenny's shoulder, "James, come and join us. We're hearing from Jenny here about what a parochial lot we are in Glasgow. She's a visitor from the Big Smoke."

Eastman joined the group and was introduced. It was clear he seemed to know almost everyone in the gallery. Jenny sipped the last of the champagne in her glass and moved it almost imperceptibly in Eastman's direction. He had been looking intently at her.

"Let me refresh that for you," he said, taking her glass and moving off towards the informal bar area, where he got into conversation with Graham about a couple of the exhibits.

Jenny detached herself from the accountants and joined the discussion between Eastman and the gallery owner. She could easily hold her own on modern art, having studied fine art as part of her degree.

It was also easy for her to hold Eastman's attention. She knew that alpha males such as Eastman love to talk about themselves, so it was really just a matter of pressing the right buttons and he was away. She kept refilling his glass, so that by the time the exhibition was winding down, it was James this and Jenny that, and he was flying, emboldened by drink.

"I think you need something to eat, James," Jenny suggested, as he staggered up the stairs from the gallery to street level. "Is there somewhere we could get a table?"

Eastman looked uncertain. Jenny realised he was sufficiently alert to be wary of being seen having a romantic meal with her. So she suggested a quick pizza in a cafe in Princes Square, which she'd scouted out earlier in the day. She patted him on the shoulder, "James, no one could think we're having a secret tryst here." Eastman seemed reassured, and said he did need to eat.

As they chatted, making their way through a decent Barolo, Jenny steered the conversation round to whether he was happy.

"James, I think there could be some synergy between us. How do you feel about exploring new ideas? 'Oranges are not the only fruit', as they say. I've some friends who're really quite liberated. There's a club in London where we could go and, well, anything goes. No single males, just couples and lesbians. Threesomes, foursomes … all very discreet; you have to wear a mask. I've a cousin – she's only seventeen – who has this fantasy about older men. I'm sure she'd love to come and – how can I put it? – join us at the club. Could you arrange a trip to London?"

Eastman looked incredulous, wide-eyed and open-mouthed.

"You know, Jenny, Scottish women, they don't talk like this. Sure, I have thoughts, and this club sounds fantastic. Is it expensive to join?"

"James, if you're worried about that maybe it's not for you. But I don't think that's right, is it? Tell me, what would you like to do there, James? I'm getting quite excited just thinking about it, aren't you? Tell me, and I'll find out if it can be arranged."

So he did. And then, on a high, inspired by the chat and the Barolo, he made his play.

"Jenny, could we go back to your hotel? I don't think I can wait until London."

But Jenny had a script to follow. She explained that her boss was in Glasgow with her, though he'd been unable to attend the gallery due to another engagement.

"I'm expected to meet up with him for a nightcap at half past ten, which is only half an hour away. James, you naughty boy, you'll have to contain yourself. But we should definitely keep in touch. You dash for your train, James. I must get along."

Eastman was in a state of confusion as they made their way to Queen Street station. She insisted on exchanging business cards in George Square, and they kissed in a perfunctory way. Eastman again seemed cautious about being seen. He saw Jenny into a taxi and ran for his train.

Back at her hotel, Jenny completed what she had been paid to do. She had Eastman's card, and now she wrote down everything she'd managed to get him to say about sex. It really was an odd thing to do, but she found she could easily remember phrases he'd used. When she finished, she put the report and the business card in an envelope addressed to a Mr Primary. She took it down to reception and left it with the receptionist, as she'd been instructed.

Colin Scott watched her do so from the mock Charles Rennie Mackintosh seats in the bar area next to reception. He'd been tailing her from her arrival in Glasgow. Attractive girl, he thought, and one who follows instructions to the letter. He would use her again.

Colin showed his "Mr Primary" identification to the receptionist and was given the envelope. Rab was waiting for him by his car.

They read what Jenny had written and concluded that James Eastman did indeed have a very vivid imagination. Back at Colin's office, he and Rab made up a letter addressed to "Carla, Receptionist, Sauna Paradisa" using much of what Jenny had written. Rab signed it "Jenny" and attached Eastman's business card to it.

5

Part of the plan was to get Alex McBain to agree to the idea of using Eastman as his lawyer, without it seeming to have come from Rab. The best way to do this seemed to be to use Sonny as the cipher. Rab knew that he would be at the Sauna Paradisa, which he ran for his father, for an early morning chat with the girls. He parked his Volkswagen Polo – Rab favoured a nondescript car – in a side street and walked past some of the local youth congregated outside the newsagents. They were respectful, hopeful of some employment in the McBain empire. Each of them said:

"Morning, Mr Donald."

No one would dare to call McBain's lieutenant "Rab".

The double doors of the Sauna Paradisa obscured what was inside from any interested passers-by on the Gallowgate, though they were unlikely to be shocked by what they saw. For all the world, it looked like a bank, with a single teller behind an armoured glass partition. A cheap maroon carpet complemented the gold flock wallpaper. To enter the massage rooms or the sauna, the receptionist had to release a lock on the side door. This was essential after the pubs had closed, when there could be what was described as good-natured boisterousness among the punters waiting for girls to become available. It wasn't so much a bank, more a cross between a betting shop and a doctor's waiting room, with the two threadbare sofas and eight hardback wooden chairs. Although smoking had been banned for years, the room still held the lingering aroma of a hundred thousand cigarettes. The sauna was in a rundown area, but it was close to a supermarket car park. Businessmen would park there – they were allowed ninety minutes – and then slip across the road to the sauna. The staff were used to hearing them explain on their mobiles that they were picking up a few things from the shops on the way home.

Rab strode in and blew a kiss to Carla, the receptionist. She'd seen years of action in the massage rooms but was now retired. Her uniform was an almost transparent wispy blouse showing off her still substantial cleavage. Face well plastered with makeup, her lipstick was scarlet, her hair a black that could only have come out of a bottle. Her job was to match the punters with girls who would accommodate what they expected from the "massage". There were a couple of girls – Morag and Zahra – who wouldn't do full sex. This caused a few problems initially, but the odd thing was that these girls were now the most popular. They gave what was described as a "handie", but their clients seemed happy to chat with them for the rest of the allotted half hour.

Carla adored Rab. She usually favoured big strong men, like McBain. Rab was a skelf compared to his boss, but he had that presence about him. She always felt safe when he was about, which was especially important if Sonny was in a mood, as he was today. He'd had a blazing row with Katrina, the girl he'd installed in his flat, and she was now in Casualty having her forehead stitched as a result of "a fall".

Carla warned Rab about what had happened, but they knew there would be no follow up, as Katrina knew better than to complain to the police. Rab said he would have a word with Sonny, to try to calm him down. Carla unlocked the door through to the back rooms and into the common kitchen, where Sonny was drinking coffee and eating a bacon roll.

Sonny was at least twenty stone. His greasy straggly dark hair was over his shoulders, and he wore a Scotland football tracksuit and trainers. His face was smeared with brown sauce.

"She deserved it, Rab. Dinnae start. She said no, and I wus desperate. I like her, though. She'll be OK."

"But she'll not be earning will she, Sonny? We'll get another girl for her slots, but this has got to stop."

"Fuck off, Rab. You cannae speak to me like that. Anyways, get another girl. I'll have Katrina to myself."

"All right, Sonny. Here's what I *can* do. I can cut your balls off and stuff them down your throat. If you want to keep Katrina for yourself, I agree she's not working here. It's too disruptive."

Sonny pulled a cut-throat razor out of his inside pocket, and in a flash, Rab opened his flick knife. They stared hard at one another, and Sonny laughed:

"Better that I jump on you and crush you to death, grasshopper. OK, I give in. I'll no' hit her again. Just don't tell Dad."

The knives were put away.

Rab went back into the reception area and saw there was a pile of incoming mail on the counter beside Carla's bookings diary. While Carla was distracted, Rab placed the envelope addressed to her among the morning post. He sat down beside her and pointed to the bundle of envelopes.

"Is that the mail, Carla? We're expecting a letter from the lawyers."

Carla looked though the letters.

"No, nothing," she said. "But here's something for me! It's no' stamped, so it must have been delivered. More porny suggestions or someone trying to save my soul?"

She opened the envelope and put James Eastman's business card on the counter. She whistled between the space in her front teeth.

"Well, well. Some tart up from London's snared a hot-shot local lawyer. She thinks we could make some money out of him. What should I do with this, Rab?"

She handed him the letter. He read it, looked up and said, "Well, see what Sonny says."

Carla shouted through to the back room, "Hey, boss man! Look at this"

Sonny waddled through and read the letter. Carla handed him the card. He looked questioningly at Rab and spread his arms.

"So?"

"Maybe you should tell your Dad about this, Sonny. Maybe this guy could be useful, if we put pressure on him. From the letter, we could honey trap him easily."

Sonny brightened, "Good idea, Rab. Dad'll be impressed. But why tell us about it?"

"Well, she's from London. Maybe it's too small beer for the London boys. Anyway, your Dad wants you to come up with new ideas. We better head up there soon. Time for morning parade! But I'll do a few checks on Eastman first. See you there in about an hour, Sonny"

6

McBain had held sway as the acknowledged crime lord in the north-east of Glasgow for more than thirty years. He held daily meetings to keep his closest associates on their toes, but in reality, there was never much to discuss. There were two sides of the "business", one of which had grown out of the other. The traditional prostitution, illegal gambling, drug dealing and money sharking generated a huge amount of cash. The organisation could recycle only a small percentage of this into the mainstream banking system, and the operations quickly built up a mountain of cash which McBain lodged in deposit boxes at a bank. Every few months he had to switch that cash with more recent cash to avoid being left with too many old notes in the bank deposits. By the 1980s the cash problem was getting out of control, but luckily, when he was on a holiday in the Algarve, he'd met a London drug baron. He was the one who had first given McBain the idea of legitimising cash through his own businesses, and he'd emphasised that it was a good idea to use respected professionals as advisers. So McBain had arranged an appointment with one of the larger chartered accountancy firms in Glasgow, and asked them to come up with a business plan. When asked about how the business was to be financed, he said he'd inherited a large legacy from a distant cousin. There were virtually no rules against money laundering at the time, so no further questions were asked.

The business plan duly appeared, together with a recommendation to use a large Glasgow legal firm and a particular bank. McBain could see how this trio were manoeuvring to cost him a huge amount in fees, but he wasn't concerned. Every new introduction, every new respected adviser added legitimacy to the operation. The lawyers set up two companies for McBain, a trading company to own pubs and betting shops, and a property investment company to specialise in joint property ventures with legitimate builders and property developers. Thus Westberry Trading Limited and Westberry Properties Limited were formed.

And when the businesses got going, how profitable they were! That was due in part to feeding cash into them from the illegal operations, but they were also successful in their own right. That led to introductions to new contacts, and the development of new skills in the McBain business, such as a company providing security services. McBain was soon being courted by local councillors who were looking for backhanders in return for giving him the nod about lucrative development opportunities.

7

Rab and Sonny were shown into McBain's office by the housekeeper. Rab saw that Joe McCarthy, known as "Mr Muscle" – the other full-time enforcer of the McBain empire – was already there.

The morning meetings first addressed problems in what McBain described as the "off balance sheet" activities. Rab and Joe were in charge of the moneylending, but such were their reputations that few dared to fall behind with payments. Sonny dealt with the saunas and the drug sellers, while McBain himself handled the buying of the drugs and monitoring the betting shops. This was generally the shorter part of the meeting.

Westberry Trading Limited and Westberry Properties Limited took up an increasing amount of time, and Rab knew that McBain was concerned that Sonny wasn't getting to grips with the complications involved in running the companies. Joe took little part in these discussions, except if a local councillor needed to be bribed or leant upon, but Rab was contributing a lot to the expansion of the legitimate operations.

Today there was an extra subject for discussion. The borders of criminal influence in Glasgow were well defined and broadly respected, and McBain ruled the north-east. However, Westberry Properties Limited had been a partner in a joint property development in Ibrox, south of the river, and Westberry Trading Limited was providing the security. There had been an incident at the development when valuable brass fittings had been stolen, and it was thought that those responsible had been from a criminal gang which controlled much of the south-west of the city, headed by the Malik brothers.

"Why did they do it, Dad?" said Sonny. "The brass was only worth a few grand."

"I think they were making a point. Maybe we should avoid getting involved in anything south of the river. For a while, anyway," replied his father.

"Fucking Pakis!" Joe McCarthy shouted. "Boss, we better teach them a lesson – this might be the start of something."

McBain had thought about retaliating, but Rab had persuaded him to be more subtle.

"No, Joe. I've asked the lawyers to contact Malik and see if he'd be interested in being part of the Canal Regeneration Partnership up here. He'll get it that we weren't muscling in on Ibrox."

"And," said Rab, "less of the 'fucking Pakis', Joe. You don't say that when you're looking doe-eyed at Zahra."

McCarthy blushed, something none of the others had ever seen, or expected to see.

There was an embarrassed silence. Sonny looked over to Rab, who gave a slight nod.

"Aw, Dad – we've got a chance to blackmail a lawyer!" Sonny looked at his father for approval.

"What lawyer?"

"Some guy called Easton or Eastman. Carla got a tip about him from some London tart."

"It's Eastman," said Rab, producing the business card. "Have you still got the letter, Sonny?"

Sonny handed it to his father. It detailed all Eastman's fantasies. "Naughty boy!" exclaimed McBain, looking up after he'd read it. Rab handed him the business card.

"James Eastman, Partner, McTavish Legal. Accredited specialist in multinational corporate finance."

"What the fuck's that?" asked Sonny. His father ignored him. Rab had his pitch ready.

"This is the type of guy businessmen use for things like taking over foreign companies or preparing contracts. He'll also have people who can save tax for you. Let's say you've got a sports shop. You can get training shoes in Thailand for a quid each. You expect to sell them for fifty quid here, but you'd pay tax on the forty-nine quid profit. What this guy can do, apparently, is set up an offshore company for you which buys the trainers from Thailand for a quid but sells them to your company here for forty-one quid, so that when you sell them for fifty, you pay tax on only nine quid. The forty quid profit rolls up tax-free in the offshore company."

McBain looked straight at Rab. "Quite a speech, Rab. Very impressive. How do you know all this?"

"I checked on his firm's website after Sonny got the letter and told me about it, and then made a few calls. I don't think it's as easy as I've said, boss, but you get the drift. It's on the edge, apparently. He's very creative, according to his website. He could be helpful to us."

"We don't sell trainers, Rab," Sonny piped up.

"He knows the offshore scene," Rab said. "There could be other uses ..."

"Remember Gibraltar?" McBain said. Joe and Rab nodded.

"Well, this can't be a set-up," he went on. "Or could it? No, there's no hook. We're not offered anything."

Sonny looked baffled.

"I think I need to meet this Mr Eastman for a little chat." McBain stood up. The morning meeting was over.

★ ★ ★

Meanwhile, as all this was unfolding, James Eastman was sitting in the First Class section of the train from Edinburgh to Glasgow and thinking over the events of the previous evening. A chance meeting with a beautiful young businesswoman and the prospect of extraordinarily exciting times ahead. He looked at the details on the card and wondered about ringing the mobile number. He thought better of it, and hid the card at the back of his wallet. By the time the train reached Falkirk he was beginning to worry. What exactly had he said to Jenny? He'd been laying it on a bit thick. Maybe it wasn't such a good idea to see her again. Things could get a bit awkward, especially at the firm, not to mention with the family. By the time he got off the train at Queen Street station he'd decided to forget all about Jenny, and was hoping she'd forget about him, and he'd never see or hear from her again. He bitterly regretted giving her his card.

God, how he now wished he hadn't bothered going to the exhibition. As he walked past the place they had parted company the night before, he thought about Jenny's card lurking in the zipped section of his wallet. A trip to London could easily be arranged. These parties she'd spoken about sounded really exciting. And the 17-year-old cousin! His thoughts were all over the place. He also had a massive hangover.

He took the lift to the seventh floor. Eleven o'clock already and nothing on the time sheet! How it controlled your life now. The firm was at the cutting edge of technology, with smart pens used to log time on bar-coded files. Eastman always wanted to be near the top of the league for time recorded as well as fees charged to clients. He continually berated his staff to log more and more time on files.

His secretary, Natasha, was fielding calls as he arrived in his office. She was petite but had a figure to die for. Eastman had been tempted, and there had been some drunken fumblings on departmental nights out, but he'd managed to resist getting involved.

"Just the priorities," he said to her when she came into his room. "Give anything routine to Paul."

"I'm fine, Jimmy boy, how are you?" Natasha countered.

Eastman groaned; this kind of banter was one of the disadvantages of having been a trainee in the firm and worked your way through the ranks. Some staff never forgot your first day. The Senior Partner had greeted him as Jimmy that day and no one would let him forget it.

"OK, OK, sorry," he said. "Protect me today. Please?"

Natasha nodded. "You've got Jonathan Black at 3.30. It's a new acquisition by the Guernsey consortium. And Kenny Richards has been pressing for the new Articles of Association."

"Fine. Ask Paul to come in."

Eastman spent the next three hours in discussion with his assistant Paul Longmuir, reviewing his draft of the new Articles and shareholders' agreements for Kenny Richards. For a working lunch, they had sandwiches brought in from Prêt a Manger, and they were just finishing off the redraft when Natasha interrupted them.

"Sorry, James, I know you said no calls. There's a strange man on the phone who insists on speaking to you now. There's something about the way he talks. He won't give me his name. He says I've to say 'Hello from Jenny's Dad'. He's really quite abrupt."

Eastman's stomach lurched, and he turned away to look out of the window.

"This is personal, guys; I'm trying to help a chum at the rugby club." He turned back and motioned Paul and Natasha to leave. He lifted the receiver gingerly.

"Hello, I'm not sure if you've got the right person …"

"You've got the right person, son. This is Alex McBain. Jenny was singing your praises and I need a lawyer. La Solera, half past twelve tomorrow."

Eastman suddenly clicked. "Is this the Alex McBain of the Westberry Group?"

"Indeed, son. But don't worry about Jenny. She's not really my daughter. Just as well for you, mind. What you suggested doing to her."

Eastman blushed and stuttered, "I ... I don't really understand ..."

"Cut the crap, you understand well enough," McBain interrupted. "You may be helpful to us, and bearing in mind what we know, you should be keen to help."

"That's blackmail, Mr McBain. I could go to the police."

McBain harrumphed, "No one's asking you for anything. I just want a chat. OK?"

"I can't see you. I'm due to be in the Channel Islands tomorrow."

Silence. Eastman could almost hear McBain thinking.

"Really? That's quite interesting. OK. Is Monday free, same time and place?"

"I'm not sure I can help you, Mr McBain. You already have a firm of solicitors acting for you. The Law Society is coming down hard on poaching clients from other firms."

This wasn't strictly true, but it was a useful way of getting out of acting for clients you'd rather do without.

"Look, son. I don't want to have to spell it out. Just agree to meet for a chat and I'll return the letter Jenny sent me. If we can't see there's anything you can help us with, we'll shake hands and you can put it all behind you."

Eastman felt a palpable relief. If McBain was as good as his word, what had he to lose?

"OK. La Solera, Monday at half twelve."

8

Eastman eased himself into the window seat for the short flight from Heathrow to Jersey. He'd slept badly and had finally got up at 4.30 and headed off for the first flight from Edinburgh to London. He was still a bit disquieted by the strange incidents of the last few days.

The previous evening he'd got back from work early, for him, at around 8 p.m. His detached Victorian home stood solidly looking onto the Botanic Gardens, just as upper middle class as you could get. The electric gates had swished closed behind him, and he'd then joined the chaos of family life with three teenagers and an unhappy wife. Anne had given up a career in accountancy to be a model mother, but the role didn't suit her. She was not inclined to return to professional life, however, nor would she start a consultancy with just a few clients, which was what Eastman thought she should now do. So they lived a mutually unsatisfied existence, bickering about trivia when they were alone, but maintaining the appearance of happiness for the sake of the children.

Some Latin and maths homework was causing problems for John, his younger son, so Eastman helped with that. His older boy, David, a keen rugby player, had been selected for the school "A" team at flanker on Saturday, so he was on a high, but Suzanne, his daughter, the eldest of the children, pointedly ignored him. She'd clearly sussed that all was not well between her parents, and she was her mother's firm ally. In fact, it seemed to Eastman that she was a bit too well informed about her parents' marital difficulties. She had sufficient Highers to go to university, but was wasting her time and his money with a Sixth Year at school to be followed by a gap year. As usual the family had all already eaten, so he grabbed a quick snack and retired to his study. He slipped off to bed at eleven. His wife had spoken only to detail problems with the cleaning lady and the gardener.

This family thing was a bit of a lost cause, but he was on the treadmill and was determined to stay with it until his younger son had completed his education. Ten more years – a life sentence. And then what?

While in transit at Heathrow, he'd phoned an old colleague who had left the life of a corporate lawyer to specialise in criminal legal aid work. Niall Welsh worked mostly in Glasgow Sheriff Court, though as a solicitor-advocate, he could also appear in the High Court. Niall had given him the lowdown on the McBain empire.

"Well, Jimmy boy, it's like Shakespeare, so it is. In the early 1970s, McBain took over the north-east of Glasgow from Gerry McNab – a free transfer, if you like. Why, do I hear you ask? Because McBain had married McNab's daughter Irene. Sonny's their only child. A few years ago there was a helluva lot of speculation that McBain was retiring to Spain after he bought a villa in Marbella, but in fact only Irene left Glasgow. Apparently there was a big family bust-up following the deaths of those kids in the fire in Dennistoun, if you remember. The McBains were blamed for that, but – surprise, surprise – there were no witnesses. Sonny's off the wall – unstable's an understatement, maybe psychopathic. McBain's had problems keeping him in check."

"OK, Niall, why's it like Shakespeare?"

"Wake up. Father and son conflicts, suggestions of treachery, madness in the family. It's all there."

"Treachery?"

"Ah, yes. McBain's nearly sixty and there are rumours about his health. In the past he was often 'on the street' but in the last year or so he's hardly ever been seen except at Parkhead, watching Celtic. The gossip is that Sonny doesn't have the brains to take over the 'firm', and that Usman Malik – you know, the guy who runs the big cash and carry on the south side – has his eye on McBain's loan book and all the rest. The cash and carry's a front, of course. He's got a lot going on right out to Pollok. So he's kind of hovering. But on the inside you've got Rab Donald, an ex-para who's one of McBain's minders. More and more, McBain relies on Rab, and he's sharp as a tack. There's the potential traitor. He might even have done a deal with Malik."

"Sounds more like Cluedo than Shakespeare, but then I didn't go to Glasgow Academy. What could McBain want with me, do you think?"

"Maybe to help with the legitimate side of his business? It's ultra respectable now, and McBain's a regular contributor to good causes. Maybe he wants to set up the McBain Charitable Foundation. That's a joke, by the way. My case is being called, James. Mind how you go."

On the flight Eastman found it difficult to concentrate on the work he was to do in Jersey. He was preoccupied trying to analyse what Niall had told him. He took a taxi from Jersey Airport to Royal Square. He always enjoyed this taxi trip, as the drive along the bay past Elizabeth Castle always seemed to be in brilliant sunshine, the sea glittering above a 1950s picture-postcard beach scene. He walked up Fort Road to the offices of Lebens, Advocates. He had a number of pressing client issues to discuss with Robert Lebens, all of which would need to be dealt with in the next two hours, as for Robert, 1.30 p.m. represented the end of the Jersey business day. Robert had a daily reservation at La Rustica, where there was a magnificent wine cellar, and the routine when Eastman was on the island was a leisurely lunch followed by a quick dash to the airport so he could get the last flight back to Edinburgh via Heathrow.

The Jersey set-up was quite unique. Being a tax haven, it was the headquarters of hundreds of thousands of trusts and companies, all administered by a small coterie of banks, accountants and advocates, which is what Jersey lawyers were called. In reality, in many cases these administrators acted in name only, as the real decisions were made elsewhere. The Inland Revenue in the United Kingdom had tried to tax the British residents behind some of them, but with only limited success.

There was, of course, a sinister side to the tax haven, as it was used by many seeking to hide resources or launder cash. But for Robert and his colleagues, so long as they carried out the required diligence, they were free to accept appointments as directors and trustees, and enjoy the fees they could charge. And that was at least £2,000 each year as a fee just for acting as a trustee, so if you managed a thousand trusts, that gave you an annual income of £2m before you even reached the office! He was definitely in the wrong jurisdiction, thought Eastman.

After dealing with business matters, Eastman and Lebens walked down to La Rustica in the main square, and over lunch they caught up with developments on how co-operation between the United Kingdom tax authorities and Jersey was progressing.

"It's not the job it was, old boy," said Robert. "I'm just thankful I'm not starting out. Compliance officers, form filling. In a few years we'll just be another state of the United States. Nowadays we rely on clients from the Levant and the colonies. No class, old boy. I'm looking for an out. Any ideas? I fancy the south of France."

Eastman thought Robert was more British than he was. He had always talked like this, from their first dealings with each other in the 1980s. He was sure Robert would never retire, and he would never leave Jersey. He loved being a large fish in a very small pond. James turned the conversation back to clients.

"I've had an approach from a new client. It just might mean some offshore work, as he's nearing retirement. It's unusual, because he's alleged to have, shall we say, underworld connections."

"Not your usual scene, old boy. But needs must. The people one has to deal with! But maybe there's an angle for your firm – and for us?"

"Who knows? I'm seeing him next week. If anything comes of it, I'll be in touch."

As Eastman was getting into the taxi they shook hands.

"May we live in interesting times, James. Who said that? Was it Mao?"

"I don't think so, Robert, and I wish you hadn't said it. That's the Chinese curse. Bobby Kennedy used it and look what happened to him!"

"Too melodramatic, James. See you soon, old boy."

On the journey back to Edinburgh Eastman's mind was buzzing with speculation. He felt sure that McBain would want to access his expertise. This was perhaps a way he could break out of his dull existence. He had never been involved in anything even on the fringes of illegal; he was fastidious about reporting even minor misdemeanours of his clients to the authorities. Maybe it was time for him to start thinking about himself.

9

La Solera, the restaurant McBain had specified for the meeting with Eastman, was a two-minute walk from Eastman's office. He knew it well as he often lunched there with clients, and the firm used it for departmental parties. Today, though, it felt different. He was hardly in the door when the head waiter Paolo scuttled over to greet him, the bling he wore jingle jangling as he approached. Eastman had never had attention like this.

"Welcome, Mr Eastman. Such a pleasure to see you again. Mr McBain is already at his table."

Paolo guided Eastman round past the small dance floor to an alcove normally used only in the evenings. A table had been set there apart from the other diners. McBain stood up. Over six feet tall, short grey hair, thin scar line, no glasses. Very expensive navy suit, white shirt, red tie, Paul Smith boots. Eastman realised he'd seen McBain lunching alone in this restaurant many times before. They shook hands.

"Paulo says you eat here quite a lot," said McBain, "so I've ordered what you usually have. And sparkling water, since we're here at lunchtime. You take a drink, though."

Eastman was annoyed at Paolo's indiscretion, but he'd learned enough about McBain's business interests and methods over the last few days to realise that generally, what Mr McBain asked for, he got. His pride was hurt, however, by the fact that McBain had evidently not noticed him lunching in La Solera previously.

"How can I help you, Mr McBain?" he asked. "I know you

use Richardson Legal for your commercial work. Has something gone wrong? I presume all this attention isn't about the mysterious Jenny, whoever she may be. I've tried ringing her, by the way. Of course, the number was unobtainable."

"Forget all about Jenny, Mr Eastman. She was a phantom. Simply a brief diversion for you, I hope, though if you really wanted to meet her again, I'm sure it could be arranged. We're here to discuss serious matters. Here's her letter, by the way, and your business card."

McBain handed over an envelope. Eastman simply put it in his inside pocket.

"Something for you to reflect on, before you consign it to the shredder, I expect. And no, we haven't kept a copy to send to the police if something unexpected happens to me, however unlikely that may be."

McBain smiled and gave Eastman a long disconcerting stare. Eastman imagined that most people found something interesting to look at on the ground in these circumstances, but he just stared back, his gaze not wavering.

"As I said, James, forget about all that Jenny stuff," McBain said quietly, holding the look. "I don't want anything to do with your inclinations, though I'm sure my son could provide any service you want, shall we say, from our wide variety of employees. No, it's your legal skills I may need. I need to diversify. No, that's not the right word. My bankers say I need to put my legal business out to tender. Now, would you be a bidder? Maybe I can get you sole bidder status. I know you could use the billings. Feeling the pressure, eh? What do you say, Jimmy boy?"

Eastman was taken aback. McBain must really have dug deep to get this level of detail about him. Fortunately, the silence was broken by Paulo arriving with their starters.

Until the arrival of coffee, Eastman was happy to josh

Glasgow talk with McBain. Football, local councillors, the Scottish Parliament, the idleness of the press. Then Paulo brought the double espressos and reached new depths of obsequiousness after asking if McBain was happy with the table. McBain said he would rather not be so close to a couple who were actually about five yards away. Paulo immediately moved them to another table, shrugging off their protestations.

Eastman sipped his coffee. McBain sat back, and again looked steadily at him.

"I think we could have areas of mutual interest and benefit. My property company joint ventures are going well, but maybe we're paying too much tax. That's where you can help, I believe. We've a new scheme about to start. I'll can Richardson, and let you do the acquisition and the development agreement. Silversmiths are acting for the funders."

Eastman felt a frisson of excitement, for this could be meaty business. He'd the firm's Partner Appraisal Scheme to think about. It was a bit like being a banker. The Board had power to make bonus payments to partners, based on fees and new business introduced. The Eastman family expenditure was such that he really needed a chunky payment from the bonus pool every year.

"How much is involved?" asked Eastman.

"Well, Rab's got the detailed figures. That's him on the left, over there." McBain pointed to two men sitting at a table on the other side of the dance floor. "He'll come to see you. I know what you need to do, so you don't need to explain. Set up the joint venture, buy the property, borrow the money, get the planning, do the contract for the rebuild, lease it out, then sell it on to an insurance company. Repay the funders, pay the tax, and pocket the profit. A real five-card trick. That's if it's an office. Different here, a bare-site development. Richardson quoted £300,000. We should get three to four mil. All these documents, all these departments with their noses in the trough. You'll be a star."

McBain sat back, looking pleased with himself. Eastman tried to remain calm.

"Since you're a new client, we'd do it on a time basis, but capped at £275,000. That's if Richardson's quote is kosher," he said.

"Don't insult me, James. We're not conning you. Full disclosure."

Silence. Eastman decided to be crafty, and pretend he hadn't checked McBain out. "Who's Rab? Your son?"

McBain grimaced.

"No, Rab's my associate. This is beyond Sonny. When ..."

Eastman was aware that McBain was unsure how to continue, so he took control. He pulled out his BlackBerry, and looked up, "Three on Wednesday, OK?"

McBain regained his composure.

"You look a bit flushed, Jimmy boy. This could be great. But mind; keep your hands off the hired help. We don't want any scandal. Our info is that that secretary of yours is married, as I think you well know."

Eastman felt those grey eyes boring through him again, but he managed to hold the gaze, keeping the thought of that moment of weakness when Sonny had been mentioned. Something he would file away for future use.

They shook hands and Eastman went for his coat. Paulo rushed across and saw Eastman to the door, wishing him a good day and looking forward to seeing him again. Quite unprecedented. Eastman enjoyed the attention, but as he turned to the main door, he noticed the two associates McBain had pointed out were looking him over, as if they were sizing him up, and then he saw Paulo whisper something to the female cashier. Was it his imagination, or was Paulo looking at him differently now? Was that look more respectful, or less?

10

Two days later, Eastman got another unusual phone call. A Detective Inspector Allensen from Strathclyde CID would like his assistance in relation to a fraud perpetrated by a solicitor in Cambuslang. The lawyer had embezzled money from his own father's estate by using a network of offshore companies, and his two brothers – well-known establishment figures – had sufficient influence to persuade the Procurator Fiscal to mount a high-level investigation. Apparently, he'd been recommended to the fiscal to give expert advice, and Eastman's senior partner had agreed that he could spare a couple of hours of his time.

With some reluctance, Eastman had agreed to call in to see Allensen that evening. He turned up at Shettleston Police Station at around 5.30, hoping to make his escape and get on the road to Edinburgh by about seven. The desk sergeant showed him upstairs to the CID area and sat him at a clear desk.

Allensen appeared carrying a red folder, introduced himself, and sat down opposite him. Eastman thought Allensen looked nothing like a policeman, and was racking his brains to work out who he looked like. Suddenly it came to him. Cary Grant! Not exactly tall, but slim, craggy features, greying hair, but with a downbeat dress sense, somewhat crumpled.

"I want you to read something," Allensen started, "and I hope it will convince you to help me."

Eastman looked quizzical.

"Delighted to do what I can, of course, but criminal work

is not my usual line of business. I know nothing about fraud, but if I can be of assistance in unravelling the corporate structure the guy apparently used …"

"You've been associating with a known criminal, Mr Eastman. I need to fill you in about your new client. I take it that's why you've been seen with Alex McBain."

Eastman was suddenly worried that this might be about his involvement with Jenny. Lawyers were gaining a reputation for being caught up in sex scandals. He simply stared at Allensen. After a pause, he replied:

"You know I'm bound by client confidentiality, Detective Inspector. Mr McBain isn't even a personal client, anyway. We may be starting to do some work for the Westberry group of companies. A very respectable business, award winning in fact. Honoured by this great city of ours. So I think I can go now, unless …"

"Don't bother me with your legal niceties. Just listen and learn about what you may be getting into. It won't take long." Allensen looked relaxed.

There was some raucous laughter from the far end of the floor. Eastman thought it was pretty shabby that Allensen had to conduct this meeting in a sectioned-off area of an open-plan office, and he told him so.

Allensen simply laid the red file on the desk.

"Four years ago, early in 2003, the Inland Revenue and Customs decided to mount a joint operation with the Serious Crime Squad. This involved establishing a business in Gibraltar, to be called Rock Transfers. The idea was to offer cheap foreign exchange transfers in the hope of gathering information about criminals and other people evading tax, as they might use the service for money laundering. It was to be a sting operation. Very – how would an educated chap like you put it? – very innovative, very ingenious."

"Very illegal, it sounds to me," Eastman smiled.

"Whatever. The Treasury were doubtful about underwriting the costs involved, but when the joint operation produced figures, they found that Rock Transfers would be profitable even at the lower charges necessary to attract business. Bankers, eh, what can you do? Anyway, banking staff were recruited to run the business, under the managing director who was a high-ranking Serious Crime Squad officer, a graduate in accountancy, who had been fast-tracked through the police system. His name was Kevin Davidson. He contacted me and asked if we had a suitable target in Glasgow. We thought at the time that McBain still had a stash of cash he'd accumulated over the early years before he set up what you call his respectable companies. We decided to use Rock Transfers to try to flush out the cash. It's millions, by the way. Davidson advertised a two-day seminar to take place in Gibraltar on the subject of 'Investing in Properties in Spain and Portugal', and it was arranged that Rock Transfers would provide Davidson as a speaker on the topic of financing from the United Kingdom. Information was then leaked to McBain via one of our undercover boys here in Glasgow that Rock Transfers might be able to help with laundering of cash from the United Kingdom."

"More illegal steps, I think. You would never have got a conviction, you know."

"Will you stop interrupting me? Anyway, we were lucky. Apparently McBain had been thinking about buying more property in Spain. He took the bait, and travelled to Gibraltar for the seminar with two of his minders."

Eastman involuntarily said "Ah" and immediately regretted it. He wondered if he'd already seen the whole Gibraltar party in La Solera.

Allensen simply continued.

"Davidson's idea was to try to interest McBain in having a

43

few drinks after the first day of the seminar, just to make a connection and see if a relationship could develop. McBain and his colleagues checked into the Grand Vista Hotel the day before the seminar. It really was a cock-up from the start. The joint operation had known exactly when McBain and his minders were travelling to Gibraltar on the Wednesday, the day before the seminar, but cutbacks had been imposed, and accommodation for the London-based four-man observation team was sanctioned only from the first day of the seminar, the Thursday. As I said, the thought had been that as the approach to McBain would be made at the end of the Thursday, no useful information would be gleaned by the observation team on the Wednesday. Davidson was annoyed, as he had wanted McBain under observation from when he arrived in Gibraltar, as McBain could be using the opportunity to make other contacts. He had only one subordinate trained in observation, a detective constable called Saunders. So Davidson decided to task Saunders with keeping an eye on McBain on Wednesday, on the basis that the four-man team would take over the next day."

"Fascinating this may be, Detective Inspector, but is there a point to this?"

"It does get more interesting. What happened next we know from the records of Saunders's calls to the Rock Transfers office. Davidson wasn't in the office – I know that's incredible, but he was at the seminar venue rehearsing – so his secretary was in charge. McBain left the hotel and apparently headed off towards the centre of town with his two associates. Then he stopped outside the Catholic Cathedral and there was some sort of argument with his bodyguards. What that was about, we've no idea. Maybe the minders wanted to sightsee, or go to the pub. Anyway, all three went into the cathedral."

"I can almost picture the scene. Can I leave now?"

Allensen continued:

"Well, all we know is that DC Saunders must also have decided to go into the cathedral. He wasn't trained for any cloak-and-dagger stuff, he was only supposed to report where McBain went. He had a directional mike, however, and it was linked to the office. So while we don't know exactly what happened inside the cathedral, some stuff was recorded on tape. I'll let you read the transcript. We managed to tidy it up – it's pretty accurate, we think."

Allensen handed Eastman the red folder and opened it at a bright yellow Post-it, pointing to where Eastman should start reading.

You probably wouldn't like me very much, Father. You might have seen me in the executive lounge at the airport. I see a lot of you priests in there. How does that work, by the way? Anyway, I'm the smart guy in his fifties, slim, fit, with a couple of younger colleagues. Something's odd, though. We're all looking at newspapers, but they're not reading. They have another job. They're watching, looking, gauging all the time. If you look at me, they clock you, and they start calculating the risk.

I've heard at second hand that although Rab and Joe are my minders, well able to turn their hands to anything to protect me, I'm the one who exudes the menace. I don't really understand that.

Oh, Father, you can't see me through the grille. I should have mentioned one reason why you might look at me and feel a bit threatened. I don't like to talk about it, but I do have a scar running from the top of my left ear to my chin. I try to convince myself that it's not there, after four operations over the last thirty years, but in bright lighting there's a faint line. Every time I cross the Kingston Bridge I have the satisfaction of knowing I'm running over the Billy Boy who caught me unawares all those years ago; running over what's left of him, that is, buried deep. Mea culpa, as you people say, Father. Yes, I remember a bit of Latin.

I grew up in Springburn. What a dump! Still is. My Dad was a locomotive engineer at the British Rail works, and that's how I got my nickname "Loco". Well, one of the reasons. I was a bit wild as a boy, though I did well at school. I passed the "Qualie" and went to senior secondary school. I was good at figures. These came in useful later.

But I began running with a local gang, and girls became an increasing attraction. Then the gangs were involved in turf wars involving territory worth nothing.

How did I get the scar? I was sixteen at the time. I guess you won't know too much about what's now called the religious divide in the west of Scotland. You never get away from it; you're either a Tim or a Proddy. I'm a Tim, and I should have kept to the rules. There was more than enough talent at St Peter's High, but this girl from Dennistoun Academy was a real stunner. I was next to her in the queue at the chippy, and we hit it off, so we agreed to meet at a cafe that Sunday evening. That's what you did in those days, you know. Oh, sorry, maybe you wouldn't know.

Anyway, it was November. Dark by seven. She didn't show up. I trudged along Saracen Street, eyes down onto the slushy pavement, hiding my shame at being stood up. I never even saw them. Three guys rushed out from the close mouth, one grabbing each arm from behind, the third swinging round to face me, wide-eyed, screaming – "Here's a message, keep away from our lassies" – as the open razor carved into the left of my face. Shock, no pain, fall to ground, six kicks, blood pooling all around me.

He hadn't even worn a scarf. I didn't know him at the time, but as I lay there I started working out how to find the razor boy and his mates.

Anyway, after that, I soon got noticed by the local big man Gerry McNab, especially when I got over friendly with his daughter Irene. I was doing a bit of minor thieving; she was in fourth year at school. I'd packed in school at sixteen. Gerry gave me a start in one of his betting shops. I knew about figures, and I was a quick learner. Accumulators, patents, trixies, all the variations, laying off, all that stuff. By the time I was eighteen, Gerry trusted me to run the shop at Queen's Cross, up near Thistle's ground.

Anyway, Father, I've been troubled lately. That's why I'm here. I *have this awful feeling of impending doom. I need some reassurance. I'm worried about my son. Family. What is it they say? Hostages to fortune. Look, maybe I'll come back. Not that I'll tell you everything. You always need to keep something back.*

TRANSMISSION ENDS

Eastman looked up at Allensen, and handed back the folder.

"That's all we know," Allensen said. "No one at Rock Transfers was listening to Saunders. When Davidson got back from the seminar rehearsal, he listened to Saunders's messages and the transmission, contacted the local police and went to the cathedral. Davidson told the bishop some made-up story that an eccentric cousin had gone missing, and had last been seen going into the cathedral. All the bishop could tell them was that one of the priests had reported a confession being interrupted. All the priest would say was that he thought someone had whispered the words "Problemo, Loco." We presume that was one of the minders, McCarthy or Donald."

Eastman now had no thoughts of leaving.

"I presume that Mr Saunders is no longer available to fill in the blanks."

"You're quick on the uptake, Mr Eastman. We'll come to the fate of DC Saunders in a bit. Davidson tried to contact him, of course. Vanished. Davidson went to the Grand Vista, but McBain and the others had checked out. When the team from London arrived the next day, they carried out an investigation and found that a Robert Donald had hired a car in Algeciras, driven it to Gibraltar and then had passed back through the border with three men in the car. The passports were all British but the names hadn't been recorded. The car was returned at Malaga Airport, and passengers McBain, Donald and McCarthy had flown to Heathrow three days later."

"So, what happened to Saunders?" Eastman asked.

"They didn't kill him, I don't know why. They've murdered people for a lot less. No, he turned up a week later at the Consulate in Malaga and handed in his resignation. We tried to speak to him, even used his family to put pressure on him, but he refused. He forfeited his salary and pension rights, the lot. But he wasn't worried about money – still isn't, as he works for McBain's ex-wife in Malaga now."

Eastman looked pensive.

"So, he's been paid to keep his mouth shut. But why? He didn't know anything of value, did he? Or maybe he did, still does, and it wasn't recorded. Or maybe he doesn't even know he knows. Yes, that could be it. As I've said, fascinating, but it's got nothing to do with me."

"Wait, look," Allensen said. "You're the very man we've been waiting for. After the Gibraltar fiasco McBain is suspicious of anyone new he comes into contact with, but he's approached you, for some reason."

Eastman looked at his shoes, remembering what had preceded McBain's approach. Allensen went on:

"Not even McBain will think we put you up to anything. Why don't you get involved with him personally? If you learn anything, pass it on to us. We're desperate to …"

Eastman thought Allensen might press him as to the reason why McBain had approached him, but thankfully Allensen didn't seem interested in that.

"Let me stop you right there, Inspector. I value my health. Thanks for your time. This is obviously one scary family." Eastman now turned to leave.

"I appreciate that," Allensen countered. "This will have to be done in such a way that McBain thinks you're after something for yourself. Let me tell you how we can do this."

Eastman was suddenly interested. He sat down, and listened

carefully. As Allensen detailed his plan to entrap McBain, Eastman thought how neatly it fitted with a scenario he himself had been developing in his own mind, ever since the meeting at La Solera.

11

Erik Allensen watched Eastman get into his Audi and drive off along the Shettleston Road, past the pubs and social clubs all with their drab concrete walls, steel doors and barred windows. The fact that they were near a police station wouldn't protect them from thieves. Even this early in the evening, Allensen could see there was already a bit of a commotion outside the Green Giant, a huge drinking club for Glasgow Celtic's football supporters, and two uniforms were intervening.

Allensen had been irritated when Eastman had teased him about his "room" at the station, saying it was more in the nature of a cubby hole than an office. He'd explained that the Division had been forced by the perennial cutbacks to squeeze as many bodies as possible into open-plan offices, but he'd managed to position some filing cabinets in such a way that he got some privacy for thinking time. Unfortunately, the cabinets couldn't block out the pungent aromas of the seemingly endless meals and snacks consumed by his colleagues at their desks throughout the working day.

The wind gusted against the window, driving rain against it out of the gloom of the early evening. Allensen decided to head for home. As he was getting into his car, he looked back at the building from the car park. The harsh strip lighting and the lack of blinds made the station look almost inviting in the surrounding greyness. Allensen knew better. Looking at his reflection in the rear-view mirror,

Allensen knew this was not how he wanted to spend the next ten years.

As he drove to his flat in Hyndland, in the west of the city, he thought about what had motivated him to join the force. He often reflected on how different it could have been, if he'd been able to follow a career path more like that of his brother Markus. In some respects he'd been unlucky. Markus had had all the breaks. He was six years older, and had passed the Local Authority qualifying exam when he was eleven. That meant he moved from Wishaw Primary to Hamilton Academy, a selective school which took the top pupils from all over Lanarkshire. It had been an ideal educational establishment, staffed by highly motivated teachers, and Markus still went on and on about how he'd been inspired to achieve. Unfortunately, by the time Erik was due to move up from Wishaw Primary, the Qualie had been abolished and comprehensive education had been introduced. He simply moved up to the local secondary school, where a bunch of time-serving teachers failed miserably to get him to achieve his potential. He was a bright pupil, but in the absence of competition and inspiration, he simply coasted along. He'd lasted a year studying architecture at Strathclyde University before dropping out, in sharp contrast to Markus who got a First Class Honours degree from Edinburgh University, and was now a successful entrepreneur in London.

After being chucked out of university, Erik Allensen had drifted into the police. Why? He still wasn't clear, although there had been an incident when he was a teenager which a psychologist might think had been a factor. His father, who worked for the Post Office as a manager, was a strict disciplinarian, and had insisted that Erik be back home every night by 10.30 p.m. One Saturday evening, when Erik was sixteen, he'd been out with his friends and had paired off with a girl from school. Her grandmother was away on holiday, she had the keys to her grandmother's cottage, and she suggested they go back there. When Erik said he had to be back home before curfew, she goaded him to the extent that he agreed to sneak back out of the house via Markus's old bedroom and meet up with her after his parents had gone to bed at their usual time of eleven o'clock precisely. All had gone well, including full use of granny's spare bed. Though the sex had been only satisfactory at best and brief in the extreme, both had fallen asleep. Erik had woken at four in the morning, made his excuses and headed home.

Erik had no worries about getting back into the house, as Markus's old bedroom was on the ground floor. Since Markus was away at university, there had been no problem exiting via the window and he'd left it open for the return. The house was part of a terrace of houses which lay in a dip facing away from the main road. The fronts of the houses looked onto a side street, and vehicle access was via a roundabout route. The rear gardens of the houses swept up to the main road, and there were gates there to enable owners to take a short cut to the centre of Wishaw on foot. Only some of the gates were locked.

As he crept along the main road towards the back gate of his family house, he noticed a suspicious-looking figure in dark clothing beside one of the windows at the rear of the Dempsters' house, two along from the Allensen home. Erik stopped and looked down towards the man – he was sure it was a man. Just for an instant, the man looked up at the main road, hearing the sound of a passing lorry. Erik ducked behind the fence. He was sure the man wasn't Mr Dempster. As Erik hurried along the pavement, through his gate and down the path, he wondered what he should do. Well, he knew what he should do, but the consequences of waking his father and explaining how he'd come to be out at that time of the morning were just too horrendous to contemplate. So he decided to do nothing. He climbed back in the window, locked it, negotiated his way back into his own bedroom, and fell asleep.

His mother woke him about nine with the news that there had been a break-in at the Dempsters' house, and both Mr and Mrs Dempster had been taken to hospital. Later it emerged that they'd been tied up and badly beaten by two men who were convinced they must have jewellery and cash in the house. Mr Dempster was so badly injured that he died two days later. Although the men had previous minor convictions, they weren't professional criminals and had decided to break in after a late boozing session at a local club. They were easily identified by fingerprint evidence.

Erik had never spoken to anyone about seeing the man at the Dempsters'. He'd worried until the trial that the man he'd seen might mention to the police having seen someone up on the road, or might even try to blame him. When the men came to court, they took the option of pleading guilty to a reduced charge of culpable homicide rather than face a murder charge, so they never gave any evidence about what had happened on the night.

Erik had always felt bad about what happened to Mr Dempster, though he suspected he'd seen the man leaving the property rather than arriving at it. Anyway, he convinced himself that must be the case. But he could never shake off the cold, gut-wrenching thought that by leaving the back window of the family home open that night, he'd put his own parents at risk.

Markus and Erik knew that their father, Harald Allensen, had been a policeman in Norway before he'd come to live in Britain. He'd married their mother in Scotland in 1946, but he'd never spoken in detail about his life in Norway and had never gone back, although Erik and Markus often thought they must have relatives there. When they were children, they used to ask their mother about their father's secret life, but she just brushed aside their questions, saying that she knew nothing about it.

She'd met her husband in London in 1945 when she was working as a shorthand typist in the War Office. They'd gone separately with friends to a tea dance at the Waldorf and had paired off there. She'd been attracted to his Nordic looks.

In 1974 Harald Allensen had died of a massive heart attack while reading the *Sunday Express* at the fireside. Erik had just dropped out of university, so he was at home, and Markus came back from London where he was starting off his career. The boys had gone through their father's papers and discovered, to their astonishment, that Harald Allensen had been part of the Oslo police department which had been charged with dealing with Norway's Jewish problem. There were newspaper cuttings among the papers about the transportation of Jewish civilians to Germany, and photographs showing the police processing the roundup at the main station in Oslo. Harald Allensen's diary disclosed that when he found out that the people involved had died in Auschwitz, he'd joined the Norwegian Resistance, and had passed valuable information on German troop deployments and the like to the British. His reward at the end of the war was British citizenship and a new life after he had testified against his superiors. He left a letter addressed to his sons explaining that he'd known that if he stayed in Norway he faced years of suspicion from former colleagues and resentment, or worse, from the relatives of those he'd implicated. He'd tried to atone for his involvement, but knew he must make a new start. Markus was largely unaffected by this revelation, but it prompted Erik to try to join the police. He'd possibly failed to stop something terrible happening to the Dempsters, just as his father had failed others in Norway.

As he turned into Dundonald Road, Allansen smiled grimly as he wondered what, after thirty years before the mast, he had to show for dealing with the detritus of Glasgow. Apart from a pension, zip … *niente*.

12

Rab was becoming a regular at the offices of McTavish Legal, though he met mostly with Eastman's assistant Paul Longmuir. McBain had brought them into two deals in place of Richardson Legal, but one, an office refurbishment, had fallen through. The joint venture for the Mollinsburn development had been progressing well. Everything was set up. A bank had identified a farmer customer in financial difficulties. His land was adjacent to the A80, the main road from the north into Glasgow, and only about ten miles from the centre of town, so if planning permission for housing could be obtained, there was a fortune to be made. The farmer had been trying to get planning permission for years, but without success. The bank had pressured the farmer into agreeing what appeared to be a generous deal, a sale at double the agricultural value of the land, which meant he could pay off his loans and have enough to buy a cottage for his retirement. The "buyer" was the joint venture between Westberry Properties and the bank. As soon as the deal was done, McBain had called in a few favours with local councillors, and planning permission was granted for a mixed residential and retail development.

Eveyone – except the farmer – was delighted. The bank stood to make a profit from its finder's fee and a small percentage of the profit on the sale. Westberry would make a huge amount, even after greasing a few palms.

The profit was going to emerge faster than usual, because as soon as news of the deal became public, three builders approached

McBain to sell the land to them before Westberry had carried out any work. McBain had held an informal auction and the successful builder was due to complete the purchase at the end of August.

Rab had been impressed at how smoothly the deal was progressing, but then he got a call from Eastman. A roads engineer had raised an objection to the plans and was insisting that a new roundabout be built to give access to the development. As the roundabout would need to be built partly on land belonging to Plettenberg plc, a neighbouring owner, this could effectively scupper the sale to the builder. Plettenberg was well aware of the value of its land, now that planning permission for the farm had been granted. Unless Westberry could buy the land needed for the roundabout, the joint venture could be left with a site of no value other than as a farm.

Rab stood over the boardroom table looking at the two plans of the site. The first showed the original layout with the access road and the second the amended layout sent by the roads engineer. Eastman pointed to the first plan.

"When we bought the farm our plan was to have the access road entirely on our site. Now that's to be changed by the planners because they think there'll be too much traffic going onto the main road from the estate, so a roundabout is needed. If we need to build this roundabout, the only place it can go is shown on the second plan. The problem is, part of that land belongs to Plettenberg. That small area of ground has become what we know as a 'ransom strip' and unless we can get it for the roundabout, the property we've bought for you reverts to its value as farmland. It's a potential disaster. I warned Alex we should make the deal with the farmer conditional on getting detailed planning permission."

"Don't be naïve, James," Rab said. "If the farmer had thought there was a real chance of planning, he would never have sold. We had to take a flier at it."

"Rab, the best way forward is for me to approach Plettenberg and see how much they want for the land. They know about the development, though, so it won't be cheap."

"That's maybe a bit premature, James. Let's see what we can do about the roads engineer. How's about you give me a copy of the letter from him?"

"Do you want the plans he sent?"

"No, just his details. I'll have someone have a word."

"Would you be using an independent consultant engineer? I can give you some names."

Rab laughed, "Well, a consultant of sorts. Leave it with me."

When Rab got into a nearby coffee shop, he called Colin Scott, and explained what had happened about the planning. He gave Colin the contact details of the roads engineer at the council. He hardly needed to explain the job. He knew Colin would easily find out the home address of the roads engineer, and would arrange to bump into him soon, probably just down the road from his home. He could be relied upon to find something to pressure a target with, just as he'd done with Eastman – he was the best. Parent, wife, kiddies, lover, boyfriend; after a little research in advance of the encounter, Colin would know how to press the right button.

A week later Rab got a call from Colin, "Sorry about the delay, Rab. This one was tricky. Ideal husband and father. He's just been passed over for promotion, though, and he's applying for a job in Birmingham. I got talking to him at his Golf Club. Don't ask how I got in! Anyway, it's going to take twenty-five big ones."

Even Rab was surprised by this amount. "Of course, he knows how much depends on this. Is it negotiable?"

"No, Rab. He's not daft. He needs that to cover the school fees down south, apparently. If you're in a rush, this is the way to do it."

"Yes, we need to move on with this. I'll clear it with Loco and get back to you."

When Rab explained the problem to McBain, he simply told him to divert £30,000 from the sauna income to Colin to cover the fee and the engineer's bung.

A few days later Rab was draining his pint as Colin came through the swing doors of the Horseshoe Bar in Drury Street, just round the corner from the Mitchell Street office. He tipped his empty glass slightly towards Colin, and Colin brought over two pints.

"How did it go? Are we clear?" Rab asked.

"One hundred per cent. I handed over the twenty-five grand, reminded him of the dangers of modern life, put my blade on the desk and told him he'd be hoping never to see me again, though I'm often in Birmingham and like to keep track of old friends. He lost a bit of colour at that. It's in the bag."

Rab got a call from Eastman later that week.

"It's the strangest thing, Rab. Never happened before. The planning authority has made some revisals to the development plan for Mollinsburn. The roundabout's no longer required provided we extend the deceleration and acceleration lanes, which we can do within our land. We're clear to complete!"

13

Sarah Plummer had a degree in politics from Dundee University. She'd joined the police as part of graduate recruitment, married another graduate in the same intake, and divorced him after an acrimonious three years because of her career taking precedence over the family hopes of her ex. She was a bright and enthusiastic Detective Constable, with red hair and a figure she kept trim at the gym. She had a good social life, but what she loved best about her life was working for Erik Allensen. When she arrived at Shettleston she'd been confused when her colleagues referred to Allensen as "Kay". It turned out that his Christian name was spelled with a "k" rather than a "c", and he'd been heard to say "it's k" so often that his nickname became Kay.

She'd been surprised when he didn't allow her to sit in on the interview with Eastman at the beginning of July. The next day Allensen had simply told her he was trying to infiltrate McBain's empire using Eastman, a respectable lawyer. He instructed that Eastman be put under observation.

"Let's see if he takes the bait, Sarah. Everyone's got a weakness."

"What bait, sir? You say this guy Eastman is squeaky clean. With so much to lose, why would he get involved with McBain?"

"Wheels within wheels, Sarah. Let's keep an eye on Eastman to see if there are any unusual contacts with McBain. Eastman claims his firm is doing ordinary legal work for McBain's companies, but I think there could be more to it. Issue a general alert to all Glasgow divisions seeking a heads-up on any sighting of McBain with Eastman."

Plummer had organised a rota to keep an eye on Eastman Monday to Friday, which was as much as the budget would stand. The annual Glasgow Fair holidays had started in the middle of July, so initially the team was a bit short-handed, but come the beginning of August they had covered Eastman's every move. Apparently he wasn't taking any holidays until later in the year. Six weeks into the operation, Plummer's team was rebelling. They were happy with the overtime, but they moaned that the observation was pointless. Plummer decided to challenge her boss.

"This is becoming a waste of time and resources, sir." She plonked herself on the chair opposite Allensen.

"He's just a boring solicitor. Arrives at the office, has meetings, goes back to Edinburgh. What sort of life is that? All we've seen is Rab Donald going into his office. Never McBain. Weeks of nothingness. We've other priorities"

"Why's Donald seeing him so often, Sarah?" Allensen asked.

"Well, sir, you told me that Eastman's acting for Westberry Properties, and, according to *The Herald* business section, they're buying a site near Mollinsburn for a housing estate. So I suppose that's a good reason for the meetings."

"Good girl. Yes, that might be the reason. Maybe. Yes … OK … could be … I suppose …"

Allensen was turned away from Plummer, staring out onto Shettleston Road. That's a bit patronising, she thought, and was about to make a face to the back of his head when he suddenly swivelled round to face her.

"It was a long shot, Sarah, but I agree it's time to wind it up. Call off the dogs. I hoped Eastman might get sucked into the McBain operation. That might still happen, though, so put the word out again, any sighting of McBain and Eastman together to be reported to me. I can then decide whether to start looking at him again. I don't know, mind. I really fancied him for this. There was something about the way he looked as he listened to the transcript."

"Forgive me, sir, but are you not getting a bit hung up on this?" Plummer pointed to her notes. "Eastman's blue chip. McBain's a crafty operator we've never got close to catching. Chances of them hooking up? OK, McTavish are doing legal work for the McBain companies, but that could just be coincidence."

Allensen said nothing, and Plummer thought she might have gone too far. He really is a bit odd just now, she thought.

Plummer knew Allensen had been married, but his wife had died of cancer five years ago. No kids. He didn't socialise with the troops. She'd seen him at the Theatre Royal once, when she and a friend had gone to a production of *HMS Pinafore*. He had been with a couple, and she'd later weaselled out of him that they were his brother and sister-in-law up from London for the weekend. Apparently, the brother was on a kind of trip down memory lane; they had put on Gilbert and Sullivan operettas every year at his school.

Occasionally Plummer thought about mentioning to Allensen that she had feelings for him which might be regarded as inappropriate, but she hadn't plucked up the nerve. Now, she simply moved back to her desk, and emailed the Eastman surveillance team that the operation was at an end.

The following Friday, McBain arrived at Eastman's office for the first time, unobserved. He was there to complete the sale of Mollinsburn. He sat, impatient, in the boardroom, surrounded by men in suits. For this meeting he favoured a leather jacket.

This was the first deal which McTavish Legal had completed for Westberry, and the champagne had been broken out. As

Glasgow had a small number of commercial lawyers, it so happened that Richardson Legal, McBain's former solicitors, were acting for the builders who were buying the Mollinsburn site from the joint venture, so there had been a certain amount of tension in the air over the last few hours of negotiation. But at 6.30 in the evening, it was confirmed that the money had moved, the last few drafting points were agreed, and all parties signed up. Represented at the settlement meeting were four parties in total: Westberry, with McBain and Rab as directors; the bank, which was the joint venture partner with Westberry (three suits); the builders (two directors), and the builders' bank (another three suits). Everyone had at least two lawyers, so it was quite a crowd.

Now it was 8.30 and, of the guests at Eastman's office, only McBain, Rab Donald and one inebriated banker remained.

Eastman turned to Paul Longmuir, "Put the guy from the bank in a taxi, Paul, and get back up here. We've still got work to do."

He moved over to McBain and Rab, "I'm sorry, guys, but Paul and I have to work on for a couple of hours on a deal due to settle next week."

This was not actually true, but Eastman wanted to get back to Edinburgh to attend a Rugby Club dinner. He was already late, but with any luck he would arrive during the sweet course, and would catch the speeches. But McBain would have none of it.

"We're all off to Sarkozy's, Jimmy boy. You owe me that. What a deal, eh? You should have asked for a percentage as a fee."

"I'd love to, Alex, but this other client …"

McBain drew him aside, "Or maybe we need a private arrangement. Why share with fifty-five partners?"

Eastman gave in. "OK, Paul, we'll look at the Craighouse

deal on Sunday. Two o'clock, Edinburgh office. You can go now."

Rab said he would drop McBain and Eastman off at the restaurant and take Paul home. When they got down to the car, Eastman saw Joe McCarthy in the driving seat.

McBain got into the front seat, and Paul, Rab and Eastman sat in the back of the Mercedes 600SE. It wasn't cramped.

Outside Sarkozy's, Joe got out with McBain and Eastman. Rab took over the driving and set off with Paul. Sarkozy's was a small French restaurant at the top of Hope Street, tightly clinging onto the edge of the city centre. Eastman had been there only once previously, but it was apparent that McBain was a regular. The owner, Nicolas, showed them to their table, complete with the customary fawning.

Joe was given a table separate from McBain and Eastman. When Eastman asked why, McBain explained that Rab was coming back and the two associates liked to eat on their own. Eastman noticed that Joe's table had lines of sight to the restaurant entrance, the kitchen and to McBain's table.

"Just like in the movies, Mr McBain. They can see whoever comes in."

"You're letting your imagination run away with you, James. Interesting that you like films, though. A bottle of the best Pinot Noir, I think, Nicolas. We've got some celebrating to do."

Nicolas moved off. McBain waved to some acquaintances at a table near the door.

"Rab will drive you back to Edinburgh, and Joe will drive your car back for you. Don't worry, he's insured. We've a few things to discuss."

Nicolas appeared with the wine and the menus. Eastman thought he was about to learn a whole lot more than he would have from Andy Irvine's reminiscences of Scottish rugby.

14

Rab Donald parked the Mercedes outside Sarkozy's. A couple of youths were hanging around outside a nearby shop. He gave them £20 and promised another £20 if the car was untouched when he came back. It was insurance.

He went into the restaurant and sat opposite Joe. He really liked him, he was a totally reliable pair of hands, but conversation was not his strong point. The football season was under way, and Joe regarded himself as a bit of an expert on tactics, managers, players and referees. Rab had heard it all before, and after Joe had forecast each Scottish Premier League result over the weekend, Rab signalled enough was enough, and that Joe should concentrate on the clientele. There really was no obvious danger here, but it was as well to be sure. A previous associate had been dispensed with after he failed to intercept a journalist who approached McBain's table.

Over his twenty or so years working for McBain, Rab had realised there was no real magic touch required to run the business, only a ruthless determination to get your own way. But that ruthlessness needed to be proportionate, and that got Rab thinking about Sonny as the heir apparent. Rab had first met Sonny when the boy was going to secondary school. Rab had just left the army at that point, and had met some nutters during his six years in the forces. He quickly recognised that Sonny had many of the characteristics of these guys, but with the added complication that he wasn't subject to any rules. So over his early teenage years, Sonny got into scrape after scrape, with his Dad always rescuing him. When he was seventeen, Sonny became obsessed with knives and guns and had used both over the years to maintain his authority over his "clients".

Rab thought about the latest mess he'd got Sonny out of. Late one Thursday he had a call from Brendan, one of Sonny's friends, saying Sonny had lost it and he'd better come out to an address in Ruchill. When he got there he found it was a house in a street abandoned for redevelopment. In the front room Sonny was circling someone lying face down on the floor, naked, sobbing through a gag made from an old tea towel. Rab could see that the man's hands and feet were nailed to the floor with six-inch steel nails.

"He's going to fucking tell us, he will, he will!" Sonny shouted as he waved an axe above his head.

"He's already cut off two of his fingers", Brendan said. "Now he's threatening to cut off, you know, his manhood."

Rab pulled Sonny into the kitchen. "What's this about? What does he know? He's a low life. What do you want him to tell you?"

"Who supplied him? Who told him to deal on our territory?" Sonny mumbled, his eyes blazing.

"OK, Sonny. I'll ask him."

Brendan came into the kitchen. "The guy was selling in the Gallowgate. Someone's supplying him, so Sonny said we should lift him and find out who's behind the competition. When we got him here, I couldn't believe it, the guy starts getting real aggressive with Sonny, saying he had connections. Connections? Sonny said we'd see how good his connections were. I think he's regretting mentioning connections now."

Rab looked back into the front room, and to the pools of blood darkening on the floorboards.

"What has he said?" Rab asked.

"He gave up some Paki shopkeeper on the south side, but Sonny thinks it's Malik, and he wants the guy to say it. But he won't, for some reason. Maybe Malik's scarier than Sonny."

"Well, that's unlikely, Brendan. None of this makes much sense. Maybe he really is freelance. I can't see Malik sending a dealer into our patch."

Sonny had calmed down.

Rab pulled him to one side, "Look, Sonny, he's a nobody. We'll dump him somewhere and call an ambulance."

Sonny popped some pills and glared at Rab. "Maybe you're right, Rab. Whatever you say. I'll just let him go and he can go to the polis, or, even better, tell everyone he fucking fooled me into letting him go! I don't think so."

"Come on, Sonny. He'll be too scared to do that."

"Well, just in case, I'll have a word in his ear." Sonny walked over and gave the lad a kick.

Rab watched from the kitchen door as Sonny knelt down and whispered something in the man's ear. Then with two blows of the axe he decapitated him.

"Job done," said Sonny then he walked out to his car and drove away.

It had taken Rab six hours to organise the disposal of the body. He was unfazed by body parts, thanks to his army experiences, though Brendan had vomited a few times. When the body was bagged up, they took it to a remote farm which McBain owned, where it was buried. Then the derelict house where the man had been tortured and killed was burned down.

Rab knew there would be much more of this if something happened to McBain. There would be chaos as Sonny got more and more extreme, and Rab knew that the Maliks of this world would eventually provoke him into doing something really stupid, something even Rab couldn't cover up. Rab was sure he himself could take over McBain's empire, but he would need

McBain's blessing, and that was not going to be forthcoming, unless something happened to Sonny.

Rab's thoughts were interrupted by Nico arriving with main courses. Rab was just resigning himself to another hour of Joe's musings on the Scottish football scene, when who should walk in but two detectives from Maryhill Division and their wives. Rab summoned Nico.

"I know, Mr Donald. Nowhere near Mr McBain. It's arranged." Nico placed his hand on Rab's shoulder.

Rab walked across to McBain and whispered in his ear. McBain simply nodded, and continued his discussion with Eastman.

McBain was in full flow.

"Well, James, I think I caught your interest over the fees. I know all about partnerships, that's why I've never been tempted to go into one. Other than the property joint ventures, of course. But they're just an evil necessity to get the inside track from the banks."

McBain tasted the second bottle of burgundy and pronounced it acceptable. They both had Tournedos Rossini, which McBain had recommended, and Eastman was sure Michael Winner would describe it as "historic". The wine made Eastman feel pretty relaxed, but he was wary of where this discussion might lead. There was a silence after the dishes were cleared away. Before the coffee arrived, Eastman decided to test the water.

"Over the years I've thought of going it alone, Mr McBain, but you know the score, you need to be in a big partnership to specialise. Yes, I could earn more as an advocate on my own, but I like the security of having other lawyers I can refer to if I think I'm out of my depth. It's a compromise."

"But what lies at the end for you?" McBain asked. "You're – what, forty-five, forty-six? In ten years you'll be finished, and you'll have nothing to sell, and no golden handshake. Then you'll need to repay the bank what you owe them."

Eastman looked up suddenly, but was unsurprised by what McBain knew. Nico arrived with the espressos.

"How much do you owe, James? Around £300,000, unless I'm mistaken. And every couple of years it goes up by £50,000 or so. That wife of yours can certainly spend it. Of course, there's the school fees and the holidays too. But if you have a couple of bad years, you'll be in trouble. Am I right or am I right?"

This was uncomfortably close to the truth. Eastman had a ten-year time span in mind for other reasons, but he was aware that his sodding pension fund was unlikely to finance a decent lifestyle for him at fifty-five or so. At the moment, it looked as if he would need to work forever.

"Well, Mr McBain, maybe Tesco Law will mean McTavish Legal will get outside investors and I'll get something for my equity interest."

The Government was anxious to open up competition for legal services to enable even supermarkets to offer legal advice, hence the name "Tesco Law". The large firms like Eastman's very much wanted this to happen, as their partners were likely to be able to sell their businesses for cash, just as the stockbrokers had done fifteen years before.

McBain leaned across the table and gave Eastman a friendly push on the shoulder.

"Come on, James. That's bullshit, and you know it! Even if it happens, the money would be peanuts compared to what your talents deserve … if you ever got it. They'd tie you in for years."

This was also true. How did McBain understand so much?

"Anyways, James, I was wondering if we could put together a little retirement fund for you. Nothing to do with McTavish Legal. Just a private arrangement between us."

Here it comes, thought Eastman. Almost exactly as Inspector Allensen predicted.

"We've had some successes business-wise, James, but they've all been based in Scotland. The thing is, I've not been using – what does it say on your card? – your international corporate finance speciality. Have I got that right?"

"Sure, Mr McBain, but the opportunities are pretty lim—"

McBain slapped his hand on the table. Rab and Joe rose as one towards the table, but McBain waved them away.

"Sorry about that, James. A bit of a short fuse. And from now on it's Alex, please? Just hear me out. This bit of work isn't for Westberry or for me, it's for a friend of mine who's a bit of a problem with the VAT man and those bastards from the Inland Revenue, about some cash he has. I know you can't get involved with anything illegal or tax avoidance. Or is it evasion? I never understood the difference."

"Evasion is illegal, Alex. If this is about cash, you should know that I've got obligations to report anything I learn about money laundering, without telling your friend I'm doing so. I could be struck off, or even end up in Barlinnie. Not an appetising prospect, I think you'll agree."

"Exactly, James. And I'd never ask you to become involved in anything like that. But my friend has a problem and you may be able to suggest a solution. I'm not asking you as a lawyer, just as a friend. All you need to do is tell me how to achieve what, eh, my friend wants."

"You mentioned some sort of pension fund for me, Alex. I take it this could be structured in any way I wanted?"

For the first time during the discussion McBain smiled, and that alarmed Eastman, for it was a strange, almost wolverine smile.

"I don't really understand terms like structured, James, but if you mean the fee would be paid wherever you like and to who you want, I'm sure we can arrange that. My friend can, I mean."

"And how much would be involved? For me, that is." Eastman asked quietly.

McBain looked wide-eyed at Eastman.

"It's a bit early for that, I think, but it would be payment by results. A basic fee and a percentage of the amount involved, or you could go for – what do you guys call it? Sad or glad? A higher percentage with no basic. It would be subject to negotiation."

Eastman fell into deep thought. McBain drained his coffee cup.

"Time to go," said McBain. "I think we should meet on Monday to discuss this further. How's your diary?"

Eastman checked his BlackBerry.

"Any time after three. Does that suit you?"

"For this we should use Westberry Drive. Joe'll collect you."

As McBain put his napkin on the table Rab got up and went to get the car. Joe came over to the table and escorted McBain and Eastman out of the restaurant. Eastman was feeling on top of the world.

Rab drove them all back to the McTavish Legal office so Joe could collect Eastman's Audi from the car park. Just as they arrived outside the building, a crowd of secretaries and trainees emerged, some the worse for wear. Eastman remembered that this was the monthly staff get-together, with booze and nibbles laid on by the partners. As Joe and Rab got out, Eastman's secretary, Natasha, saw Eastman in the car and waved at him.

"That'll be Natasha, I suppose," said McBain. "Now that I see her, I understand. She lives in Airdrie, is that not right? Rab, ask her if she wants a lift home."

Eastman started to protest, but Rab was over talking to her in a flash. She was nodding vigorously and saying her goodbyes to her friends. She climbed into the back of the Mercedes.

McBain was in the middle between them. He held out his hand to her.

"Well, isn't this a lucky chance? It's Natasha, isn't it? I'm Alex McBain."

Natasha giggled. "I've had too much Prosecco, Mr McBain."

"Alex, please! What! No champagne for the staff? Cheapskates. You should be ashamed, James. What's he like to work for, Natasha?"

"Oh, he's all right. A bit grumpy sometimes. I've stayed on far too long tonight. Donald will be mad with me."

"Don't you worry, m'dear. Rab will have you home in no time. Tell you what; to save time Joe will drop me off at Westberry Drive. Rab, you just go direct to Airdrie, and then meet up with Joe at James' house. See you Monday, James. Westberry Drive, Joe'll collect you."

At this McBain indicated to Eastman that he should let him out. He waved Joe down and got into the Audi. Eastman slid back into the back seat next to Natasha. Chanel No. 5, a revealing blouse, a pencil black skirt, stilettos. Eastman moved uneasily. The Pinot Noir had relaxed him, maybe too much.

The Mercedes set off towards the M8, joining it at Charing Cross. By the time they were passing the lights of Barlinnie Prison, Natasha was snuggled next to Eastman and by the time they reached that giant wire horse near Easterhouse, they were kissing passionately and Natasha was stroking Eastman's erection.

Rab coughed and they separated, but as the car turned off the motorway for Airdrie, Eastman leaned forward towards Rab.

"Rab, do you think ..."

"Not tonight, Mr Eastman. I don't think Mr McBain would approve. And maybe she'd regret it. If you want to go somewhere when you're both sober, we might be able to help."

71

Eastman looked into Natasha's eyes and felt her taut nipples through her blouse. She looked hungry for sex. They'd spoken in the past about passion being an unmet need. Natasha nodded.

Natasha directed Rab through the estate to her small semi-detached house at the end of a cul-de-sac.

Before she got out of the car, Natasha whispered to Eastman. "There's nothing in the diary for Mr McBain on Monday."

"Don't worry, it's social," replied Eastman.

Natasha arched her eyebrows, but said nothing. She tripped up the garden path to her front door. Just as she was about to put her key in the lock, the door burst open and an obviously irate Donald strode determinedly down the path towards the Mercedes.

"I'd better say hello," said Eastman, and opened the door. He waved to the approaching figure.

"Hi, Donald. Here she is, safe and sound. Off to the game tomorrow?"

Donald looked confused. "Not your motor, Mr Eastman. I wondered …"

"Natasha'll explain," burbled Eastman, and hastily climbed into the front seat of the car. What was he thinking about? Safe and sound? He needed a brain transplant.

15

As soon as they re-joined the M8, Eastman fell asleep. Rab noticed that the car was low on petrol so he turned into the Harthill Services. He woke Eastman.

"I need petrol, Mr Eastman. Do you fancy some water? And maybe some mints. Tell you what, I'll get one of these air fresheners, that might hide the perfume. Better safe, eh?"

After stocking up with supplies, Eastman got into the front seat. Rab thought for a while.

"You had quite a night, Mr Eastman."

"Well, Rab, it wasn't my usual Friday, that's for sure. Anyway, you're a bit of a man of mystery. Everyone's got a story. What's yours?"

"No mystery, Mr Eastman. I joined the Army at sixteen. Spent four years in Ulster. Weird, never saw a single piece of action. Road blocks, patrols, really boring. It was sideways or out for me, and some guys I knew had tried for special forces, so I thought, why not? I got myself to the gym as often as I could, built up the fitness. Never lost it, even now, twenty-odd years on."

"And then …" asked Eastman.

"Yes, well, this was '80, '81. The summer intake. Report to Dering Lines on the Brecon on the Sunday, end of June. One hundred and forty-eight of us. Based on what I'd been told, fifteen to twenty would make it. Not good odds. First up, the Combat Fitness Test. Basic stuff. A nine-mile run/walk in combat gear. If you couldn't do that, you shouldn't be in the army, never mind the SAS. But by the end of day one we were down to a hundred and thirty. Why had the eighteen bothered?

"Over the next two weeks, more of the same, but every day the distance and the weight increased. But it was no problemo for me. Then the big one, the Endurance. Total bastard. Seventy-two kliks carrying eighty pounds. I did it in thirteen hours, half an hour over the record. After that, we were down to forty.

"For a Glasgow lad, the last part was the easiest. In the jungle. Home from home, I told them. Plenty to kill and eat. Then the interrogation. Well, Mr Eastman, you're a lawyer. You know about Glasgow. Early doors, you know to keep your trap shut. Name, rank and number. Thirty-six hours. Hooded, sleep deprivation, all that shite. Name, rank and number. Two ponces, public school types. They got more frustrated than me."

"So how many made it?"

"Eighteen, me included. Proudest day, and all that."

They had reached Inverleith.

"Here we are, Mr Eastman. Back to the bosom of your family. Joe's just behind us. Two top-of-the-range motors in a row. Mind you, they're all Mercs and Jags about here. Good night, Mr Eastman."

Eastman walked up his driveway.

Joe parked Eastman's Audi in the street and joined Rab in the front of the Mercedes.

"What took you so long? I've been parked round the corner for half an hour. The cops've driven past twice."

Rab sighed, "Look, buddy, if I hadn't pulled those two apart you'd have been waiting a good bit longer. Jesus, she was hot. Our Mr Eastman is on a big promise."

"The boss was laughing about him on the way back. All he said was 'Cheeky bastard'. Mind, he disnae talk much to me."

"Well, let's see what he has to say tomorrow. You left everything secure?"

"The boss was happy to lock up himself, but I checked. God knows where Sonny is, mind. Should we try to get hold of him?"

"No, let's leave it. Look, you drive. I'm going to kip."

Rab dozed off, dreaming a dream prompted by telling Eastman about his time in the forces.

Rab's first exposure to real action in the SAS wasn't too long in coming. On April Fool's Day in 1982 the United Kingdom military were as surprised as everyone else that Argentina was launching an invasion of the Falkland Islands, a thinly populated outpost of the British Empire in the inhospitable South Atlantic. Although the Foreign Office seemed anxious to appease Argentina with a negotiated settlement, which in reality would have involved a surrender of the islands and a likely relocation of the population to Britain, the Prime Minister, Mrs Thatcher, decided that the islands must remain British and the invasion should be resisted. With what appeared to be minimal planning, a task force was despatched, and the SAS was to be given a role.

Rab participated in three operations during the conflict, and each of them soured his feelings about military life. In the first, he was part of a squad landed on the Fortuna glacier on South Georgia. When he and his mates were transferred to HMS *Endurance*, the Royal Navy Antarctic survey ship from which the SAS helicopter would take off for the glacier, they were aware right away that the crew of the survey ship regarded the SAS plan as madness, in view of the weather conditions on the glacier. Brushing aside their concerns, the order was given to go ahead, and the SAS team from 19 (Mountain) Troop landed on the glacier, the first British troops to return to the Falkland Islands.

Their stay was a brief one. In horizontal fifty miles an hour winds they managed five hundred metres in five hours, and needed to shelter in a crevasse for the night. Rab had never been more frustrated and miserable. The next day they were uplifted and returned to HMS *Antrim* in a Mark 3 Wessex. Rab was lucky to be on that because the Mark 5s involved in the rescue both crashed in whiteout conditions, though there were only minor injuries. The whole team eventually got back, thanks to the Mark 3 pilot who returned to pick up those who had been on the Mark 5s.

There was an inevitable "We told you so" from the crew.

That was nothing compared to the balls-up on his next piece of action. Rab and his squad were on a routine patrol near Teal Inlet when they spotted soldiers approaching. As it happened, this was a Special Boat Service patrol which had been dropped off a helicopter in the wrong position. Rab's team set up an ambush and challenged the soldiers. Because they were in the wrong area, they didn't know the correct response to the challenge, and one of the SBS patrol panicked and tried to creep away. One of Rab's mates shot him, the first "blue-on-blue" incident in the campaign.

At this point Rab had seen no action against the Argentines at all. Just before the invaders finally surrendered, he was part of a force sent on a diversionary attack against Cortley Hill Ridge, near Port Stanley. As they approached from the sea in their landing craft, they were spotted and a massive artillery barrage was directed at them. This had not been foreseen, so, since there was no effective artillery support for the SAS, they made a swift withdrawal.

Rab was totally disenchanted on his return to the United Kingdom, and handed in his papers at the earliest opportunity. He knew he would see more real action on the streets of Glasgow, and after a couple of weeks staying with his uncle in Springburn, he met up with Alex McBain, and had been part of his team ever since.

Rab shifted in the front seat of the Mercedes. He watched the retreating SBS man fall for the hundredth time, and then saw the widow's face glowering at him at the memorial service, then dissolving and reforming as his late mother's face. He woke with a start. They were back in Shettleston. Joe dropped him off outside the flat, muttering that he would just make sure everything was going alright at the Sauna Paradisa.

Rab thought he knew what that meant – one free massage coming up – but, as he found out later, he was wrong about why Joe wanted to go to the sauna.

Rab was a cautious man. Once he'd entered the common hallway, he stood at the foot of the stairs listening for anything suspicious. When he got to the front door of his flat, he looked for the thin black thread he always left stuck between the door and the surround. The thread was unbroken. He unlocked the door and went in.

The flat was furnished from IKEA. Rab favoured the spartan look. He listened to the phone message left for him and smiled.

16

On Monday morning, Eastman set off from Edinburgh at 6.30 a.m. to make sure he'd have an early start at the office and be there before Natasha arrived. He was unsure how to deal with the situation. He and his wife hadn't had sex for weeks, maybe months, and even then, she "succumbed" only if she'd had more than a few drinks. So the position as Eastman saw it was that he was pushing at an open door with Natasha and he might as well see if her eagerness would translate into some much needed action. There was always a danger with office romances, but he thought if Natasha agreed to some ground rules, they could work something out. No long-term commitment, no leaving spouses, just a bit of fun, since they were in sterile relationships. Yes, that might convince her.

What Eastman really wanted was a very smart, intelligent female with a great body. Natasha qualified on the smart and the body, but not the intellect. That would need to be for later. How long would he need to search, he thought? Anyway, it was ten years away. These bloody kids!

Natasha arrived at about 8.30, hung up her coat and strode determinedly into Eastman's room, closing the door behind her. No vamp today – a baggy denim skirt and a pullover and cardigan combination.

"What the hell's going on, James? Look, I was out of order on Friday." She raised her hands in mock surrender. "I'm sorry about jumping on you, but lately, Donald and I ..."

"I was at fault, too," Eastman interrupted. He swung round on his chair, looked out of the window and into the gloom of early morning Glasgow and smirked, "Should we just forget it?" Sly.

"Can I sit down?" Natasha sighed. Eastman turned back round and looked at her, feigning concern. He indicated she should take one of the chairs opposite his.

"Look, James, I don't like Alex McBain. He scares me. He scares everyone. Are you not scared of him? You never, never socialise with clients, now you're going to see him at his home. And it's not in your diary. He's supposed to be a crime lord. What are you thinking about? He runs saunas and my cousin heard that his son slashed one of the girls who wouldn't … you know. I'm really confused, James."

She started to cry, and Eastman handed her a tissue from the box on his desk.

"I know about his reputation, but the firm wouldn't … couldn't have taken him on as a client unless the Compliance Department agreed. And they gave him a clean bill of health. He was a Richardson client, for God's sake."

Natasha seemed to calm down. But then she persisted, "What about today's meeting – seeing him at his home – so the other partners don't know, maybe?" She raised one eyebrow in what Eastman immediately thought was a very attractive way. He had to put an end to this kind of talk.

"That's enough. You keep your thoughts to yourself on this. The firm's doing well acting for Westberry. We'll all do well out of the bonus pool."

"I'm not the only one asking questions, James. Paul's flatmate knows someone who works for the council. She says the planning guy who changed his mind about the roundabout at Mollinsburn has handed in his notice and is moving down south. Is that a coincidence?"

"You're pushing it, Natasha. Let's get on. We need to deal with Craighouse this morning. I need the updated draft with track changes. Paul and I worked on it yesterday."

"And what about us? We need to decide, James. Maybe we can't work together now. I could easily get a job nearer home. And Donald wants to start a family. God, what a thought! I can't do any of this."

"Look, Natasha, give me a few days to sort myself out. I felt something on Friday."

"Me too, James, you devil; but I know what you mean. Maybe we need to meet after work somewhere, and talk it through."

Later that day, Eastman was ushered into the sitting room at Westberry Drive. For all the world it looked like a small piece of Cairo had been plonked down in the north-east of Glasgow. The house itself had been built in the 1950s, but it had been completely extended and refurbished by McBain and his wife Irene, and looked to Eastman's eyes quite like how he imagined a harem would look, all rich tapestries, leather furniture and alabaster statues of leopards and lions. The security was impressive, with reinforced doors and windows as well as what appeared to him to be a sophisticated pressure alarm system.

Coffee was served by the housekeeper who soon withdrew, leaving McBain and Eastman together.

McBain sat on the edge of one of the three sofas and spoke softly to Eastman.

"We'll have a bit of a chat, I think, and then you can meet Sonny. Now, about my friend's problem. Here it is. He's got in a bank deposit – quite legally, mind – a large amount of cash. And now he wants to retire abroad. He's also got a very greedy wife, and it's possible she'd try to get her hands on it at some point. So he wants to find a way to move the cash abroad without anyone knowing about it, and then to be able to use it without it being in his name. This is what you lot do, day in, day out. Am I not right? It's in the press all the time."

Eastman coughed, "Well, Alex, starting from the other end, as it were, and assuming what you say about the source of these funds can be proved, what your friend probably needs is a Blind Trust. Well, I call them that. It's a trust which starts off with the only beneficiaries being charities, except that the trustees could add your friend as a beneficiary later. So until he needs the money, he's not mentioned in the documents. He doesn't need to sign anything, in fact, because the trustees sign a declaration on day one that they're holding the money for the charities. It works well. It's based in a tax haven. I use Jersey."

"I think you're missing a bit out, James," McBain snorted. "How does my friend get the money to Jersey and can he be sure these trustees will give him the money when he wants it?"

"That's why it's called a trust, Alex. You need to choose people you can trust. There are also some technical things we can do to give your friend reassurance and there needs to be a sealed Letter of Wishes, to cover what's to happen if he dies."

"Why? Does his Will not cover it?" asked McBain.

Not the sort of point that would immediately occur to an ordinary layman, thought Eastman. It would be dangerous to underestimate this man.

"No, Alex. It's separate. Think of it like … like the trust is a separate company. If he dies, what's in his estate passes under his Will, but what's in the trust goes to whoever the sort of board of directors of the trust decides. Again you're trusting them to act as the Letter of Wishes says."

"Could he not just say give it to who I leave my estate to, just the same as the Will?" asked McBain.

"Very neat, Alex. Yes, that would work."

"What's the technical thing, James?"

"You can have what's called a Protector. Someone in the

United Kingdom who needs to agree before the trustees can give anything to anyone. You could be the Protector for your friend."

"OK, James, I'll think about that. But the money's here in Glasgow. I asked before, how do we get it to Jersey? In theory, mind."

Eastman decided the time had come to make his pitch. He mumbled, "About this pension fund you were talking about, Alex. Do we not need to be clear about what's involved in that? This is tricky stuff. There would be a number of parties involved, not just me. And everyone will be looking for a cut. That goes up, depending on how secret, shall we say, the cash needs to be."

"I don't quite follow you, James."

"Are we talking about £1m or £10m, or more? It needs to be at least £5m to make it worthwhile."

"Well, at least £20m, maybe more. Would 10 per cent cover it?"

McBain looked straight through Eastman.

Eastman stood up. He sighed, "Sorry, Alex, £2m is nothing like it. I wish your friend all the best."

"Sit down, James, this is new territory for me. What would it take?"

"To tell you the truth, I really don't know for sure. I need to meet some people. The total cost might be as much as 50 per cent."

Eastman thought he might have over-egged it, but held McBain's stare. Now McBain stood up.

"James, why don't you find out for sure what you'd have to pay out and then we can discuss your fee. OK?" McBain held out his hand.

They shook on it.

"OK, Alex, but McTavish Legal will not be involved, nor

will either of us, directly. Can Rab be the link with your friend? Getting the cash, I mean?"

"Maybe you better explain what's going to happen, and then I'll decide if Rab can be trusted. Let's meet later this week." McBain rang a bell on his desk and the housekeeper appeared. He barked, "Fresh coffee, Sarah, and ask Sonny to join us."

Sonny waddled into the sitting room and plonked himself on most of the two-seater settee, ignoring Eastman's outstretched hand. McBain made the introductions. Sonny grunted.

McBain said that Eastman was now going to be the family lawyer, a type of *consigliere*. He wanted Eastman to explain how Wills worked, because he was thinking about putting his affairs in order. He told Eastman that Sonny's mother and he were separated, not divorced, and she now stayed in Spain. He wanted all he had to go to Sonny.

Eastman explained about Inheritance Tax and said the McBain estate problems were complicated because of Irene being in Spain. One of the Westberry companies should be exempt from tax. Eastman realised he'd already lost Sonny, and Alex was twitching with impatience.

"OK, Alex. I'll do a Will for you leaving Mrs McBain the use of the estate for her lifetime, and the capital can pass to Sonny when she dies. Hopefully there will be no tax to pay, but we have the best experts on this, so rest assured you'll pay the minimum."

Eastman now had to raise a tricky issue, "Sonny, you're not married, and you've no family."

"No chance." he declared.

"You travel with your father. What if there's some sort of accident?" Eastman continued. "Do you have other relatives or friends you'd wish to get the estate, Alex?"

McBain looked away. Almost inaudible, he said, "No relatives. A charity for poor kids. The diocese will have something."

Sonny exploded, "You're joking, Dad! What about me? Forget the Church!"

"Calm down, this is only if you go first, or you wipe out the both of us – the way you drive! Anyway, it won't happen."

Sonny sat down, and after listening to Eastman, he agreed he'd sign a Will leaving what he had to his father or the charity his father chose. It was agreed that Eastman would contact Irene about her Will, after Alex had spoken to her.

Eastman got up to leave, and to his surprise Sonny eased himself to his feet, and addressed his father:

"One of Malik's boys was in the sauna yesterday. What about the brass they nicked? Did we do anything about it?"

Alex looked pleased.

"Well remembered, son. No, we didn't. But Eastman will deal with it now."

Alex explained about the Canal Regeneration Scheme, which had been put on hold because of Mollinsburn, and why he wanted to get on good terms with Usman Malik. He asked Sonny to get Eastman the project folder and when Sonny returned with it from what Eastman presumed was McBain's office, Rab Donald was with him. He waved a greeting to Eastman.

McBain asked Eastman to meet with Malik to see if he could be brought into a consortium.

"Just let me know what the fee will be for this. It'll be a McTavish transaction. Get the file from Richardsons. We need to talk further about my friend's problems, when you've come up with some figures."

"We need a code name for your friend's transaction," said Eastman.

"Good point. Everything's a project, am I right? Well, let's call it Project Singer," said Alex. "You like the pictures, don't you?"

"What pictures?" asked Eastman, looking around. There was nothing on the walls but tapestries.

"Cinema, dummy. Bryan Singer – best director there is."

"Well, fine. It's Project Singer."

Rab was summoned and saw Eastman to the door.

Eastman got back to the office at six. He sat down at his desk, exhausted. I wonder who's fooling who here, he thought. He dictated three letters, one to Richardsons asking them to send on the file for the Canal Scheme, one to Usman Malik suggesting he arrange for his solicitors to contact McTavish Legal about a meeting to discuss Malik's possible participation in the Scheme, and one to Irene McBain in Spain. He also emailed Robert Lebens for a date to meet in St Helier.

17

Irene McBain loved being in Malaga, one of the main reasons being she was away from Glasgow. She sat on the patio beside the pool and thought through what Sonny had just told her during his weekly Sunday evening call.

She dreaded listening to his lies about what he'd been up to, but this week was different. What he'd told her was so unusual it must be the truth, and it fitted in with a letter she'd received the day before.

Her son had told her about the arrival on the scene of a new lawyer called James Eastman. When she'd asked how Eastman had met his Dad, Sonny had said it was something to do with a letter which had come to the sauna, and Rab had suggested it. Sonny often bleated to Irene that Rab was getting too influential with his Dad. Now he was worried that his Dad was going to leave everything to the church.

Irene was sure Sonny had misunderstood what Eastman had said, because in the letter Eastman had sent her, he'd explained that the church would be involved only if Sonny died without a family. Still, she was astounded that Wills had suddenly become a concern for Alex. He'd never before given any thought to this, so far as she knew. It was all very odd.

She picked up her bank statement and investment report, and immediately her mood lightened. Nothing that happened in Glasgow could affect her nest egg, and she owned the villa outright. She decided to leave Eastman's letter for another day. She wasn't thinking of departing this life just yet.

She walked back into the sitting room, rang for Tom Saunders in the staff flat and asked him to get the car as she'd be dining out. As she drove up into the hills she reflected on what she regarded as her failure as a mother.

She felt bad about abandoning her son in Glasgow, but sometimes she found it hard to accept that he was her child. She occasionally supposed that some genetic trick had been played on her, but if she really thought about it, maybe it was inevitable that a Shettleston hardman and the daughter of a Maryhill gang boss would produce someone like Sonny. It didn't make things any easier for her, though. In a way she still loved her son, although she was appalled by what he did. She felt she had to listen to him every week. He wanted her to come back to Glasgow. She was struggling to come up with new excuses.

* * *

That same evening, at Maryhill Police Station, Detective Inspector Seamus Walker was catching up with paperwork. Sunday was quiet after the rigours of a Saturday in Glasgow. He came across the memo from DC Plummer at Shettleston requesting details of any sighting of Alex McBain with James Eastman (photo attached). It was now a week since he'd been at Sarkozy's with Kirk and their wives, but there was no doubt that Eastman was the guy he'd seen with McBain that night. Damn, he thought, seeing the memo was dated two weeks previously. Confession was good for the soul, though.

He dialled Plummer's number and was thankful to get her voicemail. He gave details of the sighting, adding his apologies for the delay.

When Sarah told Allensen about Walker's message, he was

incandescent with rage, "I shouldn't have called it off. Are these guys slow readers? We've lost a week. God knows what they've planned by now. Sarah, let slip the dogs of war."

Sarah Plummer looked confused.

"Shakespeare, dammit! Resume the observation."

★ ★ ★

Meanwhile, Usman Malik sat in the office sectioned off from the ground floor of the Kanrach Cash and Carry in Kingston Street. He was a tall man, dark with a wispy beard, and in his youth he had been a fairly proficient cricketer, a fast bowler of some promise, they said at his club. But business was business and he couldn't afford to devote the hours to sport. Now he was becoming a bit portly. He knew he needed more exercise.

He had bought the warehouse from two Jewish fur wholesalers about five years before, and although the overpowering smell in the sales area was now of washing powder and disinfectant, he had never quite got rid of the faint aromas of dead fox and mink. At least that was what he thought; no one else seemed to notice, but no one disagreed with him when he complained about it.

The hubbub in the cash and carry was constant. Deliveries came in from a lane at the rear of the building, with the crates being broken down and goods either brought to the sales area by forklift truck or moved to upper floors on an ancient goods lift which screeched and groaned as it slowly progressed up and down the building. In the sales areas there was always banter between the drivers, the stackers and the checkout girls, and loud arguments between customers as to who had the best retail operation. Only the ground and first floors were used for sales, and on the two remaining upper floors, surplus goods were held in reserve. These floors also had other functions.

Malik's little office was built of cheap plasterboard to waist level, then glass to a height of about eight feet. There was no soundproofing, but that didn't matter as Malik liked to sit there listening to the clattering of the small shopkeepers loading up their trollies and arguing with his staff. Occasionally, there was a complaint about faulty goods, which Malik always dealt with personally, huddled in the corner of the unheated office, arguing over the credit to be given. It was easy for someone with his business interests to lose touch and he adored trading, both with the punters, as he had started calling them recently, and with his suppliers.

It was all a cover, of course, but, like McBain's companies, the Kanrach Cash and Carry was a profitable enterprise in itself. The real business was importing drugs from Pakistan and this was done in a number of ways. Mules were loaded up in Karachi and disgorged their stomach contents in various toilets in flats owned by Malik in the south side of Glasgow. That was for small amounts, but from time to time the clothing import side of the business would be used for a massive shipment hidden in the parkas run up in the sweat shops of Quetta, near the border with Afghanistan. Malik got a buzz thinking how much heroin could be concealed in a single container of jackets. In a way, he was sorry that his brother Imran was stuck in Quetta, but Malik was the elder brother, so he sat at the top of the chain of command.

As it happened, he had been worrying that it had been a mistake to allow these lads to steal the brass from McBain's development in Ibrox. That was the problem with acting impetuously. His father had been annoyed when he found out about it, because he thought that Malik and McBain should be able to act together, though even he agreed that McBain's son was a different matter altogether. From time to time, Malik had more drugs than he could sell in his territory. He thought that

McBain bought from London, so there could be advantages all round if he could become McBain's supplier. Economies of scale.

He carefully slit open the envelope from his solicitors. Well, well – they had had an approach by Westberry's lawyers about joining in something called the North Canal Regeneration Scheme. According to the letter, for an investment of £300,000, the Malik family could have a one-third share of the development, and the indications were that the return would be at least £2m after two years. The other partners in the consortium were to be McBain and the Hebridean Bank.

This seemed like a tempting offer, but Malik was suspicious as to why the McBain family wished to involve him. It might be something to do with his father. Maybe McBain's idea was that his father might be able to help on this. Dad was a local councillor for a ward on the south side, but he would be able to find out from the council planners what the prospects were for a profitable development on the north side. You needed to get the planners to agree for a supermarket and other retail outlets, with the minimum social housing as a sop to the locals. Yes, Dad would be keen to help, and this could have the added bonus of sounding out McBain on whether he might agree to change supplier.

Malik knew his father had met Alex McBain a few times at charity functions. He decided to discuss the letter with his father later that evening. Now his mobile rang. It was shown as an anonymous call, so he ignored it, on the basis that he could listen to the voicemail. Thirty seconds later, his mobile beeped and he listened to a voice muffled by a cloth or the like. The message was brief and to the point.

"It's a fucking set-up. Sonny cannae be trusted."

Malik sat back and looked up at the pockmarked ceiling.

Someone who knew his mobile number, but he didn't recognise the voice at all. What could he be set up for? Questions, questions, and another container of fluffy jackets coming up the M74.

18

Eastman had decided to put a proposition to Lebens in Jersey, but for entertainment during the flights over, he'd taken the files on the Canal Scheme. First he read through the file he'd received from Richardsons. The idea was to transform an area close to the Forth and Clyde Canal from a collection of pubs, fast-food shops, car repair garages and a nursing home into an enterprise business park. McBain seemed to have a particular enthusiasm for the project, and Eastman recollected from the transcript of what McBain had said in Gibraltar that he'd spoken about his youth in the area.

As it happened, Eastman had recently assisted his younger son with a school project on Scotland's canals, so he had some knowledge of the background. This canal had been built in the late eighteenth century to provide a link between the Atlantic and the North Sea. It ran from Bowling on the Clyde to Grangemouth on the Forth, and in its heyday, before the advent of the railways, its barges transported grain, timber and wine from east to west, and tobacco, sugar and coal from west to east. After the railways were built, it had gradually fallen into disuse and had been closed in 1963. Finance from the Millennium Fund had been used to reopen it for recreational use in 2002.

Eastman looked through the portfolio of photographs; the buildings immediately beside the canal had been warehousing and industrial units over the years, but many were now unoccupied and none was worth preserving. On the plans, he could see that the area McBain was interested in was a sort of peninsula, in that the canal looped round the site. There was a good wide access road, where the pubs and garages were, so there should be no problem with the planning department. Richardsons already had agreement in principle, and the local Community Council had given wholehearted support to the project. A substantial grant was likely from the European Regeneration Fund, according to the local MEP. The only area for discussion with the authorities was the mix of land use. Offices and small business units would be a huge improvement for the area, and would bring employment for locals, but McBain was pushing for some residential units on the edge of the site and a retail park in place of some of the small business units. Devoting one-third of the site each to retail, housing and business would give the greatest profit. Getting planning permission for it was the key.

In the taxi into St Helier he turned his mind to Project Singer, the theory of which was by now pretty well formed in Eastman's mind. But he needed a connection with someone who had already put the theory into practice, and was willing to do so again. He had a fair idea that Lebens knew just the person, and in any event, Eastman needed Lebens to provide the last piece of the jigsaw, the Blind Trust.

Today they had met at La Rustica; after the usual sumptuous meal, coffee arrived, and Robert looked keenly at Eastman.

"So, old boy, what brings you across to the island today, really? I don't buy that tosh about you having another meeting earlier in the day."

Eastman lowered his voice.

"Well, there is something, Robert. Remember what we talked about the last time I was over? It's, shall we say, developed. The client says he has a friend who needs a Blind Trust. I presume there's no problem with that?"

"Compliance, old boy. The bane of our lives. If the money man can jump through their hoops, it's no problem."

"There's an additional element now, Robert." Eastman whispered. "You mentioned at one time a contact in Singapore who helped out a United Kingdom client. A racing driver, wasn't it?"

Lebens put his forefinger to his lips and called for the bill.

"Back to the grindstone for us, old boy. That's the Justice Minister over there. Walls have ears, and all that. This is a bit public for us, I think."

They walked up Fort Road to the office in silence, and Lebens told the receptionist they would use Boardroom Six.

As they went up in the lift, Robert explained about Boardroom Six.

"Six is reserved for highly confidential meetings. It's swept clean every day. No bugs. Before you go in, old boy, leave your mobile phone with Anastasia. Otherwise, you'll set off all sorts of alarms. I hope you're not wired up ... Just joking!"

But Lebens looked more serious than he had ever seen him. He handed his mobile to Anastasia, who met them as they came out of the lift.

Eastman knew this was a defining moment. As he sat down, the teeming rain was swept up the window overlooking the harbour. Eastman took a deep breath.

"Robert, I have an opportunity. It's nothing to do with McTavish. I'm just a facilitator, as it were. I need your man from Singapore to create the Blind Trust. I presume he's an existing client of yours, so that should satisfy compliance."

"More or less," said Lebens. "But I'm not clear precisely what you have in mind. Maybe if you indicated how much is involved, I could say whether Mr Singapore, shall we call him, might be interested."

A hush descended on Boardroom Six. Eastman felt

confused, and Lebens just stared at him with an unnerving openness.

"I take it, old boy, that Mr Singapore is crucial to your plans?"

Eastman sighed:

"Robert, it could be £20m plus. How much might make it into the Blind Trust? The client would want to lose the very minimum."

"That depends on how greedy we are, does it not, old boy?" Robert smiled. "I can tell you Mr Singapore will give 70 per cent of face value, not negotiable. I guess your client's friend would think 60 was a pretty good return, so that leaves 10 for us to share. On £20m that's £1m each, tax-free."

Eastman spluttered.

"That's hardly fair, Robert. I'm the man with the money, or his introducer." Without really thinking, he added, "Maybe I could get a better deal elsewhere?"

"Where would that be, James? Never try to kid a kidder. I doubt you have the remotest idea how to find another Mr Singapore."

Eastman tried to negotiate.

"How about I get 75 to your 25? I'm taking the risk here!"

Lebens stood up.

"James, I think you are well out of your league here, certainly well out of your comfort zone. Mr Singapore is a respectable businessman, but some of his associates take a robust view of life. To become involved with such people, I need a good deal more than £500,000. Remember that if your client's friend fails to deliver, even if there is no loss of money to Mr Singapore, there will be a loss of face, as he sees it, and you and I will be in the firing line. So, deal at 50:50?"

Lebens held out his hand and they shook on it.

"You're a hard nut, Robert, but, as you say, I've no choice. How many yachts do you need?"

95

Lebens laughed.

"I'll need to make some calls. I'll send you the trust document next week, and the draft of the memorandum which Mr Singapore will sign. That will say the capital will be paid out as directed by your client, so we'll need his details and his Letter of Wishes. What's the Blind Trust to be called?"

"The Singer Trust. Is that name available?"

"I'd think so." Lebens stood up. "Anastasia will see you out. Don't forget your mobile. I'll be in touch. You'll get tickets for a concert or a sports match in the mail from me. That will be for your first and last contact with Mr Singapore's representative in England."

19

It was now two weeks later, and Eastman knew he would soon need to set things out for McBain. He had received the documentation for the Singer Trust from Lebens a week ago. Eastman had used Blind Trusts for his clients to carry out perfectly legal tax avoidance in the past, so he was familiar with the terms of the document – as usual, it had been completed by Robert's firm's trustee company, so there was no need for anyone in Scotland to be named or to sign. It simply recorded that the trustees held £100, and any further sums which might be gifted to them in future, for charities and, in addition, for such beneficiaries as might be included by the trustees at a later date. Who got what was entirely up to the trustees. If this document got into the hands of the United Kingdom Inland Revenue, they'd be none the wiser about who had put the money in and who could get money out.

Eastman now had to take what he knew would be an irrevocable step into crime. He needed to lay out the deal for McBain and explain how the system of *hawala* worked. He would also have to get the Letter of Wishes from McBain, so the trustees would know who was to be added to the trust and when they were to get the money. That would be a private document, never made public.

As he read over the papers from Jersey, he was distracted by Natasha coming in and sitting opposite him.

"I need to know where we stand, James. I'm happy to work

late tonight if that would help. Look, maybe we need to get away from the office. Donald's away on a course next Tuesday overnight. I could tell him I'll go out with Katie and stay over with her. You've got the Bankers' Dinner next Tuesday. We could meet up."

"Can you trust Katie?" Eastman asked.

"Definitely."

The Institute of Bankers Dinner was at the Clyde Views Hotel in Glasgow. Eastman usually stayed over for such dinners, so his wife suspected nothing when he told her about the function. Eastman booked a room at the neighbouring Gifford Hotel, and on the night went through the charade of turning up at the Clyde Views but excusing himself with his hosts due to feeling unwell.

By the time Eastman got back to the Gifford, Natasha was waiting for him in the room. She was wearing a micro skirt and a close-fitting black top. Eastman produced the champagne, and they toasted the future, whatever it might hold. Then the clothes were torn off.

Natasha was an enthusiastic but inexperienced lover, but a quick learner. They fell asleep at about two in the morning, exhausted.

The next day they stole back to the office separately. Eastman had enjoyed the night immensely, but he already knew it had been a mistake. However, if everything worked out, Natasha would be just a memory along with a lot of other burdens, and he quite fancied a month or two of illicit sex with her before things went pear-shaped, as he rather thought they would.

Eastman was sufficiently fired up by his night of carnality to face up to arranging the meeting with McBain. He was unsure whether to get McBain to drop the pretence of this being cash held by a friend, but on balance decided to let him run with the lie. To do otherwise might alert McBain to the fact that he'd learned something about his operations.

Eastman felt sure that his offices could not be bugged, but he was worried now that McBain's house might be. The experience of Boardroom Six at Lebens' office had caused him to be more careful about what he said and where. He was now using call boxes to contact McBain on his landline, not trusting his mobile or the office telephone. He arranged to meet McBain at Strathclyde Park, between Motherwell and Hamilton, in the car park near the funfair. He was confident no one could listen in to a conversation there.

McBain was clearly irritated, as he'd wanted the meeting at Westberry Drive, but Eastman insisted. When they met up at the park, they settled into the back of McBain's car.

"I may be able to help your friend, but this is very risky for me. We need to keep this tight between the two of us."

Eastman had made up a story for McBain's consumption.

"A couple of years ago one of my clients got into difficulty over a foreign exchange transaction, and put me in touch with a guy down south who was able to sort it. I met him at the time, and he said to keep him in mind if I'd any similar problems for clients in future. I've contacted him and he says 60 per cent of face value is the maximum you can get, and the cash needs to be Bank of England notes."

McBain sat quietly for about a minute. Then, "It is. Let's take a walk."

They walked round the man-made lake in silence. McBain stopped and turned to look at Eastman.

"How sure are you this will work? And what about your share?"

Eastman drew a deep breath. "I'm as sure as I can be, and the buyer is paying me, so it's 60 per cent clear. You can try it out with a small amount to start, do it by instalments or just sell it all at once. I guess instalments might be best."

"Can I meet the buyer?" McBain asked.

Suddenly, Eastman knew this was going to work.

"Don't be daft, Alex. No one knows who the buyer is. He's like Keyser Söze. You know it's all through intermediaries."

McBain laughed, "So you've seen *The Usual Suspects*, then. What a great film that is! OK, tell me how it works."

"I'll have more details for you next week. I'll be in touch."

They shook hands, went back to their own cars, and drove off.

DC Sarah Plummer watched from the cafe overlooking the car park. She'd tailed Eastman from his office but hadn't risked following McBain and Eastman as they walked round the park. In turn Rab Donald watched DC Plummer from his car. He had clocked her as soon as she drove into the car park just after Eastman. Interesting, he thought, but not unexpected.

Eastman got two tickets from Lebens in the office mail on the Wednesday. They were for a rugby league match on the next Saturday at Greenfield Stadium, near Manchester. Kick off at 3 p.m. He knew this would cause family trouble. He checked if there was a direct flight, but there was nothing suitable, so to get there in time for the game he would need to drive, leaving Edinburgh at eleven at the latest. His older son was again playing rugby for the school "A" team. Luckily, the game was to be in Edinburgh, so he could be at the school for the start but would need to slip away before half-time.

Eastman did his best to explain things to his son, who just scowled, though Eastman thought this was a bit of an over-reaction. He heard his wife and daughter muttering about priorities, and he thought to himself that if all this worked, he could be rid of the two witches sooner than they might imagine.

This was the first time he had seriously thought of walking out on his family. Which got him to thinking about Natasha, and he considered for an instant about getting her to tag along on Saturday, maybe for a bit of rest and relaxation on the way back. Donald would be at a football match, as usual. But that was too risky on a number of fronts, so he dismissed the idea.

On the Saturday he had a stroke of luck. The school rugby pitches were frozen and his son's game was cancelled. He was able to set off down the Biggar road at ten, to give himself a leisurely drive to Manchester.

It was only when he passed Penrith that he began to get nervous. Just after he joined the M74 at Abington he noticed a dark blue BMW behind him for a while, but it had overtaken him, and he'd thought no more of it. However, after Southfields it rejoined the motorway, keeping about two hundred metres behind him. When he turned off onto the M61, it disappeared.

What Eastman didn't know was that DC Plummer had switched from the blue BMW to a grey Renault at Southfields. After Eastman pulled off the motorway, she kept about six vehicles between him and her car as they followed a route which eventually led to a service station beside the Greenfield Stadium. Eastman pulled in to fill up the car and get something for lunch. As he walked back to the car, it began to snow in a desultory way. He then drove to the stadium car park and ate his sandwiches and crisps.

After ten minutes, Eastman left his car and walked purposefully across to the turnstile for the North Stand Upper, Sections A to E. Plummer watched him go in and immediately phoned Shettleston for them to arrange accreditation for her to get co-operation from the Stadium staff, if she needed to use the surveillance facilities. It seemed unlikely Eastman had come all this way to watch a rugby match.

She then made her way to Stadium Security. She found that Allensen had already arranged admission for her, though political correctness seemed to have bypassed this part of England, and she was subjected to some inappropriate comments from the uniformed security staff about her figure, dress sense and sexual orientation until she brought out her warrant card. She'd asked for some backup when she phoned Shettleston, but no one appeared and after about ten minutes she got a text from Allensen to the effect that resources were stretched in Manchester.

She commandeered the cameraman and asked him to scan Sections A to E in the North Stand Upper level. Eastman was nowhere to be seen.

In fact, Eastman had decided to stay on the inner concourse He was nervous as to who he might be meeting. The smell of the fried food combined with the sweaty bodies of the supporters was almost overpowering, but he decided to wait until the last minute before taking his seat.

The snow had been replaced by a light drizzle as the teams emerged onto the field. Plummer was able to pick out Eastman emerging onto the stand area, and she saw him sit in the middle of five empty seats. Her attention was momentarily distracted, and she didn't see someone hand an envelope to Eastman as he edged past him to sit further along the same row.

Eastman opened the envelope. It contained a programme for the match, and inside the front cover there was a typed note.

Assume you are being watched and followed. At half-time, leave, walk to Greenfield Station and buy a ticket to Manchester Piccadilly. Contact will be made on the train.

His first reaction was to look round to try to work out who was watching him, but he resisted the impulse. He simply folded the programme into his inside pocket and settled down to watch the first half of the match.

At half-time he left his seat. By now Plummer was seated at the rear of the same section, but by the time she got to the refreshment concourse, she lost him. She assumed he'd gone to the toilet, so went back to her seat. Eastman never reappeared.

When the game restarted, Eastman was already on a train

bound for Manchester. The two men who had followed him from the stadium were satisfied no one else was now tailing him, so they phoned their boss Mr Kankava to say it was safe to approach Eastman.

As the train pulled out of Salford station, one of the men, dressed in light jeans, a leather jacket and trainers, sat down next to Eastman, swept his greasy long hair from his face, and said they were getting off at Deansgate. When they got out of the station they walked up towards the site of the new Intercontinental Hotel. Eastman felt a lurch in his stomach as he watched other people doing normal Saturday things like shopping and relaxing in the cafes and bars. He began to sweat.

Then they turned into Whitworth Street. Eastman could see that at the end of the street was a sign for the car park serving the Intercontinental, under some old railway arches. He shivered as he trudged along the dark slushy street in the care of some real wide boys. This had better be worth it.

As they went through the main arch to the car park Eastman was directed to a maroon Jaguar parked in the far corner. As he approached the car his guide broke away and told him to stand by the passenger door while he rooted in the boot for an electronic gadget which Eastman assumed was to sweep him for hidden audio devices. Apparently satisfied that Eastman was not wired up, the guide opened the front passenger door for Eastman.

There was someone in the back seat, but Eastman couldn't see who it was as the partition glass was mirrored.

A voice, heavily accented, crackled through an intercom.

"You were followed, you know. We're not happy about that. Explain to me why someone from Glasgow CID tails you all the way to Lancashire in a grey Renault. You can call me Mr Manchester, by the way."

"Who's following me? Probably the Glasgow police. I've been interviewed by the CID at Shettleston in connection with a client. They want me to inform on him. I told them to get lost, Mr Manchester."

"I've used the stadium cutout before," the voice continued. "The police always go to security, so I've got a contact there. And you're right. The policewoman was from Shettleston Division. Interesting, don't you think?"

"Does this affect the deal?" Eastman shifted uncomfortably in his seat.

"Well, I can assure you that you're not going to be involved with us directly after today, so no. We're told £20m is available. It's up to you if you want to do the sale all at once or by instalments. The fewer handovers the better; all we need to know are the amounts of each payment." The voice sounded bored.

"My client would like some reassurance. He wants to know how the cash gets back into the system." Eastman asked.

"Our outlets are not your concern. All your client needs to know is that within three days, 70 per cent is deposited in his account. I presume you know the basics of how *hawala* works? Of course you do. So what's the issue about how we recycle your cash?"

Eastman was silent.

Mr Manchester continued, "Well, then, when you want to make the first payment, let me know. We'll give you two days' notice and a map reference. Be assured it will be somewhere isolated where your courier can't be followed. Your man – one man alone – brings the cash, my men count it, and your client gets his 70 per cent. Simple. Take the mobile phone on the driver's seat and the card."

Eastman picked up the mobile and the card, which had only a mobile number on it.

"Text me with the amount. I'll text back the rendezvous for the handover. I presume your man can read a map. Goodbye." The voice switched off the intercom.

A few seconds later the car door was opened. The man in the leather jacket stood waiting.

"I'm to walk you to the station," he said. "Then you'll find your own way back to Greenfield."

Eastman looked back at the Jaguar and saw it had been parked in such a way that it was impossible to read the number plate. He might just as well have been blindfolded, he thought.

His guide stayed with him until he got on the train at Deansgate. By the time he got back to Greenfield, the match had been finished for an hour and the area was deserted. He found his car looking forlorn in the car park. There was no sign of a grey Renault; in fact, the only cars left in the car park appeared to be chauffeur-driven limousines, waiting patiently for the prawn sandwich brigade to emerge from their post-match drinks with the directors.

He set off for Scotland. Just north of Carlisle he spotted a blue BMW two cars behind him. So they switched cars at Southfields, he thought. At Abington he lost the BMW, and he supposed – correctly – that his tail was heading back up the M74 to Glasgow. He got home to Edinburgh at ten, exhausted.

20

After he drove away from the Intercontinental car park, Lasha Kankava decided he would take the evening to think things over and then call Lee Yong in Singapore at midnight. That should cheer up his Sunday. Lasha owned a wide variety of businesses in the north of England, including a football club he'd bought from the administrators when it was effectively bankrupt. There were also three casinos, a greyhound racing track and dozens of small shops. The common feature was that each generated considerable income in the form of cash. It was through these businesses that the money from Glasgow would be channelled into the banking system.

Kankava and Lee Yong were partners in a Partnership Agreement whose financial provisions were obscure. How it read was Kankava put in the capital and Lee Yong put in the expertise, and the profits generated were shared 5 per cent to Kankava and 95 per cent to Lee Yong. This looked like a normal commercial arrangement, but the reality was different. This was the device by which the profit from buying dirty money was shared between them, without the money appearing to leave the country.

Kankava thought through what would happen with the McBain money, if it was £20m. He would feed the cash into the businesses as extra profits. He'd bought businesses with accumulated losses so there was no tax to pay. He would show the £20m in the partnership accounts. Lee Yong paid out £14m from Singapore to whatever tax haven McBain had chosen, so they had a tax-free profit of £6m too. Lee Yong was happy to keep his share invested in the United Kingdom, but periodically he repatriated funds to Singapore. Since these clearly came from a genuine United Kingdom business partnership, no questions could ever be raised.

When Kankava called Lee Yong at midnight, he was surprised at how edgy Lee Yong seemed to be. Never before had he had doubts about a transaction of this type.

Lee Yong had a high-pitched voice, "If this wasn't originating from Robert, I'd be doubtful, Lasha. Are you sure it's not a set-up?"

Kankava was reassuring.

"We've checked it all out. The lawyer's under observation by Glasgow CID, but we'd expect that. There's no link with us at all. We'll test his courier on the first exchange. If we get £20m, we'll invest it in the Harbour Development I emailed you about. I fancy we can pick it up cheap. Don't worry, it's become routine here."

"We need to be cautious, Lasha" Lee Yong replied. "Take no chances. If you have any doubts, abort the deal. Also, I'm getting information about your Western banks which is making me nervous. Close all accounts with British and American banks and place the funds with Oriental Bank. This is not a request, Lasha, it's an order. And so far as this Glasgow money is concerned, proceed!" The connection was broken.

On the Monday Eastman arranged another meeting with McBain. Again they met up at Strathclyde Park, and again the meeting had two observers. Eastman recounted the events of Saturday, up to the point of the discussion with Mr Manchester. Then he became imaginative. To cover up the fact that he and Lebens were sharing 10 per cent he changed the percentages of the arrangement.

"The system depends on trust between two businessmen. The one in the United Kingdom gets the cash and has some sort of arrangement with the foreign guy to reimburse him for the payment he makes to you. They share the difference. In this case, they make a profit of £6m, the £20m from Glasgow less their £14m from abroad. Simple, really. We're ready to go. We just need to know who's to be added as the beneficiaries of the Singer Trust. We need a signed list for the Jersey lawyers from your friend, and you need to decide how much is to be transferred. I guess the fewer transfers, the better."

McBain walked on in silence, and then turned to face Eastman, "I reckon you've guessed by now there's no friend. The money's mine so the Trustees need to add me as the person who'll decide how much comes out to me or my family. I've been thinking about that Will you sent me and I've decided that at the end of the day, after Irene goes, the estate goes to Sonny or, if he's no longer alive, to the Church. That's what's to happen to the Singer money as well, if I go. I went to see the parish priest to discuss this. We decided not to give Irene the estate, as she's already well-provided for, and I suppose she could remarry. I explained about the Singer money in Jersey and Father O'Rourke thought it might not be a good idea for the money to come back into this country. He suggested the International Bona Opera Fund. Nothing to do with music – 'bona opera' means good works in Latin, but you'll know that already. The fund helps poor children throughout the world; it's based in Geneva, and run by a board of Archbishops."

Eastman put on a very serious face, and said, "That can all be arranged quite easily."

McBain continued, "We're putting a lot of trust in you, James. I know you'll be on a kickback from these guys, so don't deny it. That's fine by me, but I need to be sure you're not trying to con us here. We know where your family are – don't think we'd fall for some sort of disappearing act; there's nowhere out of our reach. And don't think we don't know about Allensen's ideas. We've contacts everywhere. Can we trust you, and your trustee friends in Jersey? No doubt their snouts are in the trough, too."

Eastman shook his head, "These people are professionals. If you've any doubts, a trial run would show it works, Alex. Send five and you'll see three in the Singer Trust. Then you can go to Jersey and look at the trust bank account, if you like. I don't know what else to say. I know your reputation. I'm not stupid enough to co-operate with Allensen. OK, I'm on 5 per cent here, so that's a million quid for me tax-free. When am I ever going to get another chance like this?"

"What about Natasha, James. Does she know anything? Is she part of your master plan?"

"No, she's just a bit of fun, Alex. We're both in hopeless marriages, but there's no future for us as a couple. And she knows nothing about this."

"She's got such a pretty face, James. I wouldn't like to see her disfigured in any way. Remember Keyser Söze. And if anything happens to me, you'll have Sonny to answer to. Or Rab."

Eastman felt a familiar lurch of the stomach, "Look, Alex. There's no danger from me. Let's do the first tranche, and then you'll be convinced."

"What do we need to do?" McBain asked.

"Fix on an amount and let me know. I'll then get instructions from Mr Manchester."

"OK, I'll be in touch. I'll send Rab to see you. I'm going back to the car now. You just walk on round the lake. We won't be meeting again until this is all finished." McBain didn't offer to shake hands.

Eastman waited until he saw McBain's car pull out onto the

motorway, then headed back to the car park. As he was getting back into his car he noticed the blue BMW which followed him so much now.

Later that evening McBain and Rab discussed whether to use Colin Scott to tail Eastman, to find out if he did know more about who was really behind the cash purchase, but they decided it was too dangerous.

"That DC Plummer is on his tail, Alex. I've seen her both times at Strathclyde Park."

"If they're monitoring Eastman's calls, maybe there is a risk, Rab. But he said these guys are professionals, and they already knew he was under observation. I think we go for it."

"Whatever you say, Alex."

"The cash is a liability, Rab. It's a once and for all solution, because now we've our own legitimate side to use. But this is old money and if I get 60 per cent in a safe place, I'll be happy. Maybe with that I can think about joining Irene in Spain, if she'll have me back."

"What about Sonny?" asked Rab. "Would he go to Spain too?"

"No, Rab. Sonny would take over here, and with your help I know he could do it."

"I'm not sure I could work with him, Alex. I'm not getting any younger. I need to think about me. If Sonny and I were partners, maybe that would work."

"You know I don't like partnerships, Rab. There needs to be one boss. I'd arrange for Sonny to look after you well. You know that, Rab."

Rab looked down at McBain, slumped behind his desk. He really is looking unwell, and older, he thought, and he's losing his touch.

"Maybe we need to think this over, Alex. Meantime, do you want me to deal with Eastman and the cash? How much is to be moved?"

Rab had never had the nerve to ask this until now, but he knew McBain was set on cashing in. Most of the cash had accumulated before Rab came to work for McBain.

"There's £30m, give or take. With £18m legit in Jersey, I'll be happy to hand over. You know I can't risk getting Sonny involved on this; it's too complicated for him. He'll think I'm giving the money away. Yes, Rab, you contact Eastman and you sort it out."

"Do we move it in instalments?"

"Well, I thought at first we'd move just a bit, but now I'm not so sure we shouldn't do it all at once. I'm a bit bushed, Rab. Let's sort it out tomorrow."

Rab left McBain and met Sonny in the hall. He pulled him into the kitchen and closed the door.

"Were you listening in to that, Sonny?" he asked.

"Sure thing, Rab. Dad's sending some cash abroad and then hooking up with Mum in Spain. And I'm taking over! Good news for me, but no' so good for you. I think you're finished. You'll be gettin' a redundancy notice."

Scowling, Rab turned and left the house. But, as he sat in the Lexus, he smiled, and called a friend.

21

The next day McBain looked at the documents Eastman had sent him. The first one dealt with the situation while he or Sonny was alive. He and Sonny were to be added as beneficiaries of the Singer Trust and the Trustees were to pass capital to McBain or Sonny as McBain directed during his lifetime. If McBain died before the Trust was wound up, Sonny was able to get the cash. The second deed dealt with what was to happen after McBain's death if Sonny had died, or there was an accident involving both of them, and there was still money in the Trust. McBain added the details which Father O'Rourke had given for the Bona Opera Fund to the second deed, signed both documents, and put them in the envelopes Eastman had provided.

Rab had told McBain that Eastman had spoken to him about the importance of the letters to the Jersey Trustees, and had said that Rab must deliver them personally to him at McTavish's office. Eastman had apparently emphasised that everything needed to be channelled through him. So McBain called Rab into his study.

"Here are the documents to go to Eastman. It all seems to tie in. Tell him I've decided to move the £30m in a oner."

Rab gathered up the two envelopes. One was marked "First Letter of Wishes to the Singer Trustees" and the other, "Second Letter of Wishes to the Singer Trustees – to be opened only in the event of the death of the survivor of Alexander and Sonny McBain". He headed off to George Square, calling in to see

Colin Scott on the way. Later, he delivered the two envelopes to Eastman, who sent them on to Lebens by courier.

When he got back to Westberry Drive, Rab joined Alex in the study and they discussed how the businesses would be run if Sonny was in charge. While Alex was explaining that he would want to keep the house as his base in Scotland, even if he moved to Spain to be with Irene, and that Sonny would not therefore be moving to Westberry Drive, the housekeeper brought in a hand-written note from Eastman. It simply confirmed that he had received the drop-off details from Mr Manchester, being the time set and the map reference for the location.

Then Alex and Rab were on the laptop, googling the details on Multimap. Rab thought the location had been well chosen.

"Look, Loco. There's a long straight stretch on each approach to the lay-by, so it's easy to observe anyone tailing me. And to the east there's a roundabout with five different possible routes, so following anyone after the handover wouldn't be easy. I guess they'll head south, though there's a small airfield only about five miles away. They may switch the money onto a plane there. Who cares, though? We're giving them the money. We don't need to steal it back. Once we hand it over, I guess it's their problem. They're professionals."

McBain looked pensive.

"OK, Rab. Let's get to work. We allow five hours to get there. We go to the bank on Thursday, first thing, and empty the safe deposit. The cash's in boxes. Then straight down the M74. You can leave me at Lockerbie and then do the drop."

"How many boxes, Boss?"

"Twelve. Two point five in each. How safe is this, Rab? What do you think?"

"It looks like only Eastman is a danger. The Manchester boys are getting the cash for nothing anyway, so they've no reason to cross us. If Eastman's in with Allensen, or someone like Malik, we could have a problem."

"I'm not too worried about Eastman, Rab. You never know, though. Let's think. We're safe in the bank. If someone makes a move between here and Manchester, we'll know Eastman is a snake. Tell you what; you can be the tethered goat. Everyone will expect you to bring the cash, but you won't have it. We'll go separately to the bank. You go first, and then go to the drop, but you don't take the cash. I'll follow you via the M77 and meet you at the rendezvous just before two o'clock, and we'll switch cars. If you're picked up before you get to the drop, you'll have nothing on you."

★ ★ ★

Meantime, in his office, Eastman just couldn't concentrate on his ordinary work, so he decided to find out for himself where the handover of cash would take place. He wandered across George Square and down Buchanan Street to Borders bookshop to buy an Ordnance Survey map. He thought Mr Manchester would choose somewhere in the north of England, maybe near the Lake District.

He was standing in the travel section of Borders, looking at a large-scale map of the Lakes. He jumped as a hand was placed on his right shoulder. It was his old friend Niall Welsh.

"What's this then, young James? Planning a holiday? Surely McTavish can fund somewhere more exotic than the Lake District. Or are your new friends taking you on a trip? According to the goss, Master Eastman's life has changed. New chums, a new lady friend. Quite a transformation. Moving in strange circles, or, maybe, crooked circles? These lakes are awfully deep, James. You'll need to be careful. Just joking, of course."

"Good to see you, Niall. You know my weakness for maps. I'm updating my collection; this is a new edition. And what's all this about gossip? The Westberry companies are squeaky clean. Very go-ahead, don't you know. How's the Legal Aid side? I hear you're all going on strike."

The Scottish Executive was determined to cut the cost of publicly funded Legal Aid, and Eastman knew that a lot of Niall's income came from public funds. It was a neat way to divert the conversation away from McBain. Niall seemed to take the bait.

"Desperate times for us, trying to help the most vulnerable in society. Who knows where it'll end. When you think of the money wasted on …"

Eastman interrupted, "When it could be going to rich criminal Legal Aid lawyers? Spare me. Pull the other one. Anyway, must dash."

But Niall hadn't really been diverted. He pulled Eastman close, "Not so fast, young James. Mind how you go. These are people with no moral compass, unlike our great leader. You're way out of your league, James. Don't try to be clever. And don't deny it about Natasha. Glasgow's a small place."

Niall turned on his heel and walked straight out of the shop. Eastman felt he should go after him, but couldn't think what he would say. He joined the queue to pay for his map.

★ ★ ★

Thursday arrived. At half past nine Rab set off for the Highland Bank in the Mercedes estate, and arrived at the rear loading entrance in St Vincent Lane. He was met at the security barrier, as previously arranged. It was a double-door system, which left him in a protected area while the first armoured door closed behind him and before the second door opened. He parked in the secure internal area and was walked up to the safety deposit area by a guard, who introduced him to the duty manager. Rab handed over the security key and explained that he was there simply to check the contents of the McBain deposit and that, following a change of plan, Mr McBain was intending to call at the Bank shortly to remove the cardboard boxes from his safe deposit. He used the McBain key to access the transfer room and the guard left him. He simply waited fifteen minutes and called to be taken back to his car.

When he exited on to St Vincent Lane, he turned left onto Hope Street. McBain was waiting in a doorway; in an instant he crossed to the edge of the pavement and Rab leaned across and handed him the key. Rab then drove off, joining the M8 at the top of the town. He set off for Penrith.

McBain walked back to his hired Peugeot estate and drove round to the bank. He repeated all of Rab's moves, except the bank staff loaded the boxes into the Peugeot after McBain had signed for them. After he left the bank, he headed for the M77. He was taking the scenic route.

★ ★ ★

Lasha Kankava had decided to supervise the delivery himself, so he set off for Penrith in a convoy of two Range Rovers. There was a low-lying mist, and rain and sleet pelted on the motorway surface. This £30m was the biggest switch he had known. Kankava felt there could well be lucrative spin-offs from this, as he'd heard from his contacts in Scotland that there were other drug dealers there sitting on huge amounts of cash. He was disconcerted by Lee's hesitation about the deal, so he'd promised him he would make sure there were no hitches. The lawyer Eastman had been terrified, according to Kankava's men, so he felt he didn't pose a threat, and the client had no reason to double-cross them, because he was relying on him confirming to Lee that the cash was good, so that Lee could send the 70 per cent to Jersey. No, the only danger was from the police or a rogue element in the client's set-up.

As the Range Rovers approached Penrith the weather brightened and some watery winter sunshine started to dry the roadway. They left the motorway and headed towards Plumpton on the old Roman road. There the convoy stopped in a small hamlet and Kankava parked his Range Rover in a side street. This was the switch vehicle, so he joined his two colleagues in the other car, and then they made their way to a side road overlooking the lay-by where the handover was to take place. It was 1.30 p.m.

Kankava took out his binoculars and scanned the lay-by. Only a red pickup was parked there, with two workmen in the cab, drinking from cans and eating crisps. The signage on the side gave the name of a building company with a Lazonby address and phone number, and Kankava was sufficiently suspicious to phone the firm from his mobile, pretending to be a potential customer needing some urgent work done. Were they working in the Plumpton area, he asked? Yes, they did have two men at a job nearby. That's what they think, thought Kankava, and thanked them and rang off. He was satisfied these guys were genuine.

At about a quarter to two, a dark blue Mercedes estate approached from the north and parked at the opposite end of the lay-by. No other vehicle passed the lay-by for five minutes other than a single-decker bus. Kankava thought the Mercedes hadn't been followed. One man got out and went over to talk to the workmen in the pickup. After a brief exchange the driver returned to the Mercedes, reached in for a baseball cap. Kankava could see it was for the Baltimore Orioles, black and orange. Just then, the pickup started up and left in the direction of

Lazonby. Baseball cap, dressed entirely in black, stood casually against the boot of the Mercedes. One of his colleagues said he thought this was someone entirely different from the nervous lawyer. This guy had something, the way he walked, an assurance, a coolness. Kankava, as a former Georgian Army Captain, recognised it. He turned to his colleagues. "Ten to one on he's ex-services. Watch him carefully."

Baseball cap looked up at the approach of a grey Peugeot estate which came northwards and passed the lay-by before turning in at the far end. An older guy got out of the Peugeot, simply nodded to the baseball cap, handed him the keys, then got into the Mercedes and drove it away. Baseball cap now stood beside the driver's door of the Peugeot.

"Very clever," said Kankava. "They were worried about being picked up with the cash. Interesting ... they suspect someone. Well, time to relieve them of their burden."

The Range Rover drove into the lay-by and backed up against the boot of the Peugeot. Kankava got out and shook hands with Rab.

"No problems?"

"All going to plan, sir." said Rab. Kankava allowed himself a glance to his colleagues, who rolled their eyes. Yes, he was right again.

"Let's get on then."

Rab opened the boot and they transferred the boxes into the Range Rover. He said each box had fifty bundles of £50,000.

"OK," Kankava said. "We'll go for a drive in your car while my boys check quantity and quality. They'll phone me."

The Range Rover set off. Kankava explained that they had a facility fairly close by for counting cash. It had a bank of twelve cash machines, each of which counted and checked fifteen hundred notes per minute. To count £30m would take about two hours. Kankava suggested he and Rab go for a drink.

They found a country pub. There were a couple of locals moaning about the minimum wage, but when Kankava and Rab came to the bar, they changed tack to the problems caused by incomers owning village properties. Kankava offered them a drink which cheered them up mightily. Rab said he'd be happy with a sandwich and a Diet Coke. Kankava had a pint of Badger's Bitter and fish and chips. While they waited, they traded war stories. As they finished eating Kankava got a call on his mobile. He turned to Rab.

"OK, it's all in order. You can go now. My boys will pick me up here. Your people will be contacted on Monday."

Rab stood up. "Right, sir, I'll leave you to it. Maybe we can do more business in the future."

After Rab left, Kankava was thoughtful. Something wasn't quite right, something about the baseball cap was odd … he was too assured to be a subordinate. Maybe Baseball Cap was the real seller.

But he couldn't put his finger on it, so he wouldn't trouble Lee Yong with his doubts. His colleagues then arrived to collect him, and by the time they reached the facility – in fact, a barn on a remote farm – the cash was divided up into batches to be delivered to various sports grounds, pubs, clubs and betting shops. It would go through the books as additional income from ticket sales, bets, and so on. By Sunday morning the notes were in purses and wallets all over the north of England, and Lee Yong's partnership had an extra £30m income to book. His share was £1.5m, Lee Yong's £18.5m. Net of his payment of £14m to Jersey, Lee Yong's actual profit was £4.5m. A good day's work.

22

Rab Donald and Alex McBain were at Westberry Drive, anxiously waiting for the call from Eastman confirming that the £18m had come through.

Rab seemed distracted, "I'm still nervous about the whole set-up, Alex. As I said on Thursday, I'm fairly sure the guy in charge of the collection was eastern European, and ex-military. He's not someone you'd want to cross."

"Rab, the money was kosher. If there was a problem, I'm sure we'd have heard by now. I did wonder if the whole thing maybe was a set-up by Eastman. What are the chances of that? I don't know, I'm tired of all this. If I have £18m, maybe I'll be in Spain with Irene in a couple of months, leaving Glasgow behind forever."

"Well, Alex, you wouldn't need to worry about Sonny and me. Everything in Glasgow is going just fine. The cash is rolling in. The bookies are busy, and everyone's up to the mark with their loans. We had to make an example of some smart arse in Maryhill, and his family paid up. There's only one problem, and that's Sonny's temper. Joe called me from the Paradisa yesterday to say he'd hit one of the girls again. Apparently he was bragging to the staff about what a big man he would soon be, and the girl, Eva, had made a smart comment about what a change that would be. He'd lost it totally and punched her, cutting her lip and giving her a black eye. She can't work until it all heals up, so I told Joe to give her two weeks' pay."

"That boy, I told him about my plans but said he was to keep it to himself. What am I going—?"

The housekeeper came in carrying an envelope, saying it had been couriered by Mr Eastman. McBain tore it open. A short message.

"Lebens confirms £18m credited to the Singer Trust account. Has been invested in triple A grade bonds until you decide what you want to take out. Income of just under £1m a year."

McBain did a slow-motion jig of celebration, waving the note in the air.

★ ★ ★

Later in the day, Rab read his newspaper back at his flat. There are, on average, four murders a week in Glasgow, and Pollok had just provided another statistic. Pollok is a deprived area of local authority houses on the south side of Glasgow – its inhabitants have the worst diet, the highest drug abuse and about the lowest life expectancy in Scotland. When the motorway between Glasgow and Kilmarnock was built nearby, those on the edge of Pollok proudly flew the black flags of anarchy to remind commuters from Newton Mearns of the horrors just a stone's throw – literally – away from them, cocooned as they were in their BMWs and Jaguars. This was Malik territory.

The police had appealed for witnesses to the killing. Rab noticed that there was no mention of the murder being drug-related, which was unusual. And the journalist writing up the story was correct, for the death of Fazal Mohammed had nothing to do with disputes over drug-dealing territories. Fazal was the son of the owner of a newsagent's shop in Pollok, and had been walking back from a friend's home when he was set upon by a gang of local teenagers for no reason other than his colour. A white schoolboy from the area had been killed in a racist attack some weeks before, and his friends had determined to exact revenge. Fazal was severely beaten, and although still alive when taken to the Victoria Infirmary, he died of massive internal injuries the next day.

Opportunity knocks, thought Rab.

★ ★ ★

About ten days later, Malik received a reminder from his lawyers about McBain's offer of participation in the Canal project. He had some information from his father about it. The planners could well be persuaded to give a consortium the maximum possible retail and residential permissions. So it could be well worthwhile to join McBain on this. He thought again about the economies of scale in the wider context, if the two drug-dealing operations could be brought together. The only nagging doubt was over the anonymous call about Sonny.

Malik became aware of a bit of a commotion in the sales area. Raised voices – most unusual. He stood up sharply, knocking over his tub of coloured biros. Through the mirrored partition he could see an Asian man in a blue quilted anorak arguing with the checkout girls. The girls kept saying they could help him and he kept saying he had to see Malik himself. He was clearly infuriated and the girls were becoming alarmed. The man began screaming in a kind of high-pitched whine that Malik must see the letter he was holding.

"He must see me, he will see me." It became a kind of mantra.

Malik thought he recognised the man, but he just couldn't place him. He opened the office door and nodded to Jackie, the prettier of the checkout girls. She reassured the man he would see Mr Malik, and he calmed down. In fact, he seemed to diminish in stature before Malik's eyes, his shoulders sagging as he trudged across the cement floor, crunching the thin film of soap powder which is ever-present in cash and carry buildings. As the man entered the office, Malik held out his hand. The man ignored it. Malik gestured to the seat at the desk. The man said he'd stand.

Malik stretched out his arms as if in surrender, "Usman Malik, call me Usman. How can I help you? You don't buy from us, I think. Do you want to open an account? We give good terms."

The man spat on the floor. His breathing became shorter and shallower, almost hyperventilating.

"My name is Fazal Ali – I am the father of Fazal Mohammed."

Now Malik remembered. The boy who had been kicked to death. His father had been paraded on television with a local Asian MP, appealing for calm following these tit-for-tat attacks.

Fazal whispered, "You caused my son's death. I have a letter …"

"Now wait a minute," said Malik, stunned. "I know nothing about this at all. Who says I caused your son's death?"

"Read this." Fazal handed Malik a letter.

It was pathetic. Someone had been reading too many crime stories. The letter was a collage made from letters cut out of a newspaper. It must have taken hours to put it together. Why not just print it off in an internet cafe? When he read the first sentence – "From a good friend" – Malik thought it was a joke letter. But it was no joke.

"Your son was killed as a warning to Usman and Imran Malik. They are drug dealers whose gang stole from the McBains. Your son was in the wrong place at the wrong time. It was a case of mistaken identity. The hit was ordered by Sonny McBain."

Malik came round his desk to be beside Ali, and put his arm round him.

Fazal began to weep.

"I swear I don't know anything about this. It's a crank. It often happens, apparently, when you're on the television. I'm sorry for your loss. Could you do with some help, maybe financially?"

Fazal shook off Malik and moved to the door.

"I don't want your dirty money. And don't play the innocent. I know all about your drug outlets. No one sells that many vegetables. I'm an honest man. Keep away from my family."

And with that he walked out.

Malik sat down at his desk, and re-read the letter. Now it became clear. The Canal deal was some sort of trap. First the call, and now this. If the McBains wanted a war, that could be arranged. He would need to call Imran, maybe get some additional protection and firepower.

★ ★ ★

Meanwhile, in the city centre, Eastman was still stunned by the apparent success of the scheme. He had £1.5m tax-free to his name. Well, not exactly in his name. There, though, was the difficulty, which he had been thinking about constantly. The money was in Lebens' firm for the moment, and he had to find a way to get it into an account he could access, but of course it couldn't be in his name. The irony was his problem was now similar to McBain's – how do you clean dirty money? Lebens had withdrawn his fee of £1.5m from the Singer Trust, and had now sent Eastman a couple of emails pressing him to "deal with the Singer Trust issue".

At short notice, he decided to go to Jersey to discuss this

with Lebens, and now he sat in the taxi as it crawled along the promenade into St Helier. He had thought about setting up his own trust, but he was worried that the increased co-operation between Jersey and the United Kingdom tax authorities might mean his involvement would be discovered. No, it would be best to create a new identity for himself, and get an account opened which no one else knew about. Then if push came to shove he could disappear into a new life. The £1.5m would keep him going for a while. He'd often thought about just walking away from his present life and living a simple existence somewhere warm, maybe start a beach bar, whatever. A solicitor from Aberdeenshire had done this a couple of years ago, though he'd had pretty low-key ambitions, because he'd been traced months later working on a fruit farm in Cornwall.

The idea of walking out on everybody got mixed up with a dream he often had. He was sitting in his car at the side of a stream, in a small village, looking at a map. A woman he didn't know opened the rear door and two young children, about six and eight, got in the back and put on their seatbelts. Then she got in the passenger seat. She was blonde, about thirty-five, and he had absolutely no idea who she or the children were. She, however, was sure he was her husband, the way she talked. Just as he turned to speak to her, the dream always ended. At a party some time ago, he had met a psychologist and had asked her to analyse his dream, but she'd simply rolled her eyes, as if this were a standard chat-up line she'd heard many times before. Whatever it meant, he now had the wherewithal to make his escape.

Eastman now sat opposite Lebens in Boardroom Six. He talked in a low voice.

"This is very awkward. I need to find a home for the cash. I've read about second passports and the like, but I've no idea how to go about getting one. Can you help?"

Robert smiled, "Of course, old boy. Where do you fancy? Somewhere agreeable in the West Indies? There's a small jurisdiction we deal with. Could you produce a suitable birth certificate? Remember how it was done in *The Day of the Jackal*? The UK authorities have tightened up now, so you'll get a foreign passport."

Eastman nodded. All he had to do was tour a few graveyards and find the death of a male child who had been born around the time of his birth. He could then obtain an extract of the child's birth certificate from Register House in Edinburgh.

"Excellent! We'll deal with producing a suitable address for you; we have an arrangement that all mail for it is redirected. We'll then send any correspondence on to you. It'll take about four weeks and $50,000 to set up, and there's an annual administration fee of £2,000. I presume that's not a problem?"

"If I can use the money you have for me here for the $50,000. Is that OK? Will you then set up the new account for me?"

Lebens shook his head, "Better that you do it. Some of the Icelandic banks are offering excellent rates. There's a branch of the Kodlingski in Guernsey. Some of our clients use that. They're very discreet. When you've opened the account, I'll wire the money direct to them."

So it was agreed. After he got back to Scotland, Eastman decided to search a graveyard well away from Edinburgh, so on his way to the office he detoured to the Southern Necropolis on Rutherglen Road in Glasgow. He walked along about fifteen rows of headstones before he found something suitable. Robert Thomson, born 25th April 1959, died in infancy, 21st May 1959. He phoned Register House in Edinburgh and was told to send £30 and an extract of Robert's Birth Certificate would be sent to him. A few days later it arrived and he sent it on to Lebens.

23

Sonny had been indiscreet, boasting about how he would soon be running the McBain empire in Glasgow. News of this reached Shettleston CID by chance. A group of locals were arrested at a local club after a fracas. A girl had been ignoring her boyfriend and paying too much attention to one of the security staff. Blows were exchanged, some glasses smashed, and two people carted off to the Royal Infirmary with slashed faces. The uniforms who attended the aftermath found it difficult to get a word of sense out of any witnesses, so they simply bundled the six who were nearest the action into the van and took them to the station.

Among them was Morag Macgonigle, who worked part time at the Sauna Paradisa. She had nothing to do with the incident at all, but, unluckily for her, some cocaine had been dumped in her handbag as soon as the police arrived at the club, and now she was in trouble. Possession with intent to supply was a serious charge. However, her luck changed when DC Plummer came to interview her.

Morag was from Islay and had had a very sheltered upbringing. She'd come to Glasgow to train as a nurse, but had fallen in with a partying crowd, well up for the temptations of drink and drugs. She'd given up nursing, gone onto benefits and produced two youngsters by different fathers. About a year ago she'd pulled herself together, and given up on the drugs to devote herself to the children. Without qualifications, she'd found it a struggle to get a job, but her looks had got her into the Sauna Paradisa.

She'd met Plummer before, when she'd been checking the sauna records, so she tried to wheedle her way out.

"Come on, ye ken these were no ma drugs. Ah'm clean. Ah cannae go down for this."

Plummer said she knew Morag had no previous convictions, but she'd need to give her something in return for taking a lenient line.

"We tolerate what goes on at the Paradisa, because it keeps a problem off the streets. Maybe you've heard something from one of the punters?"

"No really," said Morag. "I dinnae encourage them to talk. I try to get it over with as soon as poss. I just give them, you know, a quick toss. Some of the other girls do more, I could tell you about that. Some weirdos."

"No, Morag, we're not interested in that. What about Mr McBain, do you ever see him?"

"Sonny's Dad? No, never. Besides Sonny, we only see Joe McCarthy. He's around a lot. Rab Donald comes in sometimes. But never Mr McBain. Of course, it's all going to change soon."

"How so? What's changing, Morag?" Plummer was suddenly interested.

"Oh, I was talking to Katrina, one of the Polish girls, ye ken. She's got to shag Sonny. Anyway, Sonny told her he'll be in charge soon. His Dad's going after his Mummy. Isnae that strange, a grown man like Sonny calling his Ma his Mummy? She's in Spain."

"Wait, wait, Morag. What exactly did Sonny say?"

"Katrina said Sonny said his Dad was going after his Mummy."

"How good is her English, Morag? Could Sonny have said his Dad was going after his money?"

"I dinnae ken. D'you want me to ask her? Is it important?"

Plummer realised she'd made a mistake referring to the money.

"No, Morag. Don't worry about it. In fact, forget it. I'm sorry you can't help us. I'll see if I can let you go with a caution. Just keep our little chat to yourself. Can't you get a proper job?"

"Not paying what I get, even after Sonny's cut. Ta for letting me go, though."

Plummer arranged for Morag and all the others to be released with cautions. She took the stairs up to the CID floor two at a time. Allensen was looking out the window, as usual. She breathlessly conveyed the news about what Sonny had said, and Allensen listened in silence. He slowly stood up, turned and smiled at her.

"Well, well, young Sarah. What do you make of that? The money's on the move, maybe? Has Mr Eastman been busy? We better have a chat. Get him in here."

On Monday morning Eastman got the call from Plummer that DI Allensen needed to chat. When asked about what was to be discussed, Plummer was evasive. Eastman said thanks but no thanks, and gave Plummer a lecture about client confidentiality. Plummer tried to force the issue, threatening to turn up at Eastman's office if he didn't agree to attend at Shettleston Station.

"Feel free," said Eastman. "Like The Ritz, we're open to all. Paying clients, of course."

The next evening Eastman was coasting along the M8 when he saw the blue lights flashing behind him. Automatic stomach lurch, followed by reassurance he hadn't been speeding. He pulled onto the hard shoulder and waited. A constable walked slowly up to the driver's side and motioned for him to roll down the window.

"Just pull up onto the raised area ahead, sir. We'll follow you."

Eastman saw the small platform about a hundred metres distant. He'd often seen it occupied by traffic cars waiting to pounce.

He did as he was instructed and the police car followed him. A figure walked along the hard shoulder, the passenger door opened and DI Allensen slid in.

"Well, well, we meet again. What *have* you been up to?"

Eastman was indignant.

"This is harassment. You can't go about kidnapping me because you want information about my clients. Clients, may I say, who have no criminal records."

Allensen smiled, "I just want to warn you one last time. We know something's going on."

"Look, Detective Inspector. I'm trying to buy a development site for Westberry near the canal. There's nothing else going on. Why don't you go after some real criminals, or try to keep hold of the few you catch?"

Allensen opened the door and climbed out. "Very funny, Mr Eastman. Don't say we didn't warn you."

And he was gone.

★ ★ ★

In Tradeston, Malik had been fretting for weeks about what to do. Eventually it had been decided that he and his father should meet his brother to decide how to retaliate against Sonny McBain. The meeting was in Frankfurt; not exactly halfway between Karachi and Glasgow, but it meant no one had to change planes and Imran didn't enter the United Kingdom. The movements of anyone from Pakistan were being closely monitored because of the terrorism threat, and the Malik operation didn't want to attract any attention from the authorities.

As they sat together in the airport cafe, Usman gave Imran

the details of the phone call and showed him the letter Fazal Mohammed had received. They discussed the offer to join the Canal consortium, and their father enthused about the potential profit which they might get, though he was also keen on the project as it would be a boost to his party's re-election prospects because of the local employment it would bring. His sons were not convinced.

The discussion became quite animated and Usman thought they were becoming the centre of attention in the cafe. In any event it was time for Friday prayers so he led his father and brother to the designated area where they joined others in the *Jama'ah*.

After completing the rituals, they found a remote seating area where they could resume their discussion unobserved. Usman and Imran were still of the view they shouldn't join the McBain project. Their father persisted trying to dissuade them from turning down the opportunity. He slammed his hand on the table in exasperation.

"Look, Usman, whoever sent the letter to Mr Mohammed would know for sure he would take it to you. If someone wanted to cause trouble between you and the McBains, this would be the way to do it. And the anonymous phone call fits with it being some sort of spoiling tactic."

Usman considered this. "But what's their motivation? And who could it be? I can't think of any other team in Glasgow who would be that clever. And there's no one from outside trying to muscle in. No, we have to respond, father."

"Well, Usman, if so, it needs to be proportionate. I've heard that there is a Muslim girl in one of their saunas. Her grandfather has written to me. She brings shame on her family, she brings shame on us all. She should be returned to her grandfather. If you arrange that, it will infuriate the McBains, but cause no lasting harm. Imran, can it be done?"

131

"Yes, father. I have an employee who is in Birmingham at present. He is due to return to Quetta next month. I will tell him to contact Usman, go to Glasgow, pick up the whore and take her back to her family. You do know what may happen to her, father. Last year in Bannu two were beheaded by the Taliban."

"That's a matter for her family. Her grandfather says she will be welcomed back. It is not our concern." He handed Usman the letter from the girl's grandfather. The brothers embraced one another, and parted.

As the Maliks were flying back to Glasgow, Eastman was looking with disbelief at a statement from the Kodlinski Bank forwarded to him by Lebens. Eastman's new identity had been established. Robert Thomson, resident at Flat 146/2 Blackhouse Road, St Mary's Beach, the holder of Passport SA195904252008 issued by the Republic of St Augustine, now had an account with the bank. In a covering letter the manager said he had been interested to hear of Mr Thomson's good fortune in inheriting a substantial sum from a relative, that a firm of solicitors in Jersey had wired funds totaling £1.46m from the Singer Trust, and the bank would be delighted to advise on investment.

24

Zahra knew she had been a real catch for the Paradisa. Homeless and penniless, this beautiful and elegant 24-year-old had walked in off the street looking for a job as a sports masseuse. She had been trained in Pakistan but her family had sent her to Scotland for an arranged marriage. Her husband had traditional ideas about discipline, and Zahra had lasted six months before making her escape. Her husband was unconcerned about her departure, expecting her to return. Zahra had quickly been put right about what really happened in the massage rooms, but she was desperate to earn money and had reached an agreement with Sonny. This had paid off for both of them. She was a big earner for Sonny, and she was saving furiously to get enough to start a university course, leaving her husband and the massage rooms far behind.

She finished chatting to Mr Macdonald, her regular six o'clock Thursday appointment. All she had to do for him was strip down to her bra and panties, and tell him about her childhood in the small village of Mirgara near Islamabad. She had confided in him about the deaths of her parents in a bombing at a political rally when she was a child, and how she had been brought up by her grandfather and aunt.

There were no other appointments for her on a Thursday, her one evening off. She was looking forward to a quiet night, though she would need to reply to a letter she had received from her younger sister begging her to return home. Zahra had been

133

surprised to receive the letter, as she had not communicated with her family since she had left her husband. She was anxious to find out how her sister had got her address.

She hurried out the back door of the sauna, and headed along Gallowgate to her flat in Thomson Street. The rain was pelting down and wind gusting behind her as she walked eastwards. Passing buses splashed the pavements. She was soaked by the time she reached the close mouth.

She heard van doors slide open and close behind her as she stepped into the close. As she turned round, she knew something was terribly wrong. The two men looked like Pakistanis and each was carrying a large suitcase. She ran as fast as she could up the two flights of stairs, but when she got onto the landing a third Pakistani man was standing nonchalantly at her door.

The man stood away from the door of her flat. He smiled, "Peace be upon you, sister."

Zahra replied, "And upon you be peace together with mercy and God's blessings."

The man lost the smile, "My name is Nazir. We must discuss your … situation. We bring news of your grandfather."

By this time the two other men had climbed up the stairs. It was crowded on the landing. Zahra looked back at them and turned to Nazir.

"What kind of news needs three messengers?"

Nazir looked enigmatic. Zahra shrugged, "You'd better come in, I suppose."

She unlocked the door and they followed her in. They had turned down with quiet laughs her suggestion that they could go in first.

There were three rooms off the small hall; a bedroom, a small combined toilet and shower room and a large sitting room/kitchen with a bay window overlooking Thomson Street.

Zahra had brightened the place up with travel posters, but the overall impression was still of dinginess. There were only two chairs in the sitting room. Nazir and Zahra sat down. The two others, relieved of the suitcases, started rummaging around in the kitchen area, then sat on the worktop.

Nazir narrowed his eyes and looked steadily at Zahra. She thought, "He's scarcely older than me. Why am I nervous of him?"

"The community in Glasgow is appalled by your behaviour. What you do brings shame on your family and on Mohammed, may peace be with Him. Your grandfather demands you return to Mirgara. Do you have your passport? Your husband said you took it when you left."

Zahra automatically glanced at her handbag on the worktop. Nazir cocked his head at one of his companions who lifted up the handbag and produced the passport with a flourish, like a magician completing a trick.

"Very well," said Nazir. "We travel tomorrow. Pack her things."

Relief was the main emotion which overcame Zahra, as she had feared the suitcases could have had a much more sinister purpose. There had been several recent honour killings of girls who had then been dismembered and packed into suitcases. She thought it might be worth while putting up a verbal fight, however.

"Nazir, my father condemned me to an arranged marriage with a psychopath. Who knows what his family will demand of me on my return? I promise to you I will leave Glasgow tonight and never work in the sauna again. Please don't send me back to Pakistan."

"You have dishonoured us by working for the McBains. Your fate is in God's hands, sister."

"As you say," replied Zahra. She saw resistance was pointless.

135

Zahra's main thought was that the important thing was to get them out of the flat before they found her Highland Bank statement taped under the table. Her family must not get to know about that. It was her possible passport to freedom. Rab Donald had advised her to put her money in an internet account she could access from anywhere in the world. "You just never know, Zahra", he had told her. She had a soft spot for Rab. He was a real nice guy, always ready to help. He seemed smarter than all the McBains put together. He said she should watch out for her husband, memorise the account details and keep no paper records. It had been a mistake not to shred the latest statement, but when she was low she liked to look at the balance.

As they were packing the suitcases, she had already thought about how to escape from Pakistan. The money in the account would see her to Dubai, and a new life there. She knew now that with her looks and intelligence she could make a go of things anywhere.

Nazir signalled that they were leaving, "You will stay at the house of my employer tonight, and we fly to Dubai tomorrow. There is a connection to Islamabad. With God's will, we shall be in the house of your grandfather the day after tomorrow."

"So be it." Zahra nodded as the two men lifted the cases. What an irony, she thought.

"What about the lease here? And the sauna?"

"It will be dealt with, sister", said Nazir.

They trooped out onto the landing, and Nazir locked the door. They were halfway down the upper flight of stairs when Joe McCarthy looked up at them from the first landing.

Joe had been sitting in his car outside Zahra's flat for ten minutes, trying to pluck up the courage to tell her how he felt. He'd had an uneventful life, if you disregarded the convictions for assault and attempted murder. After jacking in school at sixteen, he'd graduated through petty theft into what passed for organised crime in the north-east of Glasgow. Along the way he'd got involved in many a drunken rammy, and his prison sentences were evidence of his double stupidity in getting involved and then getting caught. He'd a very short fuse.

He'd married Betty Connor when they were both seventeen and she was four months pregnant. For the life of him, Joe couldn't remember what had attracted him to her. The well-built girl squinting into the sunshine in the black-and-white wedding photograph on the mantelpiece had long since disappeared into a large envelope of fat, fuelled by a non-stop diet of crisps, cakes, fish suppers and fizzy drinks. Their daughter was now herself a roly-poly seventeen, had two kids by different fathers, but was unmarried, on the social, and living in a recently renovated flat provided by the council. Rab had once told Joe his family was a sad continuation of a downward spiral, whatever that meant. Rab quite often talked pish but it didn't pay to question what he said, especially if you didn't understand it.

Joe had fallen in love with Zahra the first time he saw her. It had been that gut-wrenching moment when you see someone you think you may have met before, but who you really know you've been waiting for all of your life. It was a most unlikely unconsummated love match, and Joe was worried that the feelings were going in one direction only.

Just a few days before Zahra walked into the Paradisa for the first time, Joe had seen a photo of a youthful Benazir Bhutto in his *Daily Record*. The exiled former president had just returned to Pakistan after doing a deal under which she was granted amnesty and all corruption charges against her had been withdrawn. The *Record* had prepared a picture page feature on her life. Zahra and she could be sisters, Joe thought. Zahra's large almond eyes and slim figure had a breathtaking impact on

Joe. This was a woman quite unlike the white whale he shared a house – though thankfully no longer a bed – with.

Joe had decided finally that he must try to tell Zahra how he felt about her. There was no way he could do that at the Paradisa, so he was on his way to open his heart to her. He'd worked out what he'd say. He'd suggest that he could move into her flat, she could stop work at the Paradisa – he would square that with Sonny – and he could get a rise in his wages out of Alex McBain, and have enough for both of them. Joe was smitten.

He'd walked purposefully into the close and up the first flight of stairs. The close stairs and landings were floored with grey granite, but it was a wally close, which meant the walls were covered with shiny tiles in the old Glasgow Corporation colours. There was no natural light in the close, because although there was a cupola, the blackout blinds from the Second World War were still in place. At each landing a single 60-watt bulb was suspended from some very dodgy looking fittings attached to ancient cables which snaked uncertainly upwards. The overwhelming stench in the close was of fish suppers and cats.

Joe looked uncomprehendingly up the second flight of stairs at Zahra and the three Pakistanis. The one at the front was gripping her forearm, guiding her downstairs – she looked resigned, maybe a bit scared. Behind her were the two others, carrying suitcases. For an instant the picture was frozen.

Had it been Rab on the landing, the outcome would have been very different. Joe was on the landing below the Pakistanis. Rab would have said something like "Hi" and walked up the stairs past them. That would have given him three advantages. First, the element of surprise as he turned round on them. Second, the downward momentum attacking the suitcase carriers, who would have had their backs to him. And third,

Nazir would not have been able to use Zahra as a shield, as she was now in front of him as the party edged down the stairs.

But Joe hadn't had any unarmed combat training. He simply roared, "What the fuck's happening here?" as he charged up the stairs. All Nazir had to do was push Zahra into him to deflect the attack. Mushtaq and Shoab, the other kidnappers, dropped the cases containing Zahra's possessions, and all three set about Joe.

The granite steps were unforgiving. Joe's forehead was split open and his nose broken before the first kick hit his body. He was rolled down the stairs to the first landing where a few more kicks rained in on his curled up body. Mushtaq took out a knife, but Nazir shook his head. Joe was already drifting into unconsciousness. Zahra was sitting on the top step of the first flight of stairs, shaking uncontrollably. Nazir and Shoab lifted her up and carried her out to the people carrier. Mushtaq recovered the cases and followed them out.

There had been a lot of noise in the close, what with Joe shouting and Zahra screaming, then weeping and wailing. But no door opened in the close and no curtain twitched as the four got into the people carrier and drove off. All was quiet now on the first landing, except for some low moaning from Joe. He knew his right leg was broken and probably also his collarbone and a few ribs.

He managed to get hold of his mobile in his trouser pocket. He felt worse now, hot and dizzy. No one would help him here, people just didn't get involved. He speed dialled Rab who said "Joe, what's up?"

All Joe could say was "Five, Thomson Street" before he passed out.

139

25

Rab was sitting opposite McBain at Westberry Drive when he took the call. He stared at his mobile.

"It's Joe. All he said was 'Five, Thomson Street.' He sounded weird. Is that off the Gallowgate? I'll go."

By the time Rab arrived, an ambulance was already at the close mouth. An onlooker told him that a teenage girl returning from school had found Joe on the stairs and dialled 999. Joe was being carried out on a stretcher. Rab tried to speak to him, but the two ambulancemen chased him. Rab was told that Joe would be taken to the Royal Infirmary.

As Rab was about to get back in the Lexus, a police Range Rover drew up, blocking him in, and out stepped DC Plummer.

"What's this, Mr Donald?" she started. "Unusual, foolhardy, daring to attack a McBain man about here. Why was McCarthy here? Collecting a debt, maybe? If so, I don't give much for the mark's chances. Or maybe this was personal? Who lives up this close?"

"Not a clue, Miss Plummer," said Rab. "All these questions. All I know is my mate's been attacked. Any witnesses?"

"Hilarious, Mr Donald. This is Dennistoun, in case you've forgotten. We'll get a list of occupiers, but it'll be years out of date. You can help us on this. I'm sure my boss would be grateful."

"Let's see what Joe says. Got to go. Please?"

Rab pointed to the double-parked Range Rover.

Plummer nodded to the driver to move to let Rab out. He wound down the window and indicated to Plummer to come over. As she leaned into the car, he simply smiled and whispered, "Don't rack up too much overtime on this. We'll take care of it."

Plummer shrugged and turned to the uniforms. It seemed certain someone living in the close or visiting was involved, so she told the young constables to take statements from everyone they could find. They were to ask especially about recent arrivals, big spenders, gamblers, and anyone connected with the McBains.

Plummer then drove to the Royal. Joe was in theatre. His self-diagnosis in the close had been pretty accurate. Broken were his right leg, nose and four ribs. He hadn't realised his spleen was ruptured.

The sister in recovery told Plummer that Joe would need further surgery the next day, so the earliest she could speak to the patient would be in about forty-eight hours. Plummer returned to Shettleston and brought Allensen up to speed.

"This doesn't seem to be connected with Eastman, sir. But it is unusual, to say the least. If it turns out to be the start of a north/south dispute, we're going to be busy."

Allensen frowned. "I agree it's very odd, but I suppose it might simply be someone on a high, and lashing out at his supplier. Though McCarthy is usually a debt collector, so who knows. Put it down as an isolated instance, unless we learn more."

In the meantime, the uniforms had completed their interviews at the scene, come back to the station, told the desk sergeant there was nothing significant in what they'd found out, and gone off shift. They'd been allowed to go without writing up their reports, as the desk sergeant wasn't too bothered about someone like McCarthy being done in. He was a McBain enforcer, after all.

Meanwhile Rab and McBain were having a drink at Westberry Drive. Rab had phoned Betty McCarthy's house, but apparently the police had already contacted her and she was already at the Royal Infirmary, according to her daughter. McBain told Rab he'd spoken to his own doctor and arranged for Joe to be moved to a private clinic in Kirklee as soon as he was fit. The doctor called back to say he'd found out from Joe's surgeon at the Royal that Joe needed a procedure on his spleen which was scheduled for the next day, so the earliest he could be moved would be in about three days. He might be able to have visitors in the evening after the next day's surgery.

McBain sipped his malt and looked quizzically at Rab.

"What was he doing there, anyway? Has he got a bit on the side? It wouldn't surprise me, knowing what Betty looks like these days."

Rab shook his head.

"I don't think so, boss. He's been a bit strange recently, mind you. A bit quiet. He hangs around the Paradisa a lot. We better check the collections book, but I don't think there's anyone who owes us in Thomson Street."

McBain pulled out a red leather-bound accounts book from his desk, and they both looked over the list of borrowers. There was no one listed for that street.

"It's a mystery, for now," said Rab, "but we'll get to the bottom of it tomorrow night, probably. Meantime, I'll start asking around. The cops will be gone by now."

Rab made some calls and two hours later he had some information. A people carrier with three Asians in it had been parked outside the close that afternoon. He passed this on to McBain.

"It could be Malik, then. But why? We're trying to get onside with him. Why would he do this? What's going on?" asked McBain.

142

"Let's sleep on it," said Rab. "It may be nothing to do with Malik. I'll be here at ten tomorrow and we'll go and see Joe later on."

The next day, Zahra was due to start work at noon. At just after one, the receptionist, Carla, phoned Sonny on his mobile to tell him she hadn't appeared, and that there might be trouble because some of her regulars had booked her. Sonny was with his Dad and Rab at Westberry Drive.

Carla said that it was very strange, as Zahra had always called in if she was sick.

"Have you tried phoning her?" asked Sonny, who could be relied on always to ask the most obvious question.

"Of course, both her landline and her mobile. No answer from the landline and her mobile goes onto voicemail. Should I get someone to go round to see she's OK?"

Sonny looked at Rab and his Dad, shrugged his shoulders, rolled his eyes and mouthed, "Problems".

"No", said Sonny. "I'll go myself and see what's going on." He had a sudden desire to see Zahra tucked up in bed. He'd often wondered what it would be like to ... He pulled himself together.

"What's her address?"

He gestured to Rab to give him a pen. He wrote the address on the front of the newspaper he'd brought with him, and as he did so he repeated it.

"Two up, 5 Thomson Street. OK."

Sonny cut the connection. Rab and McBain looked at Sonny.

"Who stays there?" Rab asked.

"It's one of the Paradisa girls. The Paki. Zahra. She's no' turned up for work. What's up?"

"Really!" said McBain. "Well, Sonny, that's where Joe was beaten up. What was he doing there? I wonder. We better find

143

out. We'll see Joe later. First we go to the girl's flat. She's got some questions to answer."

When they arrived at Thomson Street, two uniforms were about to drive away. Rab knew one of them and found out they were intending to come back about six o'clock to see if anyone passing at about the same time as Joe had been attacked might remember anything. The scene-of-crime boys had gone, apparently.

When the cops drove off, McBain, Sonny and Rab started up the stairs. When they got to the second landing, the door to the left was ajar.

"Zahra, it's just me," Sonny shouted from the landing and walked into the hall. A female voice from the sitting room said "Hello" and a professional-looking woman of about thirty-five emerged holding a clipboard. She was wearing a well-cut black trouser suit and an open-necked white blouse.

"Can I help you gentlemen? Are you interested in the flat? We just got the keys back this morning. I'm just checking the inventory. I'm sure the owner would let you have it …"

Sonny started to interrupt, "No, for Christ's sake, we're looking for …"

"Well, we may be, miss," Rab cut in. "But we'd just like to have a look around. Mr McBain here might actually make an offer to buy it, add it to our buy-to-let portfolio, if the yield is right. Do you have a card?"

The lady handed one to Rab. He read out loud.

"Angela Finlayson, of Gee One Flats, 1172 West Campbell Street. Thanks. Would the owner be willing to sell, do you think? Can we look around?"

Miss Finlayson made a note on her clipboard. She looked up.

"I'm finished here. If you want to make an offer, we'll consider it. How long will you need? I've got to make some calls."

Rab walked over to the bay window and looked out onto the street. Although it was early afternoon, the tenements opposite seemed so close that it looked like night was falling already. What a depressing place!

"Oh, ten minutes will do. Leave us the keys and we'll lock up and bring them down to you. Which is your car, Angela?"

"The Fiesta, the dark blue one. Well, I suppose it's OK …" She suddenly walked over to the window.

"Maybe I should check first with the owner." To Rab, she seemed suddenly uncomfortable.

"Tell you what, Angela," McBain spoke for the first time, "I'll walk you down to your car and the boys will be at the back of us. I'll be your security."

McBain guided the woman out. Sonny had retreated to the hall, and as she passed him she handed him the keys.

As McBain and Angela left the close, the rain was battering the street. McBain said his Mercedes would be more comfortable for them to wait in, and Angela reluctantly agreed. McBain started talking about Westberry Properties, and Angela realised she might have a chance of getting some additional business out of this odd encounter. She went into full selling mode about the sales and letting services her firm could offer to developers.

McBain seemed happy to let her make her pitch at full flow for a while.

"I'll think it over, Angela. We may have some flats going up in Maryhill. By the way, what happened to the previous tenant here?"

"Well, it was a bit odd, Mr McBain. She was a lovely girl, a mature student, I think, from the former colonies, as my father calls them. She never complained about anything and always paid her rent on time. We prefer bankers' order, but she paid cash. Her lease had two months to run, and we'd have been happy to renew it. Then this morning, just after nine, her cousin came into the office and said she'd had to go back to Pakistan. Or was it Bangladesh? Anyway, he said it was something to do with a sick relative. We said we'd keep an eye on the flat for her until she came back, but he said she wanted to give up the lease and she'd cleared her stuff out of the flat. He handed over cash for the rent for the last two months. £1000. Just like that!"

"What had she to say about it? You must have been surprised." McBain looked innocently at her.

"She wasn't there. Her cousin said she was busy organising flights, so he was handling this for her. I was a bit unsure about that, but he did pay the rent. We're not doing so well just now, as you might expect. Well, you'll know all about the credit crunch. And I knew I'd a prospective tenant on my waiting list, so I just decided to accept what he said, take the money and do the inspection right away. I can get the new tenant in tomorrow, actually. The yield would be 8 per cent. Would that be of interest to you? By the way, where are your friends? What's keeping them?"

McBain stroked his chin.

"Oh, don't worry. They'll not be long. Well, Angela, that seems very straightforward about the tenant. But you said it was a bit odd. What was odd about it?"

"Up to then it all seemed fine. But then I asked him what should we do about Miss Patel's deposit. He looked totally confused. You know, at the time I thought he was starting to say "Who's Miss Patel?", but he stopped himself and asked what I meant. Well, it's £500, I said, one month's rent. Usually we send out a cheque after the inspection, when the cost of any damage has been taken off. So I asked him for Miss Patel's address."

"Interesting. And what had he to say to that?" McBain put on a concerned look.

"Where are they, your friends? They've been a long time.

Should I go back up and check?" Angela's voice sounded agitated.

McBain now looked serious, "Look, Angela, do you really see them stealing a few sticks of furniture? I know your time is valuable and you'll be … compensated for your trouble. Now, what did the cousin say about Miss Patel's address?"

"Well, he seemed thrown. He took out his mobile phone and started to dial a number. Then he put the phone back in his pocket. He looked around as if he was worried someone was watching him. Then he leaned across the desk and whispered, 'When could I get the money?' I said that could be later today, if everything was in order at the flat. He thought for a minute and asked if he could just deduct it from the £1,000 he'd brought. I told him we're not buttoned up at the back. He didn't understand that, but I think he caught my drift. So he said he'd come back this afternoon and collect it. But it had to be cash, not a cheque."

"When?" asked McBain, with a definite edge to his voice.

"Why do you want to know this? He's just a young lad. What's this all about, really? It's nothing to do with the flat, is it?"

McBain turned and looked straight at her.

"It's OK, Angela. My son is a friend of Zahra's – Miss Patel, that is. We're all concerned about what's happened. As you said yourself, it's all a bit odd. She never mentioned leaving Glasgow and she'd have told Sonny if she was going to care for a sick relative. The best thing will be for us to have a quiet word with the cousin when he comes to collect the £500."

"Maybe she's been kidnapped! Is it one of these Pakistani honour things? Maybe we should go to the police."

McBain laughed.

"I don't think it's that dramatic. And, anyway, what would you tell them? That a young girl has given up her flat and you don't know where she is. The police would pat you on the head and tell you to run along. No, we'll find out where she is."

"I see what you mean. Don't you want me to ask the cousin?"

"No – and don't let him know about us. Better if it's a surprise. Now, I need your word on that."

McBain reached inside his coat. Angela pulled back, but McBain merely pulled out his wallet.

"You've been very helpful." He counted out £1,000 and held out the wad of notes to her. She hesitated, but only for an instant, before taking the cash and starting to slip it into her handbag.

"Now you need to tell me when the cousin's due at your office. I presume you're meeting him there."

Just as she confirmed it was fixed for four o'clock, Rab and Sonny appeared and eased into the back of the Mercedes. They'd gone through all the drawers and cupboards, but there had been nothing to show that Zahra had ever existed. Then they'd moved all the furniture out from the walls just in case there was something hidden, and then Rab had said to turn everything upside down. That was when they'd found the Highland Bank statement. Rab had sighed.

"Well, Sonny, she'd never have left this. So we know she didn't go willingly. OK, let's lock up and go. Maybe Joe will fill us in tonight."

In the car, McBain turned to face Rab and Sonny and brought them up to date. Angela had meantime brought the notes out of her handbag and was counting them, ignoring the men in the back.

"Angela here has given us a lead. Zahra's cousin is collecting her flat deposit at four o'clock at her office."

"She disnae have a cous–", Sonny started to say.

McBain quietened him with a policeman's halt sign and turned back to face Angela.

"Now, my dear, you've never met us or talked to us. Is that clear? If so, you'll not get any visit at 1172 West Campbell Street from any of our associates. Deal or no deal?"

Angela Finlayson zipped up her handbag. She smilingly said, "It's been a pleasure not to meet you, gentlemen, but I'm afraid I've never heard of Mr McBain, his delightful son and the third man. So I'll be off."

She slammed the door and walked purposefully towards her car.

McBain suddenly got out of the car and ran after her, grabbed her by the shoulder, and turned her back towards him. He was breathless.

"What's your favourite scene?" he asked.

She smiled again, this time archly, "Well, well – two choices!" She unlocked the car door, got in and rolled down the window. "Where Martins sees Harry for the first time, when the light shines on the doorway, with the kitten. Or at the end, where Harry's girl walks past Martins in the graveyard." She paused, "Maybe we can watch it together sometime."

And with that she started up the car and drove off.

McBain walked back to the Mercedes and slid into the back seat. Rab and Sonny had got into the front while the exchange at Angela's car was taking place.

"That's really some lady. She likes the same scenes as I do in one of my favourite films. She called you 'the third man', Rab – would you believe it?"

"Dad, forget about your movies. What do we do now?" Sonny asked.

"Look, boss, we're not really interested in Zahra", Rab said. "Nice kid and all that, and a good earner for Sonny. But what we want to know is who did Joe in. I'm sorry, but we don't spend our time chasing skirt round the country. What's the next move, boss?"

McBain thought for a few moments.

"Let's go into town and see who turns up at four. From what Angela said, I suspect this is a bit of private enterprise, so the so-called cousin will probably come alone. We jump him as he leaves and take him out to Blanefield. Have you got a blade, Sonny?"

"Is the Pope Catholic, Dad?" Sonny pulled out a cut-throat razor.

Rab drove them into town. It was half past three when they parked in St Vincent Street. They'd a clear sight line to Gee One Flats' shopfront.

26

Zahra sat on the leather sofa in the drawing room of the mansion in Cedar Avenue. She was uneasy about how relaxed Nazir had seemed to be about how they were going to get her back to Pakistan. Her thought was, as soon as she was in a public place, she would ask a policeman or customs official for help. She was aware that in some thrillers, the kidnappers arranged for the victim to be sedated for a flight, and transported as a stretcher case, but it seemed very unlikely that Nazir would have been able to arrange something like that, involving as it must doctors and medical certificates. Just then an older man glided into the room, holding her passport.

"My name is Usman Malik. You have been my guest here since yesterday, and your flight leaves for Dubai this afternoon at 2.15. You may have thoughts of trying to escape, or of appealing to the authorities for help. Banish these thoughts from your mind. Your younger sister is being detained in Mirgara. Her continued well-being depends on your co-operation. Do you understand?"

"What do you mean? Detained? By whose authority? My sister has no part in this. Let me phone my grandfather. He will clear up this … this misunderstanding."

"Your grandfather requested that you be returned to your village, and he has detained your sister on orders from the imam there."

"But why? I left my husband, but …"

"I have no interest in your marriage. Your conduct here has outraged us, and your association with McBain must end. My daughter Fatima will accompany you on your journey."

"But what will happen in Mirgara?"

Malik looked away. "I have no idea."

★ ★ ★

Zahra, Nazir and Fatima were driven to the airport. Their luggage was checked in, and they went through Security, Fatima keeping hold of Zahra's passport and boarding card. Zahra had tried to engage Fatima in conversation, but not only did she refuse to speak, she actually recoiled from being touched by Zahra. When they boarded the plane, Zahra found that Nazir was already in the seat next to hers, so she was sandwiched between him and Fatima. During the flight, when Nazir and Fatima referred to Zahra, they did so in the third person, as if she was an inanimate object, a piece of hand luggage. Zahra's only comfort was her knowledge of the funds she had in her bank account. She was confident that in Mirgara she would make peace with her grandfather, and she and her sister would make a new life for themselves in Dubai. As the plane ascended, she looked over past Fatima to the view of Glasgow for the last time. She gazed wistfully at the tower of Glasgow University, where she had hoped to study.

★ ★ ★

Meantime, on the ground, Mushtaq was nervous. He knew he was taking a chance going back for the £500, but neither Nazir nor Shoab knew anything about it, and the whore, Zahra, hadn't mentioned it. Greed was good, especially when you had a large family back in Quetta. That money would go a long way. One of his main worries was the woman in the office, who had overawed him with her self-assurance. She was unlike any woman he had known in Pakistan. Also, the whore, Zahra, had been a bit like her. What happened to females in this country? As he waited beside the bus stop opposite the office, two teenage girls, with low-cut tops and jeans barely covering their pubic hair, leaned against the wall beside the bus stop and tried to light cigarettes. It was only mid-afternoon but they were already drunk. "Fancy a drink, darkie boy?" the plumper one slurred. "Or how about a quick shag up the lane?" said the other, screeching with laughter. Their bus arrived and the driver reluctantly let them board.

At four o'clock Mushtaq ran across the road, hoping that the woman in the office would just hand him the cash, no questions asked. A passing taxi splashed his trainers. As he entered the office, he saw the woman was sitting at the same desk as before, the one furthest from the door. The other desks were unoccupied. Mushtaq also saw a white envelope lying beside her telephone. He stood awkwardly beside the desk, and noticed the perspiration on her white blouse. Why was she nervous?

She seemed reluctant to look at him, merely pushed a sheet of paper headed "Receipt" across the desk with a cheap yellow biro pen and asked him to sign for the £500. He laboriously signed, and she indicated he should take the envelope. He counted the money carefully.

"Is everything in order?" he asked.

"Yes, please go." The lady turned away.

Mushtaq thought this strange, but he it suited him to move quickly to the exit.

As Mushtaq turned left up West Campbell Street, something made him look back down towards St Vincent Street and he saw two men finish a conversation and start to walk up the street after him.

He looked around in vain for a taxi. He quickened his pace as he approached a building which was being renovated. It had scaffolding on the side, and a narrow passageway had been constructed under it on the roadway for pedestrians to use. It was like a small tunnel, and as he entered it he saw an older man in a blue suit at the other end, standing motionless. He did not look friendly. Mushtaq decided to turn back, and walked right into Rab who immediately armlocked him.

"We need to have a little chat, cousin. What on earth have you done with our dark-eyed princess?"

Rab marched Mushtaq to the Mercedes. Mushtaq had been tempted to call out for help, but passers-by seemed to be avoiding the incident, scurrying away, and the other man had also put his arm round him, shielding sight of the mottled steel blade from everyone but Mushtaq himself.

He was sat in the back of the car, between the older man and the armlocker. The razor wielder started the engine and they set off. Nothing was said. They drove through suburbs into the country. After passing through a couple of villages, Mushtaq saw a sign for Ledburn Farm, and they drove up the farm road, past the farmhouse and up to a cottage, where there were no lights. The place seemed desolate.

The man in the blue suit turned to face him and spoke for the first time.

"Well, son, it's the end of the road for you here. Do you see that yellow digger over there? That's what we call a JCB. In a few minutes we'll start it up and dig a nice big hole. Then we'll sit you at the edge and Sonny here will carve a few slices off you. You'll bleed into the pit; we don't want any mess. You'll be brave at first, of course, but then we'll get the axes out of the shed over there. You'll tell us what we want to know after you lose your left hand, because maybe we'll let you keep your right. They do that in Africa, you know, but they have a more leisurely approach. They leave long intervals between the cutting, so you get plenty of time to regret your misdeeds."

Rab asked, "Is that in one of your films, Loco? On the guy's birthday every four years they cut off one of his limbs. What's it called?"

"No, no, that's in a book. Anyway, son, I don't want to get out of the car. It's cosy in here, isn't it? We're quite high up, and it's cold out there. The temperature drops one degree Fahrenheit every three hundred feet, but you, an educated lad, you probably know that already."

"Let's get on with it, Dad." said Sonny. "He'll no tell us unless we bleed him. Remember the boy from Castlemilk? He was one tough character. He didnae think I'd go through with it, but when I chopped off his arm, I saw it in his eyes, Dad. He believed it then. He talked and talked till he lost consciousness. By then it was too late. He's in that pit over there, what's left of him. I cut off his head just to be sure."

Mushtaq felt he was about to lose control of his bowels.

Rab put his hand on Mushtaq's forearm, "Maybe he'll tell us now, to avoid all this. What do you say, cousin?"

Mushtaq peered out at the digger, but then looked down at his shoes, saying nothing.

"Great!" said Sonny, and started to open the door.

"Wait," said Mushtaq. "What do you want to know?"

"What happened yesterday at Zahra's flat? Where is she?" Sonny asked, closing the door.

"My boss, Nazir, is taking her back to Pakistan, to her village, as her grandfather asked. We were told to clear her flat and take her to a house in Maxwell Park belonging to someone called Malik. Nazir gave me the money to take for her rent. I'm going back to Birmingham tomorrow. That's all I know."

"Is she still at Maxwell Park?" asked Rab.

"No, she and Nazir flew to Dubai this afternoon, with

Malik's sister. Shoab and I are staying with Nazir's cousin in Shawlands. Please, please let me go."

"Who's Shoab?" asked McBain.

"He's my wife's cousin. We both work for Nazir."

"All these cousins," said Rab. "What's the family business? Who's Nazir's boss?"

"Nazir's in charge. It's cash and carry warehouses, shops. We have thirty outlets in Birmingham."

"We're off the point here," said McBain. "You collected Zahra, but something else happened at her flat. What was that?"

"Oh, you mean her boyfriend? He was a madman, he tried to grab Zahra from us. He fell and hurt himself. We called an ambulance for him."

Sonny growled at this.

"Very good, cousin," said McBain. "We'll drive you back to Shawlands now, but first you can show us where you took Zahra."

"You're no' serious, Dad!" said Sonny, but his father said he'd explain later.

They drove back to Glasgow and Mushtaq pointed out the large detached house in Maxwell Park where Zahra had been taken. McBain already suspected Malik was behind the kidnapping, and seeing it was Malik's family house confirmed that. McBain gave Mushtaq a grim warning about keeping quiet about being questioned, told him he could keep the £500, and then dropped him off in Shawlands.

Sonny bleated to his father as they were making their way to the Royal Infirmary.

"Why? Why didn't we do him in? If we find out he beat Joe up …"

"Just think for a minute, son," McBain said. "Angela knows we were going to get hold of him after he left her office. We can't touch him without running the risk of being given up by her. He's not important in this. His information is, though."

McBain looked at Rab, who nodded that he agreed.

Interesting that it's Angela now, thought Rab. She certainly made some impression on the old man.

They found out from reception at the Royal that Joe was in Ward 22. They arrived at the ward just before visiting was due to start, so they had to wait outside with the other friends and relatives. Not even a powerful crime lord could get past National Health Service rules. They were the only visitors not carrying some sort of gift.

Joe's wife and daughter arrived with his grandchildren. Rab watched as McBain consoled Betty, but he could see the distrust and suspicion in her eyes. Rab suggested that it would be better if he had a quick word with Joe before the family went in, and Betty reluctantly agreed. McBain and Sonny said they'd wait in the car and they left.

When the bell rang to start the visiting hour Rab went in and closed the curtains round Joe's bed. Joe was half asleep, but became alert when he saw Rab.

"What happened, mate? Who was it? Why were you there, anyway?"

"Rab, this morphine's great. Look, I can take a shot any time."

Joe pushed the button beside his arm and sighed. Rab shook his head.

"They'll take that away sharpish, Joe. Get a grip. Betty'll be in in a minute. What's the story with Zahra? What should we tell Betty?"

"There's nothing to tell. I was going to tell her I loved her, but I never got up the stairs. The Pakis were taking her away. She looked really scared, Rab. Is she OK?"

Rab suppressed a laugh, and tried to look serious. "Loved her, Joe? You hardly knew her. Bloody hell, not in your league! Anyway, she's gone back home to God knows what. The Pakis stopped you making a fool of yourself with her. Was it the usual? Get stuck in before you think? How many were there?"

Joe lay back in the bed, took another shot of morphine and shouted, "Fuck off, Rab. Where's Zahra gone? It doesnae matter. I'll go after her. There were three of them. One older guy, the one in charge. Two younger ones, boys really. They got me off balance."

"OK, Joe. I think we know what happened. She's been taken back home, as I said. Malik's sending us a message by sending her back to Pakistan. We're not to get involved with Asians. You were just in the wrong place at the wrong time. We'll tell Betty you were collecting in Thomson Street. She doesn't know anything about Zahra, I take it?"

Joe shook his head. "No. But leave the older guy for me, will you? I'm gonna break his arms, then think about what to do to him next."

Rab patted Joe on the shoulder.

"This wasn't meant to happen. Forget it, mate, they're not local. You just get well."

Rab pulled back the curtains and found Joe's daughter Aylish was waiting beside the next bed.

"Who's Zahra?" she snapped.

Rab gripped her arm and guided her to the far end of the ward and into a store room.

"Whatever you heard, you forget it right now. And don't bother your mother about it either. It's history, Aylish. We'll deal with it."

The girl started crying.

"Some tart from the sauna, I suppose. He's been there a lot. I didn't think he'd …"

"Look, nothing happened. It was a fantasy he had. Forget it." He put his arm round her shoulder.

She pushed him away, "Bugger off. Men! You're all after one thing."

"Don't kid yourself, Aylish. To me, you're still a child." He turned and left.

When Rab got back to the car, he said he'd worked it out.

"It looks like Joe had a soft spot for Zahra, and was going to see her when he interrupted these guys taking her away. It's a weird thing to do, but it looks like a message from Malik. We know that's his house in Cedar Avenue where they took her. He's upping the ante. You can forget about him coming into the Canal project, I think. He's telling us to keep our distance, for some reason."

McBain seemed distracted.

"Joe's OK, at least. Maybe he did fall, as the Paki said. I don't want a full-scale war just now. Back to Westberry."

Rab could see that Sonny was raging inside. His father had to warn him twice about his driving on the short journey from the Royal to Westberry Drive.

Now he sprawled on the sofa opposite his father and downed his second large vodka and coke.

"I'll no' let Malik insult us like this, Dad. Everyone'll know about this in a coupla days. Soon they'll think we're a soft touch. Anyone can mess up our operations. We have to sort him out. I'll do that house, that's what I'll do."

"We're trying to get away from all of this, Sonny," McBain said. "We're businessmen. Malik's made a mistake. There's no lasting damage. We'll try to get Eastman to set up a meeting, clear the air. We don't want to go back to gang wars. We can all make money without fighting one another. Do you understand?"

"But, Dad, you'd never have stood for this when you started out. Zahra was a good girl, the punters loved her. God knows why, she was a stuck-up bitch to me. But she made us good money."

Rab joined in. "It's one girl, Sonny. Malik knew it wouldn't hurt us much, but he was making a point. Leave it."

"That's my decision, Sonny," McBain said. "Eastman can try to sort it out. I'm off to bed. Off you two go – I need to set the alarms."

In the car, Sonny started on again about sorting Malik out. He expected Rab to repeat what he'd said in the house, but now Rab took a different tack.

"Maybe your Dad's wrong not to retaliate. I didn't say this, mind. He doesn't like his decisions being challenged, as you well know. But maybe this time Malik needs a lesson."

Sonny brightened up.

"Dead right, Rab, the old man's going soft. He doesnae look so good some days. He's going away soon, to hook up again with my Mum. I'll be in charge then, anyway – we'll be a great team. I didnae mean it about you gettin' your cards. But I don't want to wait. I'll get some of the boys together and we'll torch Malik's house."

"I don't think that's a good idea, Sonny. The place is like a fortress."

Sonny pulled up outside Rab's block of flats. Rab got out and leaned back into the car.

"Your Dad said to leave it, but …" He hesitated then continued. "I didn't say this, mind, but Malik's cash and carry doesn't have much protection. Who knows what he keeps there, but if it were to go up …"

Rab slammed the car door and headed for his flat. As he heard Sonny pull away, he allowed himself a smile.

27

The three-hour wait in transit in Dubai had been agonising for Zahra, as she had so often pictured herself arriving in the emirate for a new life. Now Fatima, Nazir and Zahra waited in the arrivals hall in Islamabad for Zahra's luggage. The chaotic scenes were in sharp contrast to the orderly behaviour they had seen in Dubai.

After Zahra's case was picked up by Nazir, and they had passed through Passport Control, Fatima bade Nazir goodbye. She had a long layover until her return flight to Glasgow. She ignored Zahra, but saved a look of disdain, contempt even, for her as she was frog-marched away by Nazir and his new colleague Shokat, who had rendezvoused with Nazir at the meeting point. Zahra was bundled into the back seat of the old Mercedes 420SE beside Nazir. Shokat turned on the air conditioning, so the two-hour journey was comfortable. Soon they were in territory familiar to Zahra, and she became quite emotional, weeping quietly. No comfort was forthcoming from Nazir.

The car juddered to a halt outside the two-storey house in the main street of Mirgara. Grandfather, a wealthy landowner, had commissioned it about fifteen years previously, and it was in modern style, with large picture windows, balconies with cast-iron railings, surrounded by high walls topped with broken glass. Entry was through ornate security-controlled gates. The threat of kidnapping of wealthy citizens was ever-present in

Pakistan, and Zahra thought it ironic that she, a victim of a kidnap, was being delivered to her grandfather's well-protected house.

As soon as Shokat opened the car door, a wall of burning fetid air blasted into the car. Even in this well-to-do part of the village, Zahra recognised the faint smell of animals and excrement, from her childhood spent in a more agricultural area. She was pulled roughly out of the car, and, after security had opened the gates, Nazir and Shokat marched her up to the door of her grandfather's house. She had hoped he would be there to meet her, but it was her aunt Abida, her late father's sister, who greeted her.

"I deliver the bitch to you, may her fate be just." Nazir spat into an adjacent flower bed as he pushed Zahra into the hall and turned on his heel; Shokat threw Zahra's suitcase and handbag after her, and both men ran back to the car, which sped off, trailing a storm of red dust.

Zahra tried to embrace her aunt, but she turned away.

"Why is it so quiet? Is there no market today?" Zahra asked.

Abida looked pityingly at her.

"They knew you would be returning today, so there is no market. All the men are attending the panchayat. You are accused of sexual depravity with non-believers. Your grandfather is pleading for mercy for you. You have dishonoured the family, but, more importantly, the village."

Zahra's thought now was to get back to the airport as quickly as possible. She knew that a panchayat would impose a harsh penalty on her. In the past they had exacted high fines or donations to the community, or even excluded the accused person from the area.

"I must get back to the city. Can someone drive me there? "

Zahra looked in her handbag for her passport, but found it had been removed. She looked pleadingly at her aunt.

"They've stolen my passport. I'll need to get a replacement. Why would they do …"

Just then there was a knock on the door. Abida opened it and six village women were standing there, all wearing black chadors. They moved silently into the hall, and two took Abida into the main room of the house, whispering to her.

Zahra looked aggressively at the remaining four women.

"What are you looking at? No, sorry, look, you must help me. I have to get away. One of you must have a car …"

Just then, Zahra became aware of what seemed to be a low chant, still indistinct, and the barking of dogs. She ran upstairs and walked out onto the external balcony which overlooked the main street. A crowd of men was approaching, and now she could make out the chant:

"Let her be stoned! Let her be stoned!"

Aunt Abida joined her on the balcony, and murmured:

"All powerful God, forgive us our sins, Oh Mohammed, have pity on us."

Zahra was now shaking with fear. The men on the road had become more and more animated, but silence fell as the village elder emerged through the crowd and stood at the gate. Addressing Zahra, he announced:

"The decision of the panchayat is that you be stoned before the day ends, until you are dead. You must now seek the forgiveness of Allah. Certainly, Allah is Ever Oft-Forgiving, Most Merciful."

Abida pulled Zahra back into the upstairs hallway.

"There is no escape from this, my child. You must behave with dignity. There is no civil authority here. You have no way of contacting anyone, and no one in the village will dare question the decision of the panchayat. You must prepare yourself for death."

The chanting started again.

"Let her be stoned! Let her be stoned!"

"Where is Grandfather? Surely he will save me?" Zahra was frantic.

"He will not even meet you, my child. He has been exempted from stoning you, by a concession of the village elder. You will never see him again."

Just then, two of the men from the panchayat came through the gate, entered the house, ran up the stairs and seized Zahra. She did not behave with dignity. She screamed and yelled abuse as she was dragged to the village square, where a hole about five feet deep had been dug out. She was bundled into the hole and held down as it was filled up, so that only her head and shoulders were above ground.

The crowd went berserk, whooping and caterwauling, matched by the dogs' howling. A circle had been marked out around the hole, about 40 feet in diameter. No stoning had been carried out in the area for decades, but the panchayat had researched and found that the convention was that no one should throw from within the circle. As Zahra moaned, those at the front of the crowd saw that some men had broken off bricks from a dilapidated wall near the bus stop. They were weighing them up, staring fixedly at their target. An eerie silence descended; even the dogs sensed something, and the barking stopped.

The first few stones merely glanced off Zahra's head. Her long black hair fell over her face, mercifully covering the agony she was enduring. Some from the crowd dispersed in a mad dash for more ammunition, and then returned, hurling bricks and stones. Zahra's screaming was at a high pitch, but it was finally silenced when someone broke the circle and dropped a breeze block on her. For Zahra, it was oblivion.

The village elder held the Koran on high, and gathered the villagers round him. A new chant started:

"In the name of God, the Compassionate, the Merciful."

28

Sonny was beside himself with excitement about paying Malik back for kidnapping Zahra. He decided the sooner the better, so when he got to the Paradisa the next day, he called in Francis and Brendan, two of his enforcers. When they met up, he outlined the plan to torch Malik's cash and carry.

"All very well, Sonny," said Francis "but will it burn? How much petrol will we need?"

Sonny had burned out a flat once before, but Joe McCarthy had helped him with that. Now Joe was out of action, and anyway, Joe would never have gone against what Sonny's father wanted.

He thought back to the previous arson attack. A guy who had done some enforcing for the McBains had tried to buy himself a light sentence for an assault by informing on Sonny. Luckily, Alex McBain had retained the services of an old friend at Gorbals Police Station. Burning out the guy's flat had been a clear warning to everyone about turning police informer. It was just too bad that his sister had been staying at the flat with her kids. Seven deaths had cranked up the pressure on the McBains for a while, but there had been no direct evidence against them. How had Joe organised it?

Now Sonny remembered. Buy the petrol away from Glasgow. The cops would check all the CCTV at petrol stations in Glasgow after the fire, so send the boys away with cash to Edinburgh and Dundee to get it. And, hoodied up, walk into the garages, no motors, just to be sure. Sonny gave the orders.

"It's a cash and carry, for Christ's sake. Full of burny stuff. Get eight containers, that'll be more than enough. Today's Tuesday, we'll do it on Friday night."

Brendan and Francis had spent Wednesday and Thursday travelling all over and had collected petrol from as far afield as Dunbar and Coupar Angus. They'd selected petrol stations with no obvious CCTV, those run by small operators, and they'd paid cash, so they were sure they couldn't be traced.

The cash and carry was in an area of Glasgow Sonny knew quite well, as he'd done a project on Glasgow's docks area when he was at school. It was about the only thing which had interested him.

Tradeston lay just south of the Clyde – you could see it as you whizzed past over the Kingston Bridge on the way to the airport. On the Friday morning he drove cautiously past the cash and carry. He saw the entrance was right on the pavement, and there was no parking area except on the opposite side of the street, the site of a demolished building which had been covered over with red pebbles. It looked like someone had had the idea of developing the site for housing, as there was a dilapidated "For Sale – residential opportunity" sign hanging at an angle from the wire fence, but it was so old the telephone number had faded. Beside it was an amateurishly painted notice "Cash and carry parking – keep out".

The idea was customers parked on the red blaes site, crossed to the cash and carry, ordered and collected their goods and left them on the pavement while they brought their vans or estates across to load up. It would need to be a two-man operation here, thought Sonny, as the locals would be quick to pinch anything left unattended.

Sonny turned round the corner and parked at a meter. Looking back at the front of the cash and carry he saw an attack from there would be risky. The street was quite a major east to west artery, and in the space of five minutes, two police cars had passed by. Govan Police Station was only a few blocks away. He would need to think of something else.

He eased himself out of the car, took a sheet of paper out of his jacket pocket and walked slowly south. He looked as if he was trying to find an address. As he passed a newsagents, a down-and-out, dressed in an army greatcoat, unshaven for weeks, with long dirty fair hair, stumbled out in front of him and slurred "Are ye lost, son? Gie's a quid." Sonny moved the paper to his left hand and felt in his jacket for the blade. He looked the man in the eye, just like his Dad had taught him. "Show them you've more will than they have. Only an idiot won't back off," his father had said. Again it worked. Although the tramp was bleary-eyed, he recognised something in Sonny.

"No offence, son," he muttered and turned away.

The area had been laid out in the early nineteenth century on a grid system, with large warehouses on the north and south of each rectangular block bisected by a lane running east to west. Sonny turned left into the lane behind Malik's cash and carry. It had started to rain and the cobbles were greasy. There were black industrial wheelie bins at the side of the lane, placed at intervals of about thirty yards. The stench from them was truly overpowering, the sharp cloying smell of what might be rotting chicken, or worse.

Looking ahead, after covering his mouth and nose with his scarf, Sonny saw a large lorry parked at the back of the cash and carry and rails of puffa jackets being unloaded. The porters eyed him suspiciously, and stopped working. He decided it would look worse if he turned back, so he walked on to the delivery platform. He'd a story ready.

"I'm after the Italian cash and carry. Is it along here?" he asked.

"It's nearer Govan Cross, mate," the nearest porter said.

Sonny looked left at the delivery door. Damn! There were metal roller shutters, so no access there. However, just above the entrance, on the first floor, was a barred window. It would keep burglars out, but if it could be accessed, it might be just the ticket.

He turned on his heel and headed back to the car. They'd need a ladder to get up to that window. It would be too risky to buy one as the police might check all recent purchases. Very good, he thought, I'm learning from Joe. So, better to bring a few pallets and build up to the first floor level; there were hundreds lying on waste ground near Parkhead.

He drove back to the King James Bar in Shettleston. It was Sonny's favourite haunt. It occupied a single shopfront, the facade painted green and white, sporting the Irish tricolour above the door. It had a clientele comprising rabid Celtic supporters and other Celtic supporters. It consisted of a single huge room, with toilets in an extension at the rear, but there was a snug sectioned off from the main room by an eight-foot high mahogany and glass partition. The snug was for the exclusive use of the McBain team.

The pub had been in the Murphy family for over a hundred years, the current landlord being the great-grandson of the original owner. Sean Murphy presided over the bar and its staff like a warlord – fiercely protective of what he regarded as the Irish Catholic traditions. He was not a man to be trifled with.

Sonny had seen strangers very occasionally stumble into the bar, always tourists looking for some local colour, imagining they were in the trendy Temple Bar area of Dublin. They were met by a wall of silence from the punters, though on a nod from Sean the barman, they might take pity on them and offer, "You must be lost. There's a bus stop into town just along the road. Or I'll phone you a taxi."

It was unlikely a Protestant had ever been served in the King James. Sonny's father had told him a story, probably apocryphal, that two days after Celtic's triumph in the European Cup in 1967, at a time when he could have had free drinks in every other pub in the east end of Glasgow, the team's manager, Jock Stein, had been refused admission to the King James because he wasn't a Catholic. When challenged about this, Sean Murphy would simply say that his father had some standards.

Sonny had never smoked, but he could see that it was likely to be a major problem to introduce the smoking ban in a pub like this. The walls and ceiling were coated muddy brown from decades of exhalations from Senior Service and Capstan addicts. But amazingly, after a few grumbles, those hooked had grudgingly agreed to stand outside in all weathers feeding their habit. Now the atmosphere was a mixture of stale spilled beer, body odour and the burnt pastry smells from the pies and sausage rolls basking in the infrared rays of the heated display on the zinc bar.

Sonny knew he was safe to talk in the snug. It was unthinkable that any police would be in the pub, and the regulars knew the rules on informing. *Omertà* was the rule in the east end of Glasgow.

Francis and Brendan listened to Sonny's description of the cash and carry and his idea about how to torch it. Brendan was the smarter of the two, and he immediately explained that the plan was too risky because of the time it would take to build up the pallets. He knew where they could steal a ladder from a building site quite close to Tradeston. Sonny didn't like having his ideas questioned, but when Francis joined in, saying the fucking effort of carrying pallets around was fucking madness, he gave way. Brendan was sent off to steal the van and the ladder. It was agreed they would meet up at Parkhead Cross at midnight.

The swing door into the snug opened and Rab walked in.

"What are you two dreaming up, and where's Mr McSherry off to in such a rush? He nearly smashed into me." Rab tweaked Sonny's hair.

Sonny decided to show off to Francis. He tapped the side of his nose.

"From now on, it's need to know, Rab, and this is my operation. Things are going to be different from now on. A pint?"

Rab simply laughed.

"OK, Sonny, a pint it is. It's your show. When does the curtain go up?"

29

There was an eerie quietness at the mouth of the lane behind Malik's cash and carry. Brendan had smeared the registration plates of the van with mud before he set out from Shettleston. He picked up Sonny and Francis at Parkhead Cross as arranged, and now they began to unload the ladder and the petrol cans. All three were dressed in black and wore scarves and gloves. They looked a bit like two SAS men with a portly companion.

Sonny gave the orders and soon they were positioned on the loading bay. Francis climbed up to the barred window. Luckily it was a sash type and the lock had been left in the open position, presumably because with the iron bars no one could possibly break in. He looked in for a few minutes before gripping the bottom of the lower window. It squeaked slightly as Francis raised it and as he did he stiffened, raised his arm to silence the others, and then slowly climbed back down.

"I thought I heard voices, boss. But there's no movement on the stairs. I can see right through to the front windows, and there's loads of stuff piled up, all covered in plastic. It's a wooden staircase just there and it looks like the steps are wood, too. It'll all burn, OK. What do we do?"

Sonny smiled, "I wonder. Sing a song? What the fuck do you think we do? We get on with it. No, you get on with it and I'll be in the van. Any sign of trouble, we're out of here."

Brendan and Francis looked at one another and shrugged.

Brendan said, "If Francis hears voices, boss, we go. I'm no killin' anyone, even a Paki."

Just then a figure emerged from behind one of the wheelie bins further down the lane. It was the down-and-out who had asked Sonny for money when he was casing the area. He moved silently along the lane, his thick rubber-soled shoes gliding along the wet cobbles. It was ten hours since he'd had a drink, so he was stone-cold sober.

He looked up at the ladder propped against the wall and smiled. His voice caused all three to jump with fear, startled by the unexpected appearance.

"Boys, boys. Cut me in. There's some good stuff in there. Mobile phones and watches, I know where to get rid of that sort of gear. I can help to carry some …"

Sonny turned round.

The tramp took a backward step. He mumbled, "It's you. You were here …"

Brendan could see the anger in Sonny's eyes, and his hand reaching for his blade. Things are about to get messy, he thought. Rab or even Joe would know what to do, but they were on their own, so he'd have to think of something fast.

He turned and faced Sonny. "Hold on, boss. Maybe he can help us with the gear. We wouldn't want any of it to be *left behind, damaged*. That might confuse the cops."

Sonny failed to take the hint, "But we're no' takin' any …"

But Francis had caught on. He went behind the tramp, pointed at him and drew his finger across his throat. He then put his arm somewhat gingerly round the tramp's shoulder, and said, "Boss, he can help us all right. OK, old man, we'll get you some mobile phones. You can get a fair bit for these. You go up the ladder after my mate."

"How do we get the stuff through the bars?" The tramp was confused.

By now Brendan had climbed the thirty feet to the top of the ladder. Francis pushed the tramp up the first few rungs.

"We've got a silent saw. He's cutting the bars now. Quick, get up there."

The tramp was surprisingly nimble, and in no time was just below Brendan, who immediately said, "Here, take this box."

The tramp took one hand off the ladder to take what Brendan was passing to him, but all he got was a boot in the face. He lost his balance and fell headlong onto the lane below. Sonny was ready to finish him off with a brick, but there was no need. His head was smashed, and he was clearly dead.

"So, now we don't even need to take away the ladder," said Brendan. "It's got his prints on it. It'll look like he stole the ladder, started the fire, and then lost his balance. The Maliks won't buy that, but the cops will, at least for a while. Job done, I think."

Sonny was doubtful, "Where would he have got a ladder and the petrol? It doesnae make sense."

"But Sonny, you *want* the Maliks to know it was you. As long as the cops have nothing to come after us for, what do we care what they think?"

"Why kill this poor bugger, then? Oh, like, of course, he'd seen me. Good work, Brendan."

Francis and Brendan laboriously ferried the petrol cans up the ladder and emptied them through the window. They waited. There was no sound from inside. Francis could see that the petrol had pooled on the floor below beside a pile of plastic bags. He lit a taper and threw it through the window before sliding down the ladder.

There was a muffled pop but no immediate blast. As Sonny started the van they heard the first explosion and smoke began to emerge from the lower windows. Sonny gunned the engine and they headed south, taking a long route back through Pollok and Castlemilk where they were sure no CCTV cameras could track them. They got back to Parkhead just after two. Sonny stopped the van outside the Paradisa. He was ecstatic.

"Now burn everything you're wearing, and torch the van. Let's see what Malik makes of this."

★ ★ ★

Angela Finlayson was pondering the events of recent weeks in her flat overlooking the River Clyde. She'd heard nothing further from Mr McBain about the flat Zahra had vacated in such mysterious circumstances, and she'd a nagging concern about what had happened to Zahra's cousin. After he'd left the office she'd seen Mr McBain's son and the third man walking up the street after him. She shuddered. Still, that £1,000 had proved an unexpected and enjoyable bonus. She wondered if she should approach Mr McBain about the development he'd spoken about.

Her thoughts were interrupted by the noise of screaming sirens from the Clydeside Expressway. She went out onto her balcony and looked east towards the centre of town. Now her attention was drawn by a pall of smoke in the far distance. It brought it all back. Her father, a fireman, had been involved in two of Glasgow's worst disasters.

In March 1960 a fire broke out in Cheapside Street in the Anderston area of the city. It had started in a bonded warehouse that contained over a million gallons of whisky and rum. Within minutes of her father and his colleagues arriving at the scene, there was a massive explosion which literally blew the building apart. As the fire spread, it engulfed a tobacco warehouse, an ice cream factory and the Harland and Wolff engine works. Fed by a huge lake of whisky, the fire took a week to extinguish completely. Fourteen firefighters and five men from the Glasgow Salvage Corps lost their lives fighting the blaze.

Only eight years later, in a nearby street in Anderston, another fire broke out in another former bonded warehouse, which had been converted into an upholstery factory. Because, like many others in the area, it had been a high-security building in the past, all the windows had been heavily barred to prevent break-ins. This contributed to the gruesome fate of the employees, because these security measures made it impossible for most of the workforce to escape, and twenty-two people were burned alive. Some had been trapped in a lift between floors while others died trying in vain to break out through a padlocked fire escape.

Angela now looked over to what was clearly another very serious fire, thankful that her father was now enjoying retirement in Perthshire. She placed the fire in Govan or Tradeston. Not many buildings were occupied late at night in those areas, no hotels or the like. She turned on News 24, but there was no mention of a fire, as yet. She hoped no one had been working late in the building. It seemed unlikely, as it was now nearly one in the morning.

★ ★ ★

Usman Malik was phoned by the police at Govan and told his building was on fire. The questions came thick and fast. Was there a sprinkler system? Was there anyone on the premises?

He'd to think quickly. As well as importing drugs, Malik also arranged to bring in illegal immigrants from Pakistan, and until they got established with jobs and their own accommodation, they lived in a dormitory on the top floor of the cash and carry. It was another profitable sideline to the business.

Malik said that there was a partial sprinkler system covering the ground floor, and that all the staff left by nine. That was strictly speaking true. He was told to get himself to the cash and carry as soon as, and to contact his insurance company.

Malik had two bodyguards who lived in a flat above the double garage, in what had once been the stable block for his grand mansion. They were the reason Rab had dissuaded Sonny from trying to torch Malik's house. Now Malik roused them via the internal phone and told them to bring out the Range Rover. As they drove to the Kanrach, he called his insurers' emergency number and was told an investigator would meet him at the building in one hour. The bodyguards picked up on the situation immediately.

"What about the latest batch?" asked one. "There are four bunked down in the dormitory."

"It's in God's hands," Malik said. "You know nothing about them. If there was anyone in the building, they must have been intruders. Or squatters. We never go to the top floor, do we? My God, they had better be dead. They could give some awkward information. Never mind them, what about the consignment we got the other day?"

They had to leave the Range Rover and walk the last quarter of a mile to the cash and carry because the police had established an exclusion zone. When they got to the front of the building the smell of burning wood and plastic was all around and acrid smoke was still pouring out of the windows. They could see wisps gently rising above the slates on the roof. One of the side walls had already collapsed but it was impossible to see what was inside.

Just as they were talking to the firemen, a shout went up that there was someone on the roof. The firemaster looked through his binoculars and said he could see a small figure edging his way along the parapet below the roof, waving his white shirt. The firemaster turned to face Malik.

"I thought the building was clear," he growled. "My God! I can see arms through the bars in the top windows. There are people up there. Raise the turntables!"

But just at that moment there was an ominous creaking.

"I know that sound, sir – the roof's going," one of the older fireman said.

With a tremendous crash, the roof fell into the shell of the building, the solitary man lost his footing on the parapet and fell in a perfect dive onto the street below; the sickening thud was thankfully masked by the cacophony from the wooden beams and slates hitting the ground.

Malik was taken to the mobile police incident room. It appeared that at least two other people had been observed on the top floor. They were now buried under tons of debris. Malik was anxious to talk.

"I know nothing of these people in my building. It's conceivable they could have broken in. but why were they on the top floor? There was nothing there. Unless they were looking for lead on the roof. Could that be it?"

The firemaster and the police superintendent exchanged a look. "That's a possible scenario," the policeman said.

Malik continued. "Yes, they must have been intruders. They must have started the fire. Obviously not deliberately. Gentlemen, I am a respectable business man. My father is a councillor."

"At this stage we can't say anything for sure. We'll know more after the post-mortems, perhaps," the firemaster said.

At that point a gentleman with a clipboard joined them, and the superintendent introduced him as the insurance assessor. He shook hands with Malik.

"We're unlikely to know anything definite for a few days, Mr Malik. You'll be contacted by Head Office tomorrow about the practicalities of alternative premises and restocking. I presume all your financial records are backed up. There will be nothing to salvage, so far as I can judge."

Malik got back home at four o'clock. His father was waiting for him.

"Do we have a problem?" His father was clearly having difficulty suppressing his anger.

"No, I don't think so," said Malik. "The property is insured, we lose most of one shipment. The four from Quetta are dead. There will be questions about one of them. It seems that the body of the one who fell is intact, more or less, so they will easily see he is from Pakistan, even without a DNA test. So that could be awkward. Maybe we can muddy the waters by suggesting some sort of long-term inter-family dispute."

"Don't be naïve, Usman. Why would someone setting a fire in a building be on the top floor? No, the least said, the better. I will arrange for compensation for their families back home, to ensure that there is no loose talk leading to a connection to us."

Just then Malik's mobile rang. The same voice as before.

"You really shouldnae have lifted the girl. That got Sonny really mad. I warned you."

Malik shouted into the mobile, "Who are you? What do you want?"

But the line was dead. Malik's father stretched out his arms "What?"

"It was Sonny McBain, apparently. Now we really do have a war on our hands."

30

A detailed examination the next day of the lane at the back of the Kanrach proved to be difficult. At one point there had been a concern that the fire would spread across the lane to the adjoining furniture factory, but the wind had changed direction so the fire was contained. Because of the narrowness of the lane, however, the debris from the roof and walls which had collapsed had blocked access to the rear door, and the contractors working to clear it on the instructions of Forensics were faced with a wall of stone, wood and slate about eight feet high. The slow, painstaking process of clearing it started in the afternoon, and it was at about five that the tramp's body was found lying at the foot of the ladder, which was miraculously still in place, clearly showing where the intruders had got in.

This changed the focus of the investigation. The tramp was readily identified, being a well-known character in the area. Forensics could find no trace of petrol on him, and in any event, the beat policemen familiar with Tradeston considered him incapable of even lifting a ladder, far less organising a break-in. So, unless he'd been working with others, it seemed unlikely he was involved at all, and indeed the view was taken that he'd been in the wrong place at the wrong time. His injuries were more consistent with a fall, rather than being struck from above, but that was explained away on the basis that he could have gone up the ladder and lost his footing.

Malik had called that day at Govan Police Station as he

had been instructed, but had been told that little progress had been made and he should return the next day. When he did, he had a very difficult time with the firemaster and the police. He was told it was established that the fire had been started with petrol poured through the first floor window and that a ladder, stolen from a local builders' yard, had been found under the window next to the body of an elderly man. Malik and all his staff had accounted for their movements on the night of the fire to the satisfaction of the police, but what was awkward for Malik were the questions about the victims. The police interviewed him under caution and he had needed to get his lawyer involved. For the moment he was sticking to his explanation involving a break-in, but that did not fit with the clear evidence of arson perpetrated from outside the building, and the sightings of the four alleged intruders on the top floor.

★ ★ ★

At the same time as Malik was fencing questions about the victims of the fire, Mushtaq, who had returned to Birmingham with his £500 cash, was distraught. It transpired that the illegal immigrant who had fallen so spectacularly into oblivion at the Kanrach was his brother Javid; eight years younger than Mushtaq, Javid had wanted to start a new life in Britain, just as Mushtaq had done a year previously, and had recently arrived in Glasgow from Pakistan with three companions.

Malik had conveyed the news of the deaths of the victims to Shoab in Birmingham, and it had fallen to Shoab to tell Mushtaq that his brother was dead. Shoab said all those staying at the Kanrach had died and that Malik was sure it was in retaliation for the taking of the Pakistani woman. Malik had information that someone called Sonny McBain was responsible.

"I know this man who has killed my brother," Mushtaq started to weep.

"How can this be?" Shoab asked.

"Something happened in Glasgow when we took the woman. I must tell Malik what I know. I will need to go to back to Glasgow anyway. You can do without me for a few days."

"Of course," Shoab said. "May God go with you."

Mushtaq arrived in Glasgow to find that Malik had managed to find temporary premises for the Kanrach near Hillington. The process of restocking was under way, and the insurers had authorised an interim payment to Malik to finance the relocation. Shoab had warned Malik that Mushtaq had some information about the fire, but that Mushtaq had not given him any details.

Malik had decided to meet with Mushtaq at the new premises and when the young man was ushered into his temporary office, Malik expressed his condolences.

Mushtaq stared at the floor and whispered, "In my shame I will tell you everything which happened the day after we took the Pakistani whore. My life is pointless now. My parents will be devastated."

"But what relevance has this to your brother, Mushtaq?"

Mushtaq broke down. He apologised for his greed in trying to get the rent deposit, and went over in detail his abduction by the man called Sonny and his release. He felt he had caused his own brother's death. His only wish was for vengeance against this Sonny. He would willingly sacrifice himself in this cause.

Malik stood up from behind his desk and embraced Mushtaq.

"I will have instructions for you soon. Meantime you stay at the home of my father as an honoured guest. Your brother will be avenged."

* * *

Three weeks later Malik sat opposite DI Alfie Johnston in Govan police station.

"As you know, Mr Malik, I'm in charge of investigating the Kanrach fire, but I don't feel I'm making much progress. The report from the insurance investigator concludes that the fire was started deliberately. You'll not be surprised to learn that first suspicion fell on you, what with the history of old buildings being burned down for the insurance money. But I'm told your business had been doing well, and there seems no reason why you'd pull such a stunt. Also, no effort seemed to have been made to pretend that the fire was accidental. The insurers are satisfied it was arson by a third party."

"I know this already. The insurance company is financing my relocation to Hillington. How can I help you? Why am I really here?"

"Well, who would want to put you out of business? A competitor? Or perhaps this was personal?"

"It could be racial, of course. But I have received no threats." Malik shifted in his seat. "Should I have brought my lawyer?"

"No, you're not under suspicion. Do you have any dealings with the McBain family? There's a rumour going around that you crossed them recently. I got an anonymous tip."

"I've met Mr McBain at some charity functions," Malik said. "But we have no direct business connections, though he suggested recently that I take a stake in his Canal Regeneration Scheme in Maryhill. That hardly suggests he bears me any ill will, does it? I think someone is trying to muddy the waters."

"Maybe. Well, Mr Malik, you can go. Thank you for your help. We'll let you know when anything develops."

Malik drove back to Hillington. He wasn't surprised that Johnston had got hold of the rumour about the McBains being involved. Information was coming to him every day about how Sonny McBain was boasting about how he'd repaid Malik for kidnapping the sauna girl. He'd decided to exact revenge on Sonny McBain, but this time he wouldn't waste time consulting his father and brother.

Mushtaq had been waiting patiently for Malik to decide what to do. He busied himself helping Malik arrange the fit-out of the Hillington building.

Malik was trying to work out a long-term strategy which would leave him in control of the Glasgow drugs market. It was inevitable that Sonny McBain must be killed. Perhaps that would force Alex McBain to retire and leave Rab Donald in charge. Malik was confident that he could work in partnership with Donald.

He decided the best way would be to stage a hit-and-run. Mushtaq would be the driver. Malik set out for Mushtaq what he had planned, so there would be no apparent connection to the Kanrach fire. Mushtaq would be given a stolen car to use, and after Sonny was run over, Mushtaq would be picked up by motor bike and would be on the next morning plane to Amsterdam, connecting to Karachi. He would have to accept he would never return to Great Britain. Mushtaq was overjoyed.

Malik explained, "Sonny McBain always leaves the Paradisa after eleven on a Thursday, and walks to the King James Bar. There's a stretch of the route where a building has been demolished but a high wall has been left standing. Traffic is quiet around there. You swerve onto the pavement and pin him against the wall. It'll look like joyriders have lost control of a stolen car."

The next Thursday a car was stolen to order for Mushtaq. One of Malik's bodyguards was tasked with co-ordinating the hit on the ground, and the other with picking up Mushtaq after the "accident".

All went to plan. The road was quiet, and Mushtaq was able to pick his moment to turn ninety degrees and slam into Sonny, sending the fish supper he was carrying flying in all directions.

An hour later, DC Sarah Plummer watched as Sonny's body was lifted onto a stretcher and into the ambulance. As the door shut, Allensen's car arrived and he hurried across.

"What's known?" he said.

"Well, sir. It looks at first sight like an accident, but it's Sonny McBain. I'm sure it's an assassination. He was walking along from the sauna, heading for the pub, and – as you can see if you've the stomach for it, sir – eating a fish supper. Apparently that was his routine. The vehicle was stolen in Whitecraigs sometime after nine o'clock. The owner didn't even know it was gone."

The silver Honda 4x4 was smashed up against the wall, its front bumper distorted by the collision.

Plummer continued, "The location's perfect, as there are no properties opposite. You wouldn't expect any witnesses, but a couple in one of the flats further along saw what happened. Their flat's got a bay window and they were looking back along the road as they were waiting for a taxi. The Honda definitely swerved to hit McBain. According to the witnesses, the driver reversed after the first hit and smashed into him again, then got out, spat on the body, kicked it a few times, and was then picked up by a motor bike."

"Make sure we get the DNA from the spit. Who's told Dad?" asked Allensen.

"I've already warned the medics about that, sir. And I've sent a couple of uniforms to Westberry Drive. They radioed to say McBain just grunted and shut the door on them. Class, don't you think?"

"Whoever did this must be mad," Allensen said. "It must have been Malik in retaliation for the Kanrach fire. This is getting out of hand. I'd better phone Alfie Johnston at Govan."

"The scene-of-crime boys are almost finished here. We've

asked Whitecraigs to see if there's any CCTV stuff in their area. As usual, the one along from here's been vandalised, so no joy there." Plummer shrugged her shoulders.

Allensen asked her to come with him to see Alex McBain.

When they arrived at Westberry Drive, it was some time before the knock was answered. When the door swung open, they were confronted by Rab Donald.

"What do you want?" asked Donald. "I thought you might have more consideration."

He ushered them through to the sitting room where Alex McBain was sitting on the settee nursing a large malt.

"Sorry for your loss, Mr McBain," said Allensen, "but I just want to reassure you that irrespective of the history here we'll be doing all we can to find out how this happened. There are indications it might not have been an accident. If it wasn't, we'll need your help in getting who was responsible for this. Can you think of anyone who might have been harbouring a grudge against your son?"

Allensen had found it difficult to keep a straight face when saying this, and McBain merely looked bemused. Rab Donald gave what might have been a hollow laugh.

"Who knows, Mr Allensen? Sonny had various interests, shall we say? We'll be taking care of settling Sonny's affairs. Thank you for letting us know you'll be ... what, pulling out all the stops, is it? If we get any information which might help you, we'll be in touch. Now I think you should leave."

Allensen and Plummer were just going out the door when Allensen turned back.

"Mr Donald, I don't want a war on my hands here. Leave this to us."

The door slammed behind them.

31

Rab went back into the sitting room. McBain looked up, tears in his eyes.

"Arrange it. Get someone from London. Someone very, very good, with no … no feelings. My son's dead, and I know it. So Malik needs to suffer as I'm going to suffer. This'll need to be something special, a real message. No bodies in the boot this time."

This was a reference to something that had happened in the early 1990s to another criminal family in Glasgow. The son of a notorious gangster had been gunned down in the city's Blackhill district. Three men were suspected of carrying out the murder. By the time the gangster got to know the names of those responsible, they'd been arrested on suspicion of another shooting. One was in custody, but the other two had been released on bail.

The gangster arranged for someone the two men trusted to lure them to a meeting, thought to be at Hogganfield Loch. There they were abducted and taken to meet the father of the man they'd killed. They were each floored by a shotgun blast, and then the gangster himself completed the Mafia-style execution by putting a bullet from a .44 Magnum into the back of each victim's head.

The two bodies were thrown into the boot of a car which was left in the car park of the pub the victims used as their local.

Rab Donald spoke quietly, "If you're sure, Boss. I think Colin has heard of just the man."

★ ★ ★

A week later was the day of Sonny's funeral. McBain had told Rab that his son should be given a send-off like he'd seen in the 1960s films of London gangsters, so at great expense, a suitable horse-drawn carriage had been brought up from London, along with two black stallions. The carriage now stood outside the house in Westberry Drive.

Irene McBain had come back from Malaga and was sitting by the window in the lounge, looking out into the back garden where Sonny had so often played as a child. She was dressed in a black suit, and was wearing a small black hat with a veil covering her face. She hadn't spoken much to her husband, but was now confiding in Rab that on the one hand, she felt sorrow for the loss of her son, but on the other, an inexpressible relief that he couldn't affect her life any more. To some extent she was now putting on a show of mourning. She didn't think her husband was affected in this way at all. He'd always supported the boy's excesses – indulged him, even – and his main reaction was to see his son's killing as a personal insult. All Alex had said to her about Sonny since she'd arrived the night before was that he knew who was responsible and that it was being dealt with. Apart from that, he'd pleaded with her that she allow him to spend some time with her in Spain after everything was settled up. Irene told Rab that the prospect of that appalled her, and asked that he try to dissuade Alex from trying to resurrect the relationship.

Alex McBain, also dressed in black, interrupted their discussion as he entered the room, and he indicated to Rab that he wanted to speak to Irene privately. Rab went into the kitchen but stayed close to the connecting hatch so he could hear what was said. It was an interesting exchange.

"What does this mean for the … business?" Irene asked. "Had you put anything in Sonny's name?"

McBain grunted, "The boy was difficult, Irene. I never understood where he got that from. Your family genes … no, sorry, I don't mean that. He was flaky, unstable, but we both loved him. I was careful with him on the money side, though. I bought everything through the companies, even his flat. Apparently there'll be some money from a pension, because we paid him a salary from the trading company. I'll get that paid to you, it's about £200,000. Are you OK for cash?"

"Look, Alex. I don't need any more money from you …"

"Listen, Irene. I'm not well. I don't have that long. I'd really like to come out to Spain now. Rab can take over. I've no interest in all this now. I've made arrangements for the cash …"

Irene exploded. "Money, money, money! What does it matter now? I'm not sure, Alex, about you coming out to Spain. I can't see us as Darby and Joan playing bingo with the other expats. We need to think about this."

"You're right," said McBain. "There's some business to be attended to here anyway. But if anything happens to me, make sure you see the lawyer who wrote to you, the one called Eastman. Rab's got his details. That cash is to go to a charity run by the church. Eastman made the arrangements."

Just then Father O'Rourke appeared. He was a small dumpy man enveloped by his black cassock, with florid features surmounted by a large nose. He stared at the ground as he announced it was time to leave. Sonny's coffin had been carried out from the sitting room to the carriage. McBain and Irene stooped under giant black umbrellas as they were escorted to the car immediately behind the carriage. There were huge wreaths in white roses spelling Sonny on each side of the carriage. The horses' coats glistened in the rain, but the purple blanket with white crosses which was draped over each horse was now sodden, as were the cloths which had been wrapped round their hooves to eliminate the clip-clop sound. The black feathers attached to their heads were wilting.

Rab and Joe got into the car behind the McBains's, along with some distant members of Irene's family. No one spoke. McBain had arranged for a bass drummer to walk between the carriage and the first car, and as soon as the horses moved off the steady beat of the muffled drum started. It was a showpiece start to the day.

Father O'Rourke had been whisked off from Westberry Drive so that he was at the entrance to his chapel to receive the carriage. Lining the steps were twenty of the undertaker's staff, each in formal black jackets and striped trousers, holding their top hats in front of their chests.

Rab and Joe followed Alex and Irene into the chapel, but sat at the back alongside Eastman and Paul Longmuir. It was clear to Eastman that McBain had been determined that the service would be traditional, but with a hugely personal element. The congregation included the great and good of Glasgow, as McBain's influence was felt all over the city. There were councillors, bankers, lawyers, accountants, and directors of all the football clubs. The police were represented by the chief constable. Through his football connections, McBain had got to know a number of high-profile supporters, including actors and entertainers. There was an excited babble of conversation as a well-known actor appeared with a young partner; he must have flown in from his tax-haven home to pay his respects. Just as the doors of the chapel were being closed, Eastman noted the arrival of Detective Inspector Allensen and DC Plummer.

Father O'Rourke delivered the eulogy, which Eastman thought was perhaps a little too complimentary, though he actually knew very little about Sonny, having met him only once. Then the priest announced that a well-loved Glasgow lass would sing a song specially adapted for the occasion, and a diminutive figure in a short black dress moved to the front of the gathering. She'd only had two hit records and that was decades ago, but she still had a huge following. In honour of Sonny, she said she would sing "Abraham, Martin and John".

Eastman cringed. He'd never been at a Roman Catholic funeral, and this was not what he'd expected.

The xylophone player tinkled the introduction. Eastman was struggling to see the relevance to the McBains of a song composed as a tribute to the assassinated Abraham Lincoln, John F. Kennedy and Martin Luther King. The first three verses were as originally sung by Dion, each ending with the assertion that the good died young. Eastman and Paul exchanged puzzled looks – "good" and Sonny McBain were not exactly synonymous.

During the bridge before the last verse, however, Eastman suddenly saw where this was going. Instead of the fourth assassinated politician Bobby Kennedy walking over the hill with his brother John, Abraham Lincoln and Martin Luther King, the congregation would be invited to envisage Sonny rather than Bobby in their company. And that was exactly what the tiny chanteuse delivered.

Eastman felt a bit nauseous, but everyone else burst into applause. Father O'Rourke gave the singer a hug, lingering perhaps a little longer than was really necessary, and then announced that after the interment, refreshments would be served in the Clyde Views Hotel, and that everyone was welcome.

Eastman and Paul decided they would go to the burial. As they came out of the chapel they saw the horse-drawn carriage for the first time.

"Whatever next?" Paul said. "Will we have a volley of shots at the graveside? Like Robert Burns?"

The rain cascaded down on Barmulloch Cemetery as the crowd gathered at the open grave. It was like a scene from any number of Hollywood epics with the added elements of late morning mist and the rumble of traffic from the nearby motorway, which almost drowned out the final words of comfort offered by Father O'Rourke.

The wake at the Clyde Views soon degenerated into a rammy thanks to Sonny's friends taking advantage of the free bar. Some of the girls from the sauna were there, and a number of mourners seemed anxious to get to know them a lot better as quickly as possible. Morag Macgonigle was being chatted up by about four older men and it looked like Carla was taking bookings. There was talk of keeping things going at the King James, after the Clyde Views bar closed at four. Eastman and Paul left as soon as they decently could.

32

It was three weeks after Sonny's funeral when Benny Jankovicz got a call on his pay-as-you-go mobile. The caller wanted to know if he could help with removals.

Benny was a careful man. He'd come to London from Tel Aviv in the late 1990s. He felt he'd slipped easily into the Jewish community in Golders Green, and a distant cousin had found him a job as a settlement clerk in the back office of a multinational stockbroking firm based at Canary Wharf. The travelling on the Northern and Jubilee lines was a bit of a bore, but Benny was happy enough reading crime novels on the way to and from work. Physically, he was stocky, just over five foot three, and possibly verging on the overweight. However, he kept in good shape, and most of the bulk was muscle. He was swarthy and had black curly hair, just beginning to thin slightly on top. No spectacles.

Benny thought that his work colleagues regarded him as a bit of a nonentity, but from his quarterly staff assessments, it was clear that his superiors thought him diligent and trustworthy. Their only negative comments in these assessments related to his rather frequent absences due to illness or family commitments. He was happy to take unpaid leave for the latter, and since he always seemed to catch up on his backlog on his return, he always qualified for an above-average bonus on his rather modest salary.

He never socialised with the other staff, using the excuse of having to look after elderly parents, and that was sufficient to dissuade his co-workers from pressing him. Benny rather thought they seemed relieved that he did not join them.

In his previous life Benny had been part of the Israeli Defence Force and he'd been the most accomplished sniper in his unit, their Designated Marksman. He'd left the army after Israel began to use Russian mercenaries in the Gaza Strip. It wasn't a matter of principle for Benny, but one of economics. The mercenaries were being paid six times what he earned, and they paid no tax.

Rather than become a mercenary himself, which was a very dangerous business, Benny calculated that the best financial return was to be got from assassinations, and that was also the best way to preserve your anonymity. He calculated that although some targets would be well guarded, with patience and careful planning, the risks could be minimised. He'd read all about the history of contract killing and was appalled by the amateurishness of most of the attempts. A single shot from a distance of 1000 yards would be his *modus operandi*.

To get into business in this area, though, you don't advertise in the *London Evening Standard*. Benny had made a number of criminal contacts while in the Force and one Bosnian had come up trumps with the name of a crime boss in the East End. Benny had contacted him after he settled in London and, by using the Bosnian as a referee, he'd been entrusted with a contract, which he'd carried out quickly and efficiently. Since then, he undertook five or six contracts annually, at a standard price of $100,000 each. Hence the frequent absences from work, and the build-up of the Swiss bank account.

A small amount of his work was abroad, but Benny preferred to operate in Great Britain. There was still a call for work in Northern Ireland, but Benny knew that the chances of his identity being compromised were much greater there, as there were so many undercover operatives.

For work in England Benny had bought a blue Ford Transit van. He noted, wherever he went, the registration numbers of all blue Ford Transits, and at weekends made up new number plates for the van. He always had at least thirty sets of plates for the van, and he could switch the plates in less than a minute. Benny knew that at some time he would inevitably make a mistake, and the number plate of the van would be captured on camera or noted down and reported to the police. To ensure confusion, Benny used at least three different sets of plates on each operation.

Do-it-yourself hadn't figured much in his life, but Benny was a quick learner. In the lockup he rented in Clapham, his printing and metalwork skills were tested in making up the number plates and adjusting the van. He created small sliding windows on each side, to give him the ideal lines for taking shots from his preferred seated position.

★ ★ ★

Benny got up from his desk and moved over to the window overlooking the Isle of Dogs. The caller repeated his question, "We need to organise two removals. Can you help?"

Benny was a bit of a pedant. "It should be 'Will I help?' Never mind. Always happy to oblige." He rang off.

The call was a coded message. The arrangement was that Benny would collect a package from a mail box shop. In it were details of the name and address of the target, and a $100,000 bearer bond. The deal was, if Benny couldn't carry out the contract, the bond was to be returned to the mail box shop, and a message aborting the contract would be posted by Benny in the *Standard*. This had not yet happened.

The next day Benny picked up the package. For the first time, Benny was asked to carry out two contracts and the value of the bond was doubled. It looked to him to be a difficult assignment, but he was happy to take it on. Anyway, he'd never been to Scotland.

Benny arranged to take a week off from the following weekend. It was a quiet time in the Stock Market, so his superiors were prepared to agree. He got up to date by the next Friday, and then set off for Glasgow.

The van was well-equipped, a kind of mini office and bedsit, as Benny never checked into a hotel or bed and breakfast, always paid cash for petrol, and, before he set off, he bought all the food he would need for the trip. He always found a quiet spot to park the van overnight. He arrived in Glasgow in the late Saturday afternoon, and parked the van two streets away from the address he'd been given, near Maxwell Park on the south side of the city.

When he'd driven past the target's house, he could hardly believe his luck. The street was in a sort of valley and there were two streets running parallel to it on the side of a hill to the south-east of the house. This meant that Benny would have a clear line of sight from the next two streets to the target's front porch, depending on how the houses on the higher streets were staggered; and he would be firing with the sun behind him. As he drove along, he noticed a 4x4 with two Asians in the front seats, just outside the drive of the house. Obviously, Mr Usman Malik needed protection.

Benny had planned to park overnight in different outlying areas. He'd decided on Greenock for Saturday night, Loch Lomond for Sunday and East Kilbride for Monday. He'd calculated that he'd have worked out how to carry out the hit by Monday, so it was likely he would be on his way back to London on Tuesday. Every evening he changed the number plates on the van.

On the Sunday, Benny just drove around the area, familiarising himself with the roads in Maxwell Park. He realised that all traffic was funnelled out of the district by one street, so it was essential he be well away before anyone realised how the hit had been carried out.

Benny thought things over on the Sunday evening, and decided his best chance of a clear shot was as the first target walked out of his front door. But the wind from the west in Glasgow was quite strong and he'd have to factor that into his calculations. The best outcome would be to find a way to get the target static.

On Monday morning Benny got into position on Beech Avenue by half past seven. He watched the postman arrive at Malik's house at about a quarter past eight. Malik left the house at about 9.30. Benny could see a possible solution to the problem. He drove off and parked near Hampden Park in the south of the city. In a post office he bought a large envelope and picked up a Recorded Delivery form from the display. Back in the van he addressed the envelope, and filled up the Recorded Delivery form, using a fictitious name and address as the details of the sender. He then drove to Castlemilk and parked near another post office. He looked out for a suitable courier.

Twenty minutes later a teenage boy wearing a lime green shell suit sauntered along towards the van, idly kicking a can. He had a shaven head and didn't look like a respecter of authority. Benny leaned out with the envelope and a £10 note.

"Look, mate, I'm in a rush and there's a queue. Post this recorded delivery for me and you keep the change."

The boy looked doubtful, eyed the note, and said "Twenty."

Cheeky sod, thought Benny, but gave the boy another note.

"First class, mind, or I'll be back."

The boy grabbed the cash and ran into the post office with the envelope.

At midnight Benny returned to Maxwell Park, but left the van some streets away from the target's house. He walked along Cedar Avenue, and tied some ribbons to four trees he knew would be visible from Beech Avenue. These were his windage flags.

On Tuesday morning Benny drove to the spot he'd picked out in Beech Avenue, between two red sandstone villas, looking down at Malik's house. He'd parked the previous day on the next street up. He loaded his Steyer SSG, sighted the porch through the aperture, checked how much the windage flags were moving, and in which direction, made the appropriate allowance for the wind, and waited.

The only traffic on the street seemed to be cars loaded with children in smart uniforms. Benny had seen none of this in Castlemilk, and assumed that this area must house only those attending fee-paying schools. A few joggers passed by, eyeing the van with more attention than Benny had been aware of the previous day.

The postman was on time. He walked up to the gate where the two Asians were lounging about, smoking. They obviously knew him, as there was some desultory conversation. He walked up the drive and rang the doorbell. Malik appeared, there was a discussion and Malik looked behind as his 15-year-old son approached with a pen, and made to sign for the letter addressed to him. Benny shot the boy square on the forehead. A perfect, clean hit. Now came the difficult part. He was instructed to wait until Malik clearly realised his son was dead and then shoot him too. This might have meant a second trip if Benny couldn't get another shot off, but Benny had reasoned that Malik wouldn't dive for cover, but would stay with his son and probably look up to where the shot had come from. Benny had seen that happen so many times when he'd shot Arab terrorists. A colleague would usually try to help the target, which put him right in the frame for a double hit. And so it proved here. Malik cradled his son in his arms and looked up towards Beech Avenue, at which point the SSG burped and it was all over.

33

Govan Police Station was in uproar. A shootout had been reported in Maxwell Park, and firearms were being issued. When he saw the address of the property involved, Detective Inspector Alfie Johnston realised this was probably gang-related, as the division had been warned to expect some retaliation from McBain following the death of his son. Alfie phoned Erik Allensen.

"It's happening, Kay, a shooting at Malik's. Meet me there."

Allensen commandeered a squad car and was crossing the Townhead interchange westwards on the M8 at one hundred and ten miles per hour when a nondescript blue Ford Transit van passed heading eastwards on the other carriageway. He paid it no attention.

Johnston and Allensen met up and stopped at the road block just along from Malik's house. One of Johnston's colleagues briefed them.

"It's a mess. Mrs Malik was able to get out of the house by the rear and she's in that ambulance. Before collapsing, she said her son and her husband were shot when signing for a letter from the postman. The two Asians with handguns are the husband's bodyguards. No one knows if the postman's armed. It's a standoff, but we've got them covered."

Just then, the Chief Inspector from Govan, trained for hostage situations, spoke on a loudhailer.

"Everyone listen up. We have the area surrounded by armed

officers. No one is shooting their way out of here. Take off your tops and shirts, put your hands on your heads, and walk slowly towards me."

The two Asians stood up slowly from behind the hedge at the front of the house. They had removed their tops and shirts as instructed. A third figure rose up from behind the porch wall. He'd also removed his blue postman's shirt which was now billowing across the front lawn.

"Now, all three of you lie down on your fronts, keeping those hands on your heads."

Everyone complied and armed officers rushed forward, handcuffed them and bundled them into separate vans. An ambulance made its way to the front door to collect the victims. Johnston and Allensen ran across to the porch, but one look was enough for them to see this was a murder enquiry.

Scene-of-crime officers were now chasing everyone out of the area as they began the task of reconstructing what had happened. Then Johnston and Allensen returned to Govan Police Station to question the suspects.

The Asians were saying nothing until they had a solicitor present, but the postman couldn't stop talking. On the way to the station, Allensen and Johnston had discussed the similarity of this to the shooting a few months earlier of a stockbroker on his doorstep in a small town near Aberdeen, and they had the postman down as prime suspect until they listened to his description of the shooting for about two minutes. Johnston called the Southern General Hospital, where the bodies had been taken, and was told that the injuries were quite inconsistent with a handgun, and it appeared that only high-velocity bullets could have caused the damage.

"A professional, then," Allensen said.

"We better cordon off the area pronto. He must have fired from a house on Beech Avenue or maybe from Cedar. Or maybe from the street. Unlikely, though. Let's get back there, Kay."

Allensen shook his head, "Not my bag, I think I'd better get back to Shettleston. Find out if the grieving father has been letting out contracts. This is getting serious."

The inquiry at Maxwell Park was painstaking. No house in Beech Avenue or Cedar Avenue had been broken into, but two residents had remarked that a blue van had been in the vicinity over the last few days. The following day from about 7 a.m. the area was flooded with officers questioning passers-by. At about a quarter past eight a constable stopped a jogger.

"Do you use this route every day, sir?" he asked.

"Sure," replied the jogger.

"Did you notice anything unusual yesterday at this time? Maybe a strange van?"

"As a matter of fact I did. It had a very unusual number plate for Glasgow."

"How so?"

"Well, I don't think any vehicle with the number plate KB05FTP is going to last long in Glasgow, is it?"

The constable radioed Johnston. "Unbelievable, sir. KB – King Billy, FTP – Fuck the Pope. We've got him."

Johnston was initially confident of tracing the driver, but his euphoria was short-lived. It transpired that the owner of the van with that registration number was a removal firm in Brixton and the van itself had been en route from Newcastle to Cardiff over the last weekend. Hours were spent examining the CCTV footage from all the major routes out of Glasgow on the Tuesday afternoon, but they lost sight of the van as soon as it reached the junction at Newhouse. Benny had then kept off motorways heading back to London.

The investigation into the recorded delivery letter was equally unproductive. The postmaster at Castlemilk remembered the boy paying the fee with an English twenty-pound note, but was only able to say he was about fifteen years old. The police appealed for the boy to come forward, but the boy decided to keep his involvement to himself. There had been something in the tone used by the driver when he'd said he would be back. The boy thought it would be as well if that didn't happen.

Benny had made a mistake with the number plate, but had got away with it. He was a careful man.

★ ★ ★

For the next few weeks the newspapers were full of details of the double assassination, and speculation was rife about tit-for-tat gang warfare. The press had quickly linked the death of McBain's son to that of Malik's son, and there was unanimity that the hit must have been carried out by a professional. The *Daily Telegraph* had sourced details of other professional hits from its United Kingdom-wide archives, and listed eight assassinations in the previous three years which had similarities to the Maxwell Park hit. Nobody at Benny's employers spotted how some of the dates coincided with Benny's unpaid leave.

McBain was interviewed by Allensen and Alfie Johnston, but it was a waste of time. Johnston, whose case it was, put money on the street in an attempt to get information, but the usual snouts knew nothing. The only people in Glasgow involved in the contract had been McBain, Rab Donald and Colin Scott. The investigation was widened to London, but no information was forthcoming, and after a month other priorities took over.

Malik's father decided to wind up his involvement with Glasgow. It was all just too painful for him. He stood down as a councillor, and sold the Kanrach business to a friend, who also took over the contacts in the drug supply chain. Imran wanted to avenge his brother, but his father said he was forbidden to do so, realising that McBain was capable of unimaginable retaliation for whatever the Malik family might do. The whole Malik family moved from Glasgow to Birmingham. Glasgow was now wide open to the McBain operation.

34

Angela Finlayson sat at her desk in Gee One Flats and looked out at the traffic in West Campbell Street. Business was very quiet and it looked as if she wouldn't meet the target necessary for her to get her bonus. She considered for the umpteenth time phoning the police about what had happened with Zahra's flat. She'd read about Sonny McBain's death and then the shootings at Malik's house, and was sure there had to be a connection with Zahra. She was fixated on the money McBain had given her, and wondered whether there might be more where that had come from. So, better not to involve the police, but maybe contact McBain. She could do with some cash and maybe her silence was worth something. She decided to write McBain a letter.

The letter was deliberately ambiguous. She remembered McBain's excitement about the fact that she'd referred to one of his colleagues as "the third man". She was interested in films, so maybe she could get to meet McBain by suggesting they go to a showing of a classic. She leafed through the *Glasgow Herald* and saw there was to be a David Lean week at the Cosmo cinema. McBain would be bound to like *Doctor Zhivago*, she thought. So she wrote in her letter about how she'd read about his loss. She'd met Sonny only the once, so she hadn't come to the funeral. She'd sensed she and McBain shared an interest in films, so would he like to go with her to the Cosmo to see *Doctor Zhivago*? To tempt McBain, remembering how he'd asked about her favourite scenes in *The Third Man,* she mentioned the two scenes in *Doctor Zhivago* which were her favourites. Just before the interval, the revelation that Tom Courtney's character, Strelnikov, has survived and is now a communist leader, when his red-flagged train thunders past the siding where Zhivago and his family are waiting to go on to their country dacha. Then, at the end, when Zhivago's half-brother, played by Alec Guinness, is startled when he sees that Lara's daughter is carrying a balalaika. Yes, that should tempt him.

When McBain received the letter, he was excited. He hadn't had any relationship with a woman since Irene had left him. Maybe he could have a few months with this attractive young woman who obviously shared his interest in films. If something more developed, he wouldn't resist.

He and Angela met up at Sarkozy's for a pre-theatre meal before going to the Cosmo. Rab and Joe were in position as they'd been for McBain's dinner there with Eastman. McBain had warned them to be more watchful than ever, as there was a widespread belief that McBain was responsible for the assassinations of Malik and his son, and even the Glasgow underworld had been aghast at the killing of a young boy. Angela had been collected from her harbourside flat by Rab.

McBain and Angela seemed to get along well enough at the restaurant, and Rab and Joe sat on either side of them at the Cosmo. McBain noticed that Rab seemed to enjoy the film, but Joe snored loudly throughout. As they left the cinema Angela pointed at Rab and Joe.

"Do we have to have the two stooges with us all the time? Why not come back to my flat? The view of the river is fantastic."

McBain had taken the precaution of getting a full report on Angela from Colin Scott before he'd agreed to meet her. It was just possible she could be the bait in a trap. The report had revealed nothing suspicious, but McBain was still wary.

"OK, but Rab will check out your flat first. You never know. There are some strange types about that area. Footballers and the like." The development had attracted some highly paid Rangers and Celtic players as tenants, and there had been a few riotous parties reported in the press. Everyone laughed nervously as the Mercedes headed for the Clydeside Expressway and the new flats built opposite what had been the Glasgow Garden Festival site. When they arrived Rab took Angela's keys and disappeared to look round her flat. He came back and he and Joe escorted McBain and Angela to her door.

"OK, boys, I'll phone when I need you."

McBain winked as Rab and Joe left. They knew they'd have to stay outside guarding the flat. It might be a long night.

Angela took off her jacket.

"Make yourself comfortable and I'll fix you a drink," said Angela. "How about a Bowmore?"

"Fine," McBain said. He looked east towards the city centre, then west down the river past the shipyards towards Dumbarton. "This is quite a place."

Angela handed him a glass.

"It's great in the summer; facing south gives me the sun on the balcony all day. I can just see East Kilbride in the distance. That's where I grew up – in a soulless new town. I love looking at the tower blocks there and thinking how lucky I am to have escaped."

McBain sat down on the black leather sofa and Angela perched on an armchair opposite. There was an awkward silence which both broke at the same time. They both stopped and laughed.

"You go first." Angela said.

"Well, I really enjoyed the film and it would be great to see you again, if you'd like that. It's a long time since I was courting, but I think we get on. What do you think?"

Angela uncrossed her legs and sat back on the armchair.

"We both like films, that's for sure. Would I be a gangster's moll, do you think? I quite fit the bill. I've been reading all about you in the papers, obviously."

McBain tensed up.

"I'm a businessman, Angela, not a gangster." McBain was suddenly nervous, wishing he wasn't here in a compromising situation. "Thanks for the drink. Maybe I'll be in touch." He drained his malt and stood up.

"Not so fast, Mr McBain. I think we've a bit of business to discuss. You were generous when we met at Zahra's flat and I think you need to be again. I've been putting two and two together and this is how it looks to me. For some reason, the Zahra disappearance, whatever that was, provoked Sonny to torch Malik's cash and carry. I actually saw that from my balcony. Then Malik got his own back by getting Sonny killed, and you got his son killed in front of him before he was shot too. I'm sure the police would be very interested in my theory. No doubt they've a good idea about how things went after the fire at Malik's, but I know how it all started. Obviously, I'm happy to keep quiet about this, if we can come to … an arrangement."

McBain walked round the sofa, punching Rab's number into his mobile. He was looking out of the window, with his back to Angela.

"I don't know what you're talking about, Angela."

His heart was thumping, but he kept his cool. He assessed the situation quickly. Random thoughts. What had happened to the nice Angela? He would like to throttle her now, but they'd been seen together. He was fairly sure she was an amateur. Colin Scott would have found out about any police connection. So it was unlikely she was wired up. Anyway, he hadn't said anything incriminating. Best to play her along for now.

He spoke into the mobile, saying he should be collected now. He turned to face Angela.

"I'll discuss things with Rab. We've a few developments where we need an agent. It would be well paid. Why don't you come to Westberry Drive tomorrow evening? We can discuss figures then."

"OK, Mr McBain, but I'm thinking about, say, £10,000 per month, for, say, two years? Cash, of course."

"We'll see you about six, then," McBain walked towards the door.

"Just remember that if I have an accident a letter goes to Govan CID, Mr McBain. I'm not stupid."

McBain slammed the door. He walked down the corridor towards Rab and Joe. Suddenly breathless, he stumbled and reached inside his jacket for his medication. His chest seemed to be imploding. That bitch, he'd had hopes of a soulmate. He coughed as he passed out, falling on the floor about five yards from where Rab and Joe were waiting.

Rab could see that McBain was having some sort of attack. He'd some medical training from his Army days but he simply called the ambulance. He and Joe carried McBain back into Angela's flat. She became hysterical, babbling about not really meaning it, which caused Rab to look up quizzically. McBain had turned ashen gray, his breath shallow. The ambulancemen got him to the Western Infirmary within seven minutes, but he was dead on arrival.

★ ★ ★

McBain's funeral was a much more restrained affair than Sonny's. Those attending looked a lot more nervous, and there was no knees-up at the Clyde Views. Irene was accompanied by Rab, which was a pretty plain indication of who was favoured to take over the McBain empire.

Such as it was. The reason the bankers attending were edgy was that the Hebridean Bank had been forcibly amalgamated with a rival and their inspectors had taken a close look at the Westberry accounts. These had been found to be in the red because the properties had been consistently overvalued. The local bank manager who was responsible for the Westberry accounts had been suspended. In effect, the Westberry companies were insolvent, and the bank was appointing an administrator to both Properties and Developments.

That left the sauna, the loan sharking and the drug dealing. The last two were cash businesses, and Rab had the loan book and the supply chain under his control. Irene had expected to find that the sauna was owned by a Westberry company, as Alex had told her that everything was in the companies, but it turned out that it was rented from Sean Murphy of the King James Bar, and he was happy for Rab to take over the lease. So, seamlessly, and without any financial cost, Rab Donald took over what was left of the McBain empire.

Irene and Rab sat in McTavish Legal's waiting area before being shown into a Boardroom. Eastman had arranged for them to meet a Mr Gloag, who dealt with the administration of estates.

Mr Gloag seemed a bit disorganised but he explained that Irene would receive the income of the estate during her lifetime, and on her death the capital would pass to the Glasgow Diocese of the Catholic Church. Because she was still married to Mr McBain when he died, there should be no inheritance tax, but anyway it looked like the estate consisted only of the house and car, so it was under the limit, valued at about £300,000. Because interest rates were so low, she might only get about £7,000 a year. Was that going to be a problem?

Irene had £5m in investments and a house worth £2m in Spain, so she laughed. No, it wasn't going to be a problem. Could she just give the Diocese the money now?

Yes, of course, said Mr Gloag, and in that case there would certainly be no tax to pay. As soon as the house and car had been sold, the money could pass to the Diocese. Would she want the endowment to be in her husband's name?

No, she said, let's make it anonymous.

Joe drove Irene and Rab out to Glasgow Airport after the meeting. Joe's nephew Patrick had just returned from a stint in Afghanistan and had had enough of the Army. Rab had been keeping an eye on the lad and had suggested he be recruited as a minder, so the bodyguards now were Joe and Patrick. Rab sat in the back of the newly rented BMW 4x4. New regime, new vehicle.

Outside the security gate, Irene shook Rab's hand.

"I won't be back, Rab. Alex always liked you. It's right you should take over."

"Don't be a stranger, Irene, and if you need anything, don't hesitate."

Irene did hesitate.

"Rab, you know, it's all been a bit odd, don't you think, the way things happened? First Sonny, then Alex. And where's all that cash Alex used to talk about? I phoned the Highland Bank but they said the deposit boxes were closed. Alex mentioned something about it the day of Sonny's funeral, but I can't remember what it was. I phoned Eastman about it, as I think Alex said he'd made the arrangements, but he said he only dealt with the Wills for Sonny and Alex."

Rab smiled, "Don't dwell on it, Irene. It's in the past. You're well looked after. But if you're ever short, let me know."

He turned and left.

35

Allensen had pleaded with his colleagues that his leaving do on his retirement should be low key. The superintendent would make the presentation in the office, there would be a toast with some cheap cava, and that would be that. The office had been brightened up for the occasion, but in a rather unenthused way. A single banner – "Happy Retirement" – and a few red, yellow and black balloons, a tribute to Partick Thistle, the team Allensen always claimed to support in order to avoid antagonising Rangers and Celtic supporters in the force. As he'd always been regarded as stand-offish, there was no real enthusiasm among the staff at Shettleston to prolong the celebrations, so by 7 p.m. Allensen was in a taxi heading for La Solera with Sarah Plummer, recently promoted to Detective Sergeant. She'd insisted that on such an evening, he mustn't just head back to his flat. He'd agreed reluctantly.

At the restaurant, over coffee, talk soon turned to work.

"You must be pleased, sir. You leave on a high. The McBains and the Maliks are history. We'll never stop the moneylending, drugs, prostitution, but with Rab Donald running things, well, it could be a lot worse."

"No more of the sir, Sarah. There's always unfinished business, isn't there? But at least Sonny is out of the way. He was a psychopath."

"What are you really going to do, sir? Sorry – what do I call you now? – Mr Allensen is too formal, and Erik just doesn't seem right."

Allensen called Paolo over, and asked for the bill. He placed his hand on Plummer's shoulder.

"Well, Sarah. After this evening it won't be an issue. I'm not one to be coming back to the office to tell you how to do your job, or, even worse, to tell you how it used to be done. So this is goodbye, not *au revoir*."

Sarah Plummer's stomach lurched, and she did her best to conceal her disappointment. There was to be no happy ending after all.

★ ★ ★

John Gloag contemplated the six Iron Mountain boxes which had been delivered to McTavish Legal. They were the contents of Alex McBain's filing cabinets at the Westberry Drive house and should enable him to trace any assets McBain had, to include in the Inland Revenue account he needed to lodge. Not that there would be any tax to pay, as Irene McBain had signed away her legal rights in the estate to the Diocese, which was a charity. All Mr Gloag had to do was lodge the list of assets in court, sell the house and car, collect any money due, and, after the McTavish Legal fee had been deducted, send what was left to the Diocese.

He sighed as he thought of the time it was all going to take to go through all this junk. No doubt there would be life policies long ago paid out, building society passbooks from decades ago, and Inland Revenue forms galore. This was not an efficient use of his time. He preferred to pretend to be preparing trust accounts while admiring the cleavages of the secretaries. Better to get a trainee to do this. He really couldn't be bothered.

He phoned Paul Longmuir.

"Hi, Paul. Your lot can't be that busy, what with the credit crunch. Maybe I can poach your trainee to go through McBain's papers. After all, the work came from your boss".

As it happened, Longmuir was happy to agree because new work had dried up and he was being constantly pressed by Frances, the trainee, for something to do. So the Iron Mountain boxes landed on the desk of Frances, with an instruction to extract and list anything she thought relevant to McBain's estate.

Frances was a very bright girl. She attacked the task with relish. Her enthusiasm diminished with every box, but after two days she had listed the items she thought were important. She emailed the list to Mr Gloag, and copied it to Eastman and Longmuir.

Before Rab delivered the Iron Mountain boxes to McTavish Legal, he had been careful to put to one side all documents he had found at Westberry Drive which referred to illicit activities and also anything to do with the cash which had been laundered to the Singer Trust. Or he thought he had done so. But tucked into the envelope containing an old Prudential Life policy was a copy of the letter which McBain had signed to the Trustees, which had directed that if both Sonny and he died, the money in the Singer Trust was to go to the Bona Opera Fund.

Frances had found this and included it in her list, with a note that there was nothing else in the boxes about the Singer Trust, but it was interesting that the beneficiary in the letter sounded like a charity, and that since a charity was to receive McBain's estate, it looked like there might be a connection.

Eastman fired off an email to Frances as soon as he had recovered from seeing the reference to the Singer Trust on the list. He thanked her for her work, asked her to give him a copy of the letter and to give all the papers back to Mr Gloag. He then phoned Gloag and told him to ignore the Singer Trust, as everything was going to charity anyway. But while Gloag was a lazy sod, he was a competent paralegal and he was not convinced.

"Sir, we need to make sure the deceased had no interest in the Trust, and that he hadn't gifted any funds to it. Admittedly, it's just a Letter of Wishes, but he says the funds should go to him or his son, and only to the charity if they're both dead. I think we'd better check this with the Jersey lawyers."

Eastman hesitated. He knew Gloag was correct and he also knew that McBain was only a discretionary beneficiary, so even if Gloag got the information from Jersey, it would make no difference.

"You're quite correct, John. Of course we need a letter from Lebens. As it happens, I've had dealings in the past with them, so if you give me a letter to them asking for the details, I'll make sure you get a reply right away. I know you'll want to wind this one up quickly."

He phoned Robert Lebens and explained what had happened. Robert assured him that he would deal with Gloag's enquiry himself and there would be no reference to Eastman's involvement in the Singer Trust.

Later that afternoon, Natasha brought in the letter from John Gloag for Eastman to sign.

"Just fax it to Robert, darling. Can you stay later?" He looked meaningfully at her. Eastman was now concentrating in keeping his place in the partnership and enjoying as much of Natasha as he could. He'd rented a flat near the office where he and Natasha now regularly met up after work. Natasha was beginning to suggest they should move in together, but Eastman was stringing her along meantime.

The next day Natasha brought in the faxed reply from Lebens. It confirmed that McBain had been one of a number of discretionary beneficiaries in the Singer Trust, but had never given anything to the Trust, nor had he received anything, either income or capital. The letter added that the Trust had recently been wound up. Eastman was sure this would satisfy Gloag, and sent the letter to him. Gloag later confirmed that he could now complete McBain's estate.

Meantime, Rab Donald was sitting opposite Colin Scott in the investigator's office. He reassured Colin that there would be no change in the working relationship following McBain's death, though it looked like it was going to be some time before new companies could be set up for property developments.

"Everyone's affected by the credit crunch, Rab," Colin said. "I suppose the loan book will be building up. I can always help with the collections. Back to the old days, eh?"

Rab smiled. "Of course, Colin. We'll need your ... expertise in the difficult cases. And I've a job for you now. Remember the girl you did a report on for Alex, just before he died? In fact, he'd just left her flat when he had the heart attack."

"Angela Finlayson? Of course. Quite a looker. Were she and Alex ... you know?

"Maybe. But something's nagging at me. Something she said when we took Alex into her flat and called the ambulance. She said she didn't mean it. Odd, don't you think?"

Colin thought for a minute, "Oh, I see. You think she said something to upset Alex, that stressed him out and he had the heart attack. Maybe she'd just dumped him."

Rab stood up, "Possibly, but it's a loose end. I really need to know what she meant. Your report mentioned elderly parents. Could that be something to prod her with? There didn't seem to be anything else."

"Consider it done," Colin said as they shook hands. "Rab, if it was anything more sinister, do I use my own judgment, or report back?"

"I'll leave that to you. There are funds available for a specialist, if that's necessary, but I think you should be able to handle it."

Colin spent the next weekend in Perthshire, where he visited the small village of Comrie, home of Angela Finlayson's parents. He got some excellent photographs of them in their garden and attending a country show in the local park.

On the Monday evening, he called at Angela's flat. After he rang the bell, she'd obviously looked at him through the peephole. She kept the door closed and asked who he was and what he wanted. He gave his name as Detective Constable Brown and quoted her parents' names and their address, saying he needed to talk to her about them. She'd made him show her his fake CID warrant card before she let him in.

She was clearly upset.

"What's happened to Mum and Dad? Has there been an accident?"

Colin drew the photographs from his pocket. "I just want to be sure I've got the right person. These are your parents. Correct?"

"Yes. What's happened to them?"

"Don't worry, they're fine. For the moment, that is. I just need to ask you a few questions about the late Alexander McBain. You were a friend of his, I'm told."

Angela was confused, then wary.

"Should there not be two of you? Let me see that card again."

Colin nodded.

"You're right, of course, I'm not really a policeman. I'm a friend of a friend of the McBain family. You upset Alex just before he died. What did you say to him? Before you think of lying or doing anything stupid, look closely at the photos. Comrie's a long way from Glasgow, you might think. But these were taken yesterday. Someone could get there and back in four hours, even if they also had to do a bit of – what might I call it? – business while they were there. Now, what did you say to Mr McBain?"

The threat to Angela's parents was only too clear. She thought about what had happened to the Maliks. Tell him everything? On the other hand, McBain couldn't have said much before he collapsed. She decided a little of the truth might satisfy this man. She just wanted him out of her flat.

"I work in a flat-renting agency. One of our tenants left suddenly, an employee of Mr McBain's son. It was all to do with some Pakistanis. Then people started getting killed. Mr McBain and I were just talking about it."

Colin tore one of the photos in half.

"I don't really think that was all. You said you didn't mean it when they brought Mr McBain into the flat. Didn't mean what?"

For the life of her Angela couldn't think of a single thing to say. Her mind blanked. Colin turned to leave.

"Wait," she said. "I asked Mr McBain if the police would be interested in a theory I had. That everything was connected to the Pakistanis."

"And what did Mr McBain say to that?"

Angela looked down at the floor.

"He said we might come to an arrangement. He didn't want any more trouble. He was going to give me a job."

Colin looked sceptical.

Angela gave in. "OK, I asked him for money to keep quiet about it. A lot of money."

"And do you want money now? Are you thinking of going to the police with your theory? It's all water under the bridge now, isn't it? Or maybe you're thinking of selling your story to the papers?"

"No, no, none of that! I just want to forget all about it."

"A very wise choice, if I may say so. But just to be perfectly clear, some of Mr McBain's associates are concerned to preserve his good name. If there's the slightest suggestion that you've been blabbing about your theory, there will be consequences. Clear?"

Angela turned and looked out at the Clyde.

217

"Crystal. Please leave me alone, and my family."

The door slammed behind her.

Colin reported the exchange to Rab.

"She's terrified. No worries there. Case closed."

36

Three months later Irene looked out of the picture window of her villa in Malaga as Tom Saunders flopped onto the sofa. When he first came to work for Irene, some four years previously, Saunders had happily settled into the post as driver and general handyman, and had kept a distance from his employer. Recently, though, they'd become friends, mainly because of McBain's death, and Saunders had felt confident enough to ask Irene if he might leave as he hoped to move in with his friend Juan. They'd taken on the lease of a beach-front club together. Saunders sipped his orange juice and spoke.

"It's really decent of you to let me go, Mrs McBain. Juan and I are excited about the new bar. Will you come to the opening?"

"I don't see myself as a gay icon in pink chiffon," Irene said. "Maybe a full leather outfit? But no, Tom, I wish you well but I won't be a regular at the Off Set Club".

She continued to stare out of the window.

Saunders frowned, "You never asked how I came to be here. I expect Mr McBain told you a bit. I was working in Gibraltar for the Serious Crime Squad. It was really dull until we were told to target Mr McBain. I was just a pen pusher, really, but my boss asked me to keep an eye on Mr McBain for a few hours until the professionals arrived. I'd had a bit of training, and was equipped with a clever piece of kit which recorded from a distance. I don't suppose it matters now that Mr McBain has gone but I recorded

Mr McBain's confession to the priest, and I was able to listen in. It was a very scary confession. I should never have gone into the cathedral at all. I'm not surprised you left him."

Irene turned round, "You heard his confession? Did he say anything about me?"

Tom shook his head, "Nothing really, except about how he'd met you, how he really loved you, and how worried he was about Sonny. It was all about his history, as if he was trying to justify his life. Some of it was very violent. Anyway, I lost concentration for a minute and then I noticed his minders had moved. I hid the kit between two kneelers under the pew, and tried to get downstairs to the exit. They were waiting for me at the foot of the stairs. I'd no chance.

"They knocked me out with something, and the next thing I knew I was in a bare room, sitting on a metal chair. Chained to a radiator. I couldn't move, and I had earmuffs on. They were really ticklish. I was kept awake for ages. If I dozed off, one would come in and slap me awake. No one spoke to me.

"After God knows how long, the two minders came in – I now know it was Joe and Rab – they came in and hooded me. They must have brought in a basin because my shoes and socks were removed and my feet were placed carefully in cold water. After about two minutes, I could hear an electric switch being turned on and off. I got the message.

"They removed the hood and unchained me. I was taken into an adjoining room and sat on a bed. It was a kind of motel with two bedrooms. They'd cleared all the furniture out of one room to hold me in, and this other room was packed with beds and chairs. I never understood that. It was weird.

"Still Joe and Rab said nothing at all. Then Mr McBain came in and asked me if I'd seen the film *The Usual Suspects.*"

Irene groaned at this. How many times had she heard about that film? She'd never watched it, though.

"It was his all-time favourite, apparently. I said I hadn't, so he explained about this character Keyser Söze. I was confused, as you might expect, but I soon realised what this was all about. Apparently, Mr McBain liked to model himself on this guy. What happens in the movie is a gang of Hungarians try to muscle in on Söze's operation. To intimidate him, three of them break into his home, rape his wife, and hold the family prisoner until Söze returns. When he comes back, he sees his family all distressed – his wife can't look at him. To show Söze they mean business, one of the gang slits the throat of one of the children. Söze draws out a pistol and kills two of the gang, but the last gang member's grabbed another child, a little girl, and he's holding an open razor to her neck, just nicking it to draw blood. He's really confident he can use her as a hostage to escape.

"What Söze does next is stunning in the film, apparently. He shoots all his children and his wife, having been shamed, as he sees it. But he lets the last intruder go. This is so the Hungarians will get the message that he's not to be trifled with. He waits until his family have been buried, then he exacts revenge. But he doesn't just kill the last Hungarian. For each of the three gang members, he kills their children, their wives, their parents, their brothers, sisters, nephews and nieces. Again, I got the message.

"After Mr McBain had finished, he said the best thing would be for me to tell them everything I knew about Rock, the seminar, the whole operation. If not, they'd have to kill me, very painfully, and then make my body disappear. And that would just be the start of it. I thought about my parents and my sister. It was no decision, really."

Irene shivered, "He'd have done it, you know …" said Irene, her voice breaking. "There was a family in Glasgow. No connection with the gangs, except a nephew turned police informer. Their house was petrol bombed, three kiddies burned to death … That was when I finally left."

"Mrs McBain, I'm not surprised. Maybe it's just as well I told them the lot, except the bit about the directional mike and actually listening in on the confession. I suppose I'd been so amateurish they thought I was just observing. They asked who'd been the liaison in Glasgow, so I told them about Detective Inspector Allensen. When I finished, Mr McBain just patted me on the shoulder and said I'd be leaving the police service and working for someone he knew in Malaga from now on, at an increased salary. And that's how I ended up here, delivered by Joe and Rab, with a warning to tell you nothing. I felt like a child. The last thing Mr McBain said to me was that I was to remember Keyser Söze."

Irene gathered up an envelope from the table and handed it to Saunders. It contained $5,000.

"I hope this will help, it's a wee minding, as we say in Glasgow. By the way, did you ever hear of a lawyer called Eastman?"

"No, Mrs McBain. I've never heard of him."

★ ★ ★

At that moment, in Glasgow, the said Eastman was nervously looking through his bank statements online. He was working through the credit crunch as best he could. McTavish Legal had had to make some staff redundant, and it looked like his share of profits might be less than half last year's. His finances were in a dire state, but he would get by. He now had his escape plan.

He glanced at the note from John Gloag, confirming that the administration of Alex McBain's estate was now complete and the Diocese had received a cheque for £320,000 after expenses. Father O'Rourke himself had been co-opted onto the committee set up to administer the legacy and he'd sent an invitation to Eastman to attend a reception at the Glasgow City Chambers to meet the other Board members and Monsignor Bertolini, a representative of the International Bona Opera Fund, who was on a goodwill visit to Glasgow.

Normally, Eastman wouldn't have thought of going to such a dull occasion, but his curiosity about what had happened to the Singer Trust money got the better of him. He knew he should put as much distance as possible between himself and the Singer Trust, but a weird professional pride wanted to know if it had all worked out. The Bona Opera Fund should have received about £18m.

At the City Chambers he sat through two tedious presentations before the gathering broke up for coffee and biscuits. Father O'Rourke guided him to meet Monsignor Bertolini and they sat down at a corner table.

Bertolini had perfect English. He explained that the Bona Opera Fund was based in Geneva and acted as an overseer to the individual bodies working in each developing country. Eastman saw a way to enquire about the Singer Trust.

"So, if the Fund in Switzerland were to get a large endowment from a donor, is it shared out among all the countries, or can the donor specify where it's to be used?"

Bertolini looked coy.

"Well, if we were lucky enough for that to happen, it would probably be shared out."

Eastman decided to take a chance.

"Did I not read recently about a single donation of over $25m this year?"

"No, Mr Eastman. You didn't read about that because there have been no donations to the Fund for more than five years. Our funding at present comes wholly from the Vatican."

Eastman looked pensive.

"Sorry, I must have confused your Fund with another Swiss charity. There are so many!"

"Not so many that I would not know about such a donation, Mr Eastman, and I do not. Now, you must excuse me."

Eastman walked down the marble staircase with Father O'Rourke.

"I suppose the Monsignor could just have been keeping a confidence about big donations?"

"No, Mr Eastman, if the Monsignor says there was none, there was none. He would have been more circumspect if he'd wanted to keep a confidence."

Eastman felt he should ask Father O'Rourke about what he'd discussed with Alex McBain about the Singer Trust, as he was sure the Geneva Fund had been put forward by the Father, but would he break such a confidence, and, anyway, why draw attention to this at all? He was in a labyrinth of confusion as he walked back across George Square to his office. He remembered he had a current transaction on with Robert Lebens, and he had an excuse to go to Jersey in connection with that. He would take the opportunity to try to find out what had happened to the Singer Trust money.

★ ★ ★

A few days later, Eastman sat opposite Lebens in La Rustica. He was unsure how to raise the question of the distribution from the Singer Trust. He knew Lebens would be reluctant to say too much about it.

"Something strange happened recently. We just completed the administration of a client's estate. It went to a Scottish charity, and I was invited to meet some of the people who look after the funds. They'd brought along the international director, who's with the Swiss organisation which was to get the money from the Singer Trust. I asked him about it, in a roundabout way, but he was adamant they'd got nothing from you. How can that be?"

Robert looked annoyed, "What are you suggesting, James? Of course the funds were transferred to Switzerland in accordance with the Letter of Wishes. I have all the documentation."

"Was there any change to the original Letter of Wishes?"

"No, everything was done as your client originally wished."

Eastman suddenly had an inspiration, "May I see the Letter of Wishes?"

"Very irregular, old boy, but in view of the, er … history, I'm sure I can stretch a point. Come back to the office."

Eastman sat in Boardroom Six. Lebens' secretary brought him the papers for the Singer Trust. The Letter of Wishes was clear enough. But the organisation which was to receive the capital should Sonny and Alex both die wasn't the Bona Opera Fund, but something he had never heard of – Cadzow Global Provision SA – with an address in Zurich. It looked to Eastman as if McBain had changed his mind about the beneficiary, or the first page of the Letter of Wishes had been switched after McBain had signed the second page.

He sat back, thinking furiously. How had it been done? He trusted Lebens implicitly, so the switch had to have been made in Glasgow. He thought of the sequence of events after he'd taken instructions from Alex McBain and sent him the Letter of Wishes. Rab Donald had brought the Letter of Wishes after McBain had signed it, so, unless, McBain himself had changed his mind, or Sonny had been involved, it looked as if Rab had switched the first page of the Letter.

He asked to see Robert before he left. He decided not to alarm him by voicing his suspicions about the switch.

"I know I'm pushing it, Robert, but I now see that the money's gone in accordance with the Letter of Wishes. The trouble is, I'm fairly sure – no, I'm certain – that McBain changed his mind about who the beneficiary should be after I saw him. I'm just curious to know why. I'd like to find out a bit more about Cadzow Global. I've got the address, but do you have any more details about them? Who were their lawyers, bankers and so on?"

"Sorry, old boy. You're trying to cross a line. I've been too indulgent with you. But in fact there's nothing to tell. We got instructions by email to send a bank draft to the address you see before you. It's a small legal firm in Zurich. That's all I know."

★ ★ ★

Eastman was surprised to get a call from Sarah Plummer on his return to Glasgow. She wanted to talk to him about the Proceeds of Crime Act. There were apparently some issues relating to McBain's estate which the Crown Office in Edinburgh wanted to raise, after they had learned from the Court papers that McBain had left a substantial sum. He told her McBain's estate had been wound up, and anyway McBain had never been convicted of any crime. She insisted on seeing him, and he decided the police had been at McTavish Legal's office often enough, so he would call into Shettleston on his way home.

When Eastman spoke to the desk sergeant at Shettleston he said he'd a meeting with Detective Constable Plummer; he was told she'd been promoted, and was now a Detective Sergeant. He was shown up to the same area where he had originally met Allensen. Plummer was sitting at Allensen's old desk.

"So he got a room at last," Eastman said.

Plummer looked blank.

"Kay, your boss. He's been moaning for ages about his quarters, hasn't he? Where's he billeted now? Has he been promoted too?"

"Detective Inspector Allensen has retired, Mr Eastman. He'd put in the years. He lives in Portugal, now."

Sitting down, Eastman had the strangest feeling. He looked across to the chair from where Allensen had interviewed him, and tried to picture him. What had it been about Allensen that had unnerved him at the time? Something about the way his eyes sparkled, and a kind of knowing look from time to time, that was it. As if he was a step ahead. And now he was living in Portugal. Not the usual retirement destination for a modestly paid policeman. Odd.

"Anyway, Mr Eastman, we're not here to chat about my former colleague. The Crown Office have a large file for your client Mr McBain, though as you said on the phone, he was never convicted of any crime. Crown Counsel feel that we can close the file if we know his estate has gone to a charity and, according to the Will you lodged in court, that will happen on Mrs McBain's death. We're unhappy that she'll get the income, maybe for years, and the charity might end up with nothing. Crown Counsel also mentions she has other legal rights in the estate."

Eastman sighed, "If you'd only said this on the phone, it would have saved me a journey. Mrs McBain gave up her rights under the Will, and also her legal rights, and all of Mr McBain's estate has already gone to charity."

"Apart from your fees, presumably." Plummer smiled.

Eastman stood up, "The labourer is worthy of his hire, as your boss, sorry ex-boss, no doubt advised you many times. I recollect he was fond of quotations. Are we done here?"

Plummer showed Eastman down the stairs and opened the door into the public area. As he crossed over the threshold, he looked back at her.

"I don't suppose there's any chance of getting Kay's address from you. I really liked him, and I'm pretty sure you did too. Are you still in touch?"

227

Plummer slammed the door behind Eastman. As he looked back through the security glass, he could see her mouthing "Fuck off!" On an impulse, he gave her a wink.

When he got back to Edinburgh that evening, he joined his wife watching television rather than go off to his study, as he usually did. His mind was awash with theories about what had happened, and he knew he couldn't rest until he found out what had really been going on since his ill-advised encounter with the classy London tart in the Art Gallery. So to his wife's utter consternation, after *News at Ten* and the Scottish news, he turned to her.

"Look, darling, we've been in a rut for months. We need some time to ourselves, away from the children, work, the office, all these distractions. Remember the holiday we had before we got married, in Wengen? We really enjoyed Switzerland. Work's pretty slack at the moment, and I know I can organise a goodwill visit to Swiss lawyers to cover the cost. How about it? Business class, and a long weekend in Zurich. Sightseeing, shopping, relaxing, trips on the lake, the whole nine yards. What do you say?"

"Who'd look after the children? Oh, I suppose I could dragoon Mummy into doing it. Funnily enough, she's been suggesting we do something like this. Yes, James, let's do it."

The next day Eastman faxed a letter to the lawyers in Zurich who had received the Singer Trust funds from Lebens on behalf of Cadzow. He explained his involvement in international transactions and his requirement for assistance with Swiss Law from time to time. He would like to explore areas of mutual interest, and as he would be in Zurich in a week's time, could they spare him half an hour on the Friday or Monday? They faxed back that the senior partner, Mr Bidermann, would be pleased to see him at three o'clock on the Friday.

37

Eastman was in the waiting room at the offices of Gruenschildt Partners in Bahnhofstrasse in Zurich. His wife was shopping for presents for the children. The decor in the offices was starkly functional, all leather and dark wood. There was no board listing the companies for which Gruenschildt acted as registered office, as is usually displayed in lawyers' offices in most jurisdictions.

A matronly secretary walked Eastman to Mr Bidermann's office. Eastman was immediately impressed by Bidermann and his young assistant, who sat at right angles to his boss, effectively on the end of the mahogany desk. Both wore immaculate dark suits, white shirts and discreet club ties. There was no dressing down in Zurich. Bidermann was about fifty-five years old, gaunt with greying hair and thick black designer spectacles. His assistant was of similar build; they could have been father and son, but they were not. Both had faultless English.

The three exchanged information about the current economic climate and the opportunities there were, particularly for Swiss investment in the United Kingdom. The consensus seemed to be that UK companies in financial services were undervalued, and that some Swiss banks might take the chance to acquire these businesses.

Eastman took the opportunity during a lull in the conversation to raise the real reason for his visit.

"Mr Bidermann, I have a particular interest in one of your clients and would very much like to make contact with the principals of the company. My correspondents in Jersey were involved in the winding up of a Trust earlier this year, and its assets passed to your clients Cadzow Global Provision SA. I had a peripheral role in the matter, and my understanding had been that when the Trust was wound up, the funds would pass to the Bona Opera Fund, a charity run by the Catholic Church from Geneva to benefit orphans in the Third World. There seems to have been, how can I put it, an element of confusion in the giving of instructions, and I've learned that the funds came here. I haven't been able to find any trace of Cadzow in any register of charitable organisations; it may be that Cadzow carries out the same role as Bona Opera, but I would like to be reassured on that. Can you help me with this? Perhaps you could ask the directors of Cadzow if I might meet with them?"

Mr Bidermann grew thin-lipped.

"As I'm sure you are very much aware, Mr Eastman, I am bound by client confidentiality. I cannot and will not break that and I am puzzled as to how you obtained information about a body you think is a client of ours allegedly receiving funds. Maybe other lawyers are not so strict about confidentiality. In any event, thank you for taking the trouble to come to see us, whatever your motives may have been."

"I quite understand," said Eastman, "but if there's anything you can help me with, please contact me. Maybe the principals behind Cadzow will be prepared to give me the reassurance I'd like. I'm staying at the Hotel Baur au Lac until Monday, thereafter you can get me in Glasgow."

Eastman shook hands with both men. He exited the offices somewhat disconsolate. He did not expect to hear anything from Gruenschildts. The trail appeared to be at a dead end.

Hermann Klopfer was Bidermann's assistant. He had worked for the firm for fifteen years, and recently he had begun to have doubts about the morality of a lot of the work

Gruenschildt carried out. The news that somehow a charity had lost out on $25m troubled him greatly, for he was a Roman Catholic.

Once he was back at his desk, he logged on to the client system and reviewed the file for Cadzow. It didn't seem to him that orphaned children in the Third World were likely to benefit from the $25m which had been channelled through Gruenschildt's account. He decided an anonymous note would be best.

Eastman had gone back at the Baur au Lac, and was on his third gin and tonic in the cocktail bar overlooking the lake. His wife was chatting in an excited way about what a lot of good the weekend was doing for their relationship. Now she whispered that she'd bought something special in the lingerie shop which would be guaranteed to spice things up later. Eastman summoned the waiter and ordered another round.

The staff in the Baur au Lac were ultra-professional. They knew all the guests by name, so when the envelope for Eastman was handed in at the porter's desk it was brought immediately to the cocktail bar rather than left for him in his room.

The porter wore an immaculate uniform which Eastman thought would not have looked out of place in the Court of Czar Nicholas in St Petersburg. He carried the envelope on a silver tray and presented it to Eastman, who waited until the porter had withdrawn before opening it slowly. His eyes widened. The typed note was unsigned:

Please destroy this immediately. The person whom you seek is Erik Allensen, Villa Norvege, Armacao de Pera, Algarve, Portugal.

Eastman spent the rest of the weekend trying to piece together what had happened. It was like a Chinese puzzle. He just couldn't work out how McBain's funds had ended up with Allensen, the very man who had warned him off getting involved with McBain in the first place. He could see how dangerous it would be for him to go to the Glasgow police about Allensen having the money. His own role in the money laundering would undoubtedly come to light. Anyway, what would be the point? He decided to try to put it out of his mind. After all, he himself was sitting with an unattributable £1.5 million in the bank

But a week later the whole issue still nagged at him. He decided to surf the net to see if there was anything he could learn about Allensen. He googled Erik Allensen without any result. He then widened the search to Allensen only, restricted to the United Kingdom.

The unusual spelling of the surname helped. From the seventy Google search results, he picked out a reference to a Markus Allensen. A high-flying businessman educated at Wishaw Primary, Hamilton Academy and Edinburgh. It seemed likely that this was Erik Allensen's brother. If so, there was a chance they would both have been at the same school.

He tried the Friends Reunited website under Hamilton Academy, and while there was an entry for Markus, there was nothing for Erik. He then went onto the Wishaw Primary website, and, again, Markus appeared but there was no individual entry for Erik. On a hunch he entered the details of each person involved with the McBain empire. There was an individual entry for a Robert Donald, and Eastman drilled down to look at that. Robert had been a member of the football team which won the Lanarkshire Primary Schools Football Cup in 1965, and there was a link to a photograph. Eastman enlarged the photograph, which had the names of some, but not all, of the players detailed below. And there, standing proudly to the left of the goalkeeper, were the full backs, none other than the named Robert Donald and the un-named but clearly unmistakable Erik Allensen.

At his villa in Portugal, Allensen hauled himself out of his pool, dried himself off, and sat down at his laptop. The email he'd received from Plummer was unanswered, for he was unsure what to say in response to her account of the interview with Eastman. She'd said that when she told Eastman that he had retired, his initial shock had immediately been replaced by a look of suspicion. She'd also mentioned that Eastman had asked for his address.

Plummer was also angling for an invitation to his villa.

He decided to walk down to the local hotel for the buffet lunch. It was a constant round of golf matches, eating out and socialising with the other expats. He needed to give some further thought as to how to deal with shaking off Plummer's interest in him and Eastman's curiosity. Maybe inaction was the answer.

As he entered the restaurant his golfing partners called him to join them. There was an unfamiliar lady at the table. She introduced herself as a journalist doing a piece on recently arrived residents in the area.

"Erik, I've told her you're our man of mystery," Tommy Jones said. "She's intrigued. We all are. You've got to come clean with her. Source of funds for that lovely villa, all that stuff." The others laughed.

"Well, it's all evidence of expenditure, not of income. But to set your mind at rest, there's no mystery. My gratuity paid the deposit, and I've a big lifetime mortgage round my neck. I did have some luck when my company shorted some major investment houses, and the bets came off. When the share prices collapsed, we cleaned up. And the total irony is, I borrowed the money to do it from one of the banks involved!"

"And your company would be Wishaw Investments, I presume?" the journalist said.

"You have done your homework, miss. Those public records

are such an intrusion. Yes, Wishaw Investments is my company. But everyone here has his own investment vehicle, so there's no story for you here. I'm a simple retired cop with a decent pension."

"Yes, I've done some background on you. Wealthy retired policemen inevitably attract attention. But the odd thing is, unlike many, there's never been any suggestion of your being involved with organised crime. Maybe you did just get lucky that one time."

Allensen frowned. "Interview over, I think, and anyway, I'm sure you've got lots to do. Don't let us detain you."

He stood up and indicated the discussion with the journalist was over. She flounced out of the restaurant.

The others said they thought he'd been a bit abrupt with her, but Allensen laughed it off.

"Sorry, chaps, but I just don't hold with journalists. Idle sods, they always misrepresent you. You all know the trouble they can cause."

After lunch he wandered back to the villa. For the tenth time that week he reviewed the spreadsheets showing the Wishaw Investments' transactions, and the Profit and Loss Account and Balance Sheet prepared on his instructions by a retired accountant living in Tavira. Markus had recommended the accountant, as he'd represented him in disciplinary proceedings at the Institute, and got him off on a technicality. Everything looked watertight.

He decided to walk into town to get a British newspaper. As he made his way along the broken pavement he looked at the parched grass and the clay football pitch surrounded by broken fencing. In the distance was a block of flats which would not have been out of place in Shettleston. Poverty existed next to opulence around here.

Suddenly, there was the familiar sound of a police siren which jolted him. He wondered why.

38

Eastman had arrived in Armação de Pera unannounced. The look on Allensen's face when he recognised his visitor had been thunderous, but he soon recovered his composure. He offered Eastman lunch.

Now they looked out to the south over the cliffs which fell away at the foot of the Villa Norvege. They'd enjoyed a couple of beers after some sandwiches and now sat in the shade beside the pool.

"Well, here you are, James, what the hell do you want? I don't really think we've much to discuss, do you? Happy to give you lunch, of course, for old time's sake. But I don't think I need a lawyer. And, by the way, if you're wondering about how I can afford all this, let me put your mind at rest. Do you know how many deals it took me to accumulate what I have now? Nine. And I have all the contracts. You can see them if you like. It's a whole new world out there. Structured products, they call them. Covered warrants. But you know how they work, don't you? You can double your money in a minute if you call it right. And I did, as you can see. Started off with my gratuity, £50,000. Nine contracts doubling up. You do the maths. That's £20m, give or take. All tax-free, legit, and accepted by the authorities here."

Eastman eased himself back in the steamer chair.

"Yes, I thought that would be your story. That or options contracts. But let me tell you how I see it. I've learned a lot about you in the last couple of weeks. It's amazing what you can pick up once you can see the woods behind the trees.

"You've got an older brother, Markus. I never met him, but he dealt with one of my partners. I think he put you onto me. You see, for years you'd been trying to work out a way to get at that cash McBain had. My guess is you saw it as your due for the years slaving away for a fraction of what your brother earns. And you got to know about it from your old school pal, Rab Donald. Don't deny that, at least. I have the photo of both of you from 1965.

"If I'm charitable – what a laugh! – I'd say Rab's been a police informer working for you, but I doubt it. I think you and he got together after the Gibraltar fiasco and decided to use someone like me as the patsy to move the money. Come to think of it, maybe Markus thought up the whole Blind Trust idea. Maybe not the actual idea, but he'd have known I'd be able to come up with something. As soon as Rab found out about McBain's heart condition, you knew you had to move. The only problem was getting rid of Sonny, wasn't it?

"But I'm getting ahead of myself. To get me involved, you set the honey trap and I fell right in. The genius of it all was I thought I was manipulating everyone to get my share of the action, but I was being played like a fine violin. The tricky part for you was making sure Rab could switch the Letter of Wishes, but because I was part of the conspiracy, it never occurred to me that Rab might be working against McBain.

"To make sure the funds ended up with Cadzow you had to eliminate Sonny. Again, this was genius. You and Rab somehow got Malik to provoke Sonny into burning down his premises, knowing he'd retaliate. Rab's on the spot, geeing Sonny up, and you're leaking information to Malik. And when the inevitable happens, Rab's right there to arrange for Malik's assassination. And Alex McBain was bound to drop down dead at any time.

236

"So at the end of the day, Rab's got control of a huge swatch of Glasgow, including much of what Malik had, and you're sitting here with the £18m."

Allensen took a swig of his beer.

"It's a great story, James, but you can't prove one single bit of it. And, as I've said, there's a clear paper trail in Wishaw Investments accounts, starting with the £50,000."

A car horn sounded. Eastman stood up.

"I think that's my taxi, Mr Allensen. Covered warrants are like a carousel, you know. One contract goes up, the other goes down. My guess is Wishaw got the money from Cadzow, and then got subsidiaries to buy both put and call contracts with the money, starting with just £50,000. It's a no-loss situation, you don't care that you lose on one of the contracts, because the winning contract washes the money clean. Then you just destroy the contract you lost the money on. With a co-operative accountant, you can easily produce a set of accounts which look legitimate."

Allensen looked serious.

"Good luck in the rest of your career, James. You've seen how easily things can go awry. I'd stick to corporate law, if I were you. I don't know what you made on the Blind Trust, but I suspect you don't want that to be made public."

They shook hands.

★ ★ ★

Two weeks later, on a Saturday morning, Eastman returned home from watching the schools rugby match his son had been playing in. He enjoyed reading the *Telegraph* after lunch. He turned to the Business Section.

Although the FTSE had fallen nearly four hundred points, the largest single-day points fall since it was launched in 1984, this wasn't the biggest story of the day. The main article revealed that the Icelandic Government had seized control of the country's largest banks in an attempt to fend off wholesale economic collapse. The banks' shares had been suspended, and there had been widespread panic in the tiny state.

Speculation was that people who had money deposited with Icelandic banks in the Channel Islands faced major losses as a result of the crisis, because they might not benefit from deposit protection schemes. The administrators of these banks could not say how much was available to pay out, or when customers would get their money back. The only reassurance offered was that they would be working for orderly repayment of deposits. The head of the United Kingdom Serious Crime Squad had announced that as it was suspected that these banks had been used for money laundering, the Guernsey authorities had decided that banking secrecy rules were to be waived, and the Squad had been invited to work closely with all the administrators, in collaboration with the Inland Revenue, to verify the source of funds in respect of which claims were made.

Suddenly Eastman's plans for the future looked less assured.